I0561779

# MERCENARY
## THE KINDRED CHRONICLES
## JODI KENDRICK

SOULGATE PUBLISHING

# PROLOGUE
## MYST INNYS

"STAY THE EXECUTION, IF you want a public abdication. Send them both into exile." Erevan ap Brodin y Draighdoine interrupted his father's meeting.

Brodin, current king of Myst Innys, sent his clerk away as Erevan approached him.

The clerk bowed. Without a glance in Erevan's direction, he left the room through the plain side door.

"I did not expect you for several days," Brodin said to his eldest son.

"I came as soon as the decree for the execution was made public. You can't allow it."

Brodin lifted a brow. "You no longer have weight on the council's judgment. And I follow their decrees."

"You have the power to veto them; do not allow this to happen."

Brodin studied him with a shrewd eye. "And you will voluntarily abdicate."

Erevan's gut twisted as he observed his father's masked gaze.

"You wanted me to make a public declaration. I will do it, on the condition they are both sent into exile. No executions."

"Neither of them deserves your concern, Erevan. Or mine. The stolen artifacts have not been returned. He insists there were no other tomes or valuables; however, our inventory is incomplete."

Erevan swallowed his shock at his father's cool words.

Brodin went on, "You will make the announcement and return to the academy."

"I will publicly renounce my right to your seat of rule, then find what was taken."

"I would send the Retrievers after them."

"No. The Retrievers would put them to death, especially if there is any resistance."

"Why do you care if they die? They betrayed you."

"Why don't you care? They're your blood."

"That's irrelevant. They've proven themselves to be undeserving." King Brodin strode toward his desk, pushed a few documents across its surface. "Perhaps this little request to retrieve the stolen valuables yourself is just what you need to learn a few life lessons. Living outside of the kingdom for a time will make you understand how fortunate you are to serve it in your own way."

Erevan stiffened but held his tongue.

"It will take some time to smooth things over with the Council. They are quite ruffled over the thefts and deceit. Negotiating with your abdication will go a long way to soothing their concerns, though both will take some time. But this will be a positive step toward regaining your honour."

"I understand." Erevan grit his teeth. Time, and much public spectacle. He swallowed his humiliation as he stared at his father.

"I shall resume my work now, if you've nothing else to request?"

Erevan offered his father a curt bow before leaving the room.

*Is this a mistake?*

# ONE

## AELOZIA

'*Shhhevonnnnh.*' The dark voice whispered her name from somewhere deep within.

Limbs trembling and heart racing, she faced a great fiery beast.

Gasping, her gaze darted to the dead, caught as they escaped from the destroyed house.

Murdered.

She knew them. All of them.

Her kin.

With a sob, she tore her gaze away, seeking, head spinning.

Her hands, too small for the weapon she wielded, struggled for a firmer grip.

There!

She ran toward her sister, who knelt over their bleeding mother.

Nearby, her brother battled a foe double his size. She ran forward to help him.

He glanced in her direction before he fell.

'*Shhhevonnnnh.*'

Scalding winds stopped her just steps before she could reach him, encircling her, blocking the sight of her dying brother, and then of her mother as she turned to see her.

*The beast ascended with snapping jaws; wings extended with menace. Heat wavered from it, glaring at her with a terrible yellow eye, shot with a hard onyx pupil.*

*"Destroy them!" Its terrible voice rumbled through her head, erupting like an ancient volcano. The crash of responsibility peppered back down on her, layering more and more until she buckled under the weight of it.*

*Falling to her knees on the rocky soil, she cried for her mother, her father, and her small brothers.*

*The terrible voice screamed as her body jerked, pain ripping through her chest.*

*The swirling vision of fire broke enough for her to see her mother's hand extended in her direction, claw-like and twisting a beam of light aimed straight at her.*

*She screamed under the onslaught of pain as her mother's power burrowed into her. "Mother!"*

*Her sister knelt, eyes wide, tears streaming down her face.*

*Their mother snarled at her, and she lifted her hand.*

*The second stream of power, although weaker, was too much.*

*'Shhhevonnnnh.'*

Siobhann woke with a jerk, dragging air into her lungs.

"Hold still, I'm almost finished," the craggy voice of healer Bruner barked at her.

She was face down on a table, naked from the waist up.

Disoriented, she closed her eyes as pain continued to sear through her.

Not through her heart, but across her back.

*Not the farm.*

Her gaze sought her pack. It slumped between a chair and the wall where she'd left it. It didn't appear to be tampered with.

Air hissed through her teeth as she drew a deep breath.

"Stop fighting my magic and this will go faster."

Siobhann forced herself to relax as much as possible under the onslaught of the healer's ministrations.

"I can fix those for you too," the healer said. "The night terrors. For a fee, of course. I'll give you a discount since you're already spending good coin here. Tell your friends about my excellent work."

*Excellent work?*

"I don't need a dreamwalker," Siobhann huffed a laugh, then grunted as a particularly sensitive area twinged.

"Relax!" The healer moved to the other side of the table.

Siobhann swallowed another retort.

"And yes, you do need a dreamwalker."

"What do you know?" Siobhann snarled as her body curled around another pain point.

The healer's hand slammed down on Siobhann's shoulder, forcing her back down on the table. "Plenty. Seen it all the time on the front with soldiers that did too many cycles on and off the battlefields."

*Darya.*

"I'm not a soldier."

"Aren't you? Soldier, warrior, mercenary—whatever. All the same. Hold still, this part is going to hurt."

Siobhann nearly laughed at that, but didn't have time as the healer's magic ripped through the muscles in her back.

She had no breath.

*Ashiel, this hurts more than the goddess-damned injury!*

"I think I've traced most of the poison, though judging by the faint scars and traces of several other healers' magics, I suspect you may be on the verge of a death wish. Perhaps you should let me attend to those night terrors, mistress."

"I'll have spent quite enough coin here, thank you."

"But I'm worth it. Make sure you tell your friends. Discounts for groups and loyal customers." The healer's dry hands smoothed down Siobhann's spine and back up again. Mistress Bruner gently squeezed Siobhann's upper arms, signalling the end of the treatment. "There, that's the last of it. Mind you, the muscles will be tight for a few days. I've left a lingering spell to work on the deeper tissues while you sleep."

The old woman shuffled toward her work bench. It looked much the same as her sister's did. And her mother's had.

Siobhann dry swallowed the unexpected lump in her throat, as she reached for her chemise and eased it over her head.

The dream was coming with more frequency, and always the same.

That day. That day that she didn't ever want to remember.

Dipping into the leather coin purse secured at her waist, she extracted several silvers and placed them on the healer's workbench.

The healer grunted acknowledgment and placed a bound jute satchel next to the coin. "Complements. Tell your friends—,"

"Excellent work. I know," Siobhann grinned at the woman, testing the flexibility of her back muscles. "And thank you." She snatched up the satchel, guessing that it was a sleeping tea.

"For the healing, and for the dreams. If you change your mind, you know where to find me."

"I do." She pulled on the rest of her gear, buckling her weapon belts in place. At last, she pulled her cloak on, securing it with the brooch.

"Ah, I thought as much. You're one of Donnen's." The old woman nodded at the circular brooch bearing a jet raven with claws and beak extended.

Siobhann raised a brow. "I am."

"As I said. Mercenary, warrior, soldier. All the same."

Siobhann snorted. "Hardly. Warriors and soldiers have causes and orders. Mercenaries just have coin."

The old woman snorted right back. "I know Donnen Kember. There's more to you lot than that." She pushed the silvers back across the bench toward Siobhann. "On the house. I'm sure Donnen will make good use of those."

"I—,"

"I won't tell him you came to me. Knew him a long time, I did, so I know what he's like." The woman's heavy lid descended in a wink. "Still, tell your friends—,"

"Excellent work. The best in Millhaven." Siobhann winked back and stowed the silvers back in her purse as she turned toward the cottage door.

"Mistress. Mind the tea, would you?"

Siobhann turned at her serious tone, glancing back at the old woman's earnest expression. "I will. Thank you."

She considered the healer's words as she retrieved her horse's lead, petting and nuzzling his grey muzzle. "All better, Odyn."

With a glance toward the nearby rooftops and trees, she noted that her usual shadows weren't there. Her ravens.

*Likely returned to the aerie now that we're on respite.*

Smoothing her hand along Odyn's long neck, she noted the dried blood crusted on the saddle and his flank. "I'll have Roan clean you up as soon as we get home. I promise."

He nudged her shoulder.

"Yes, and extra oats, too." She mounted him and patted his muscular neck. "My good boy."

Before she had the chance to nudge him with her knee, he turned toward home.

# TWO

WEARY, WITH A NAGGING itch deep in the knitted muscles of her back, Siobhann McLeighan sighed with relief when she sighted the familiar faded sign of her favourite tavern. Its sigil—the Rose and Star—direly needed paint, and the afternoon sun continued to burn away any pigment it had left.

Still, her heart lifted to see it above the door. Dropping her gaze to the solid wooden door, she caught her warped reflection in the brass oil lantern beside it and quickly schooled the whimsical expression she saw looking back at her.

Hardened mercenaries didn't grin with whimsy. They grinned. Just not with whimsy.

"Are ye going to stare at the damned door or open it?" a gruff voice broke her mental wandering.

Goddess, she was tired.

She scowled down at the diminutive form of a fellow traveller, just as dust weary as herself.

Shoving the door open, she strode inside toward the counter without waiting for her eyes to adjust. She didn't need to.

The pungent scent of alcohol stung her nose and made her eyes water. But as soon as that first assault faded, other sensory details replaced it.

"You're back." Arlyss said from behind the barrier. "And in one piece. That's good. The usual?"

The particular spices Arlyss used in her stew teased Siobhann's nose. Her mouth watered and her stomach growled over the low murmur of the other patrons.

Siobhann gave her a curt nod before turning to claim her seat by the corner window, in a nook that contained two small tables. A bench ran the perimeter of the nook and single chairs were set on the open side for extra guests.

Her scowl deepened.

Siobhann's spot was occupied. Her gaze flicked over the figure as she turned toward the other table in the nook. In the darker corner, away from the window.

The hair on her body rose. Her gut tightened as she bypassed the stranger.

*Dark. Broody. Power. Danger.*

The space in the nook was charged. Like when a magic user was about to execute a spell.

She didn't remove her gear before settling on the bench, facing the open space of Arlyss' tavern, though she ensured her weapons were accessible should she need them in a blink—despite Arlyss' rules of absolutely no violence in her establishment. She propped her booted foot on the opposing chair beneath the table and eased her back against the wall, careful not to strain the healing wound on her back.

Semi-relaxed, but ready.

Her gaze swept the patrons.

*A handsome man in my bed tonight would be nice.*

To ease the tension in her shoulders, she rolled them as she studied her neighbour, occupying *her* usual spot.

The stranger ignored her, head bent over a map stretched out on the table, illuminated by the sunlight filtering in through the window. A wine glass was set next to a nearly empty platter.

His long, dark hair obscured his face, a cloak draped his broad shoulders and his long legs took up the space below the table.

*Promising. Now if he'd just look up.*

With her attention on her neighbour, the ions in the air intensified, affecting the surface of her skin.

She glanced at him as she shifted on her seat, trying to dispel the sensation. Her gaze then swept the rest of the patrons. No one else reacted to the charge in the air.

Arlyss approached, bearing a tray with Siobhann's dinner and ale. "Here you are, luv." She placed the dishes on the table between them. "Mission successful, then? I'm surprised to see you here without a scratch. Unless, of course, you've already been to see Domini Kember?"

Siobhann grinned up at the innkeeper. "And risk another tongue lashing?" She took a long drink of the dark ale to wash the road dust from her throat.

*Home.*

"Ah, your sister then?" Arlyss frowned. "Must have been serious enough to want to avoid Domini Kember."

"You're not wrong." Siobhann shifted her posture, easing the ache in her back. "Third little bastard dropped out of nowhere and swiped my back. It'll take a while to mend, but no, I stopped by a healer back in Millhaven along the way. The job was in the opposite direction from where Darya lives."

Arlyss shook her head. "You're like a bloody cat. One of these days…"

"I know, I know." With a roll of her eyes, Siobhann laughed and winked at Arlyss before taking another drink from the tankard. "Let Dea know I'm back so we can resume her lessons when she's ready."

"I'm surprised she's not in here already, pressing you for your latest tales."

"Boy?"

Arlyss shrugged, "Who knows? Maybe?" She turned to Siobhann's neighbour then. "Can I get you anything else, sir?"

His dark hair fell away from his face as he raised his head. The soft glow through the window illuminated his profile.

Siobhann gasped, a whisper between her lips.

A jet brow that looked as though an artist arced and slashed inky paint to accent the thick fringe of black lashes around his dark eyes. A straight nose at opposing angles to the strong jawline that descended to frame the most beautiful lips she'd ever seen on a man.

The curl at the corner of his mouth drew her focus.

A shiver trickled down her body with tiny snaps as she considered what it would be like to place her own lips to that delicate spot.

She blinked, sucked in another breath and jerked her gaze away.

From her periphery, she continued to observe. He straightened. The curl of his lip drew upward in a little smile as he dipped his forehead in thanks. "More wine, please."

The sound of his voice with its slight accent, teased her spine. The timbre of it slid downward in a far, far too pleasant way.

*Very promising.*

Arlyss reached for his goblet, bobbed, and whirled away to fulfil his request.

He turned his head, meeting her gaze. He dipped his forehead in the same respectful way he'd offered Arlyss. "Madam."

Her breath hitched a third time.

*Perfection.*

*Oh dear Goddess.*

Fantasies bombarded her brain, battering and tumbling down through her heart, straight to her lower core.

She blinked.

*Goddess, I haven't reacted to a male like that since I was tumbled into womanhood and was falling in love with every squire and knight that smiled at me.*

Her tongue slid across her lower lip, reminding herself she had lips...to speak with. "Sir." She replied, mouth gone dry.

Besides, she reminded herself, she usually preferred bearish men with impressive beards that spoke with a voice that could carry across a battlefield.

Usually.

Not this—this beautiful, elegant stranger who was neither bearish nor sported a silky beard.

Still. Something about him whispered to the deepest part of herself. Whispered indecipherable words of power and danger.

She scoffed.

He spoke.

She blinked. "What?"

"You know where I might find him?"

She'd been still staring at him.

He stared back, brow arched. The attractive corners of his mouth had tightened and weren't quite so enticing.

Coherent thought returned.

"Kember," he said.

"Do you mean Donnen Kember?" Arlyss asked, setting the replenished wine goblet on the table.

He nodded, claiming the cup. As he tipped his head back to drink, the long silky hair framing his face swung back like a show curtain, revealing something new and precious.

Siobhann's eyes swept the details. Golden markings along his hairline and down his throat, disappearing beneath a high collar. Her gaze lingered on the muscles of his throat as he drank before sliding back up and finally noting his ears.

Their tips poked through the black satiny strands and braids.

Tips.

*Elf.*

She reviewed what she'd already seen.

Golden markings down his face and throat.

"What do you want with Donnen?" Siobhann demanded.

Arlyss' attention shot to her face at her tone.

The stranger replaced the emptied goblet on the table.

"Just a little conversation." He turned his attention back to the map he'd been studying.

She stiffened at his dismissal, twinging the sensitive wound in her back, which flared her temper.

Ignoring the subtle cues, Arlyss said, "Will you take him home with you then, Siobhann?"

*A moment ago, I'd have been all for it!*

*Now?*

She glanced at the visible tip of his ear as he ignored the women.

*Not bloody likely.*

*Elves. Arrogant. Stuck up. Dangerous. Sly.*

*Don't trust an elf. Especially not a bloody noble one!*

Grimms taught her that.

And there was no doubt. With markings like that? That one was royalty.

She turned to the cooling food and sighed. Arlyss' beautiful stew was already congealing and despite the growl of her stomach, Siobhann's appetite was concentrated elsewhere.

She dipped her spoon in the food, too distracted to actually taste the aromatic spices.

What the hells is an elf doing here? A royal elf? And looking for Donnen?

There was no way she was going to let this guy—elf...could elves be guys? —anywhere near Donnen, not without vetting him for herself first.

Not a chance.

"Siobhann?" Arlyss prompted.

"For a fee, I'll consider it. I am a mercenary after all, and the guildhall needs upkeep."

He turned toward her again. "A mercenary. You."

"Yeah, what of it?"

His gaze was one of mild interest as it slid over her, triggering the fine hairs all over her body to rise again despite her aversion to the man—elf. It was probably some Elfy woo-woo that made her feel like that.

Or so she told herself.

His gaze lingered on her hips.

"What?"

"Exquisite ax. May I?" His long fingers twitched in her direction.

"No. Nobody touches Sally and Trish except me." Her left hand moved protectively toward Sally, exposed to his view. Her right covered Trish, resting on the other hip, just in case.

"Sally and Trish?" The corners of his mouth curled.

Arlyss slid between the tables, creating a barrier between Siobhann and the stranger. "How about I pack your stew in a clay pot? You can send it back with Dea tomorrow after her lesson."

"If Mister—what's your name?"

"Erevan ap Brodin."

"If you're not in a hurry, sir, I will just finish my dinner. The clay pots always leak in my satchels, which are a nightmare to clean."

Arlyss rolled her eyes, stepping back out of the narrow space between the tables, muttering. "You should have told me they leak. I'd have packed them differently. Anyway, I have some pies for you to take home to the boys." She wandered back to her post at the bar to tend several newly arrived patrons.

The boys—meaning the men at the guildhall where Siobhann lived.

Arlyss was the only one that ever got away with calling them that, thanks to her heavenly pies. The guildhall was an assorted collection of fierce warriors, and trackers, and other miscellany of individuals who lived together, economizing their skills.

Mercenaries.

Like herself.

Siobhann's second family.

As she ate the last spoonful of her stew, her gaze slid back to her neighbour, curiosity growing.

*What does he want with Donnen?*

She couldn't see enough of his markings to determine which Elven clan he was from.

Nor could she imagine any reason he, or any elf for that matter, would be here, on the war-riddled frontier of the Aelozian Empire she called home.

A shadow fell over her table.

She glanced up into a handsome face staring back at her with a flirtatious expression.

*Now that's better.*

Obviously a warrior in serious need of a bath. Blond hair pulled back into a thick queue, broad shouldered, corded muscles in his arms, heavy pack.

"This seat taken?"

Handsome, but not original.

She was about to shift her foot to slide the empty chair out for him when there was a crash behind him. His head snapped to the side in search of its source. A dark spot scurried along the fair hairline behind his ear.

She shuddered and pulled the chair tighter to her table.

"It is." She dismissed the louse-ridden traveller to resume her meal.

He grunted and turned away.

When she finished her food, she slid off the bench and rose, scooping up her bowl and tankard. "Ready, sir?" she tossed over her shoulder as an afterthought.

The stranger in her spot nodded.

As he began rolling up his map, she turned and approached the counter, setting the dishes atop it for Arlyss, and slid a double-headed coin under the foot of the tankard, out of sight.

Arlyss glanced over from her position, drawing another tankard for someone else. "Just give me a moment." She handed off the ale, wiped her hands on her apron, then disappeared into the kitchen. She reappeared a few moments later with a small crate of the treasured pies and handed them over to Siobhann.

Everyone was going to be extra happy to see Siobhann again. She balanced the crate on one hip as she turned to leave. "Tell Dea; sunup."

Arlyss nodded.

Siobhann hadn't heard the elf move, but she felt his presence behind her.

She strode toward the door and pulled it open.

His hand locked in place on the edge of the door above her head, holding it open for her to pass through.

Startled, she glanced back and up at him before stepping out into the noisy street and away from the tingling sensation that swept her with his proximity.

EREVAN AP BRODIN LET the woman's sure strides carry her several paces ahead of him so he could study her.

In the low light of the inn, her copper hair shone under the lamplight. He recalled her green eyes, which sparked with curiosity, and the delicate skin beneath the sprinkling of freckles that turned a rosy shade when her ire rose.

Her soft, full lips and low voice enchanted him. He enjoyed looking upon her.

He had no idea what to make of her naming of the pair of exquisitely made light axes she wore at her hips.

Sally and Trish.

Who in their right mind would name such beautiful weapons thus?

She must not know what she had.

A dwarf would certainly set her straight.

His gaze fell to her swaying hips, the axes secured at either side.

Distracted by the sway, he found himself admiring her shapely anatomy below her narrow waist.

Erevan blinked. His gaze shot up and swept the street in case anyone noticed him admiring her posterior.

He cleared his throat and forced his gaze to remain level and well above her head as he followed her around the corner to the livery.

He handed the stable boy a coin and waited for Kelstorm to be brought to him.

She led her grey gelding out of the stable a few moments later. Stopping some distance away, closer to the road, she murmured to her companion.

"I know, I know, Odyn. I promised you'd relax here for the night. And I thought I was going to have a nice tumble in bed tonight before heading home, but we have a little job to do."

The horse nickered.

"I'll make it up to you," she promised.

Kelstorm nudged Erevan as the stable boy handed him his reins.

"My apologies for disrupting your evening plans, madam." He joined her by the road.

She didn't answer. But the tense set of her shoulders was enough to let him know she'd heard him.

Rather than answer, she led her horse out and mounted, setting off.

Growing used to the rudeness of humans, Erevan mounted Kelstorm and followed.

# THREE

Erevan had braced himself for the expected barrage of questions.

Questions about himself, about his people, about his dealings.

It hadn't come.

They passed several trees uprooted during recent storms, already dragged to the roadside by previous travelers. He glanced at the sun, a breath above the distant western tree line, where one tree in particular had a familiar crook.

He stared at the back of the woman's flame-haired head as her horse cantered before him, kicking up road dust. Her pack and saddle bags were well worn. The pommel of a spare short sword jutted from the centre of a bedroll. A quiver of raven-fletched arrows and a maple bow slung from one side, within easy reach. The box of pies hung from the other.

His keen eye picked out several semi-obscured leather-wrapped dagger handles and a few slim, notch-handled throwing knives that lined the wide leather belt around her waist.

The axes secured at her shapely hips shone under the waning sun, swaying with the rhythm of her horse.

A seasoned fighter.

He had questions of his own.

What kind of magic did she have that caused his aura to tingle the moment she came too near?

The way she'd studied him, and the sharp turn of her demeanour when she interacted with him.

*Because I'm Elvenkind.*

His hands tightened on the reins. Kelstorm grumbled. Erevan instantly eased his hold.

He often encountered distrustful reactions during his travels. But what he had not encountered, ever, was a woman like her.

But he was new to *this* region. *Perhaps she isn't unique among her people at all?*

Still, he couldn't account for the energetic reaction. The frizzle that whispered to his power.

"What do you want with Domini Donnen Kember?" she finally asked again, with a glance over her shoulder at him.

"I'm not in the habit of discussing my affairs with strangers. I will pay you for your guidance when we arrive."

Her horse stopped at a bend where a narrow trail jutted off into thick woods. Erevan stopped next to her, meeting her scowl.

"Since you haven't bothered to ask, I'm Siobhann McLeighan, loyal Kindred mercenary. I don't care about your affairs, sir. I care about what your intentions are for the Domini." Her fingers loosened on her reins as one hand eased toward Trish.

Or was it Sally?

No matter.

Still ridiculous.

He suppressed a sigh as he met her glare.

Neither of them had made any effort with introductions.

*Any point in bothering now?*

Her gaze flicked to his throat.

A threat?

The corner of his lip curled.

Her scowl deepened, but her fingers never twitched toward whichever weapon she was ready to embed in his neck.

One way to stop him from muttering an incantation. Not that he needed one to access his power.

To his benefit and a serious problem for everyone else.

He brushed aside thoughts of his family before they could catch hold.

Even though the woman's hand rested near an ax, he decided she'd use a throwing knife.

What spells could *she* use against him? Reflexively, his gaze flicked over her features and other assets, recalling she'd been looking for a man to share her bed just hours before.

*It would be a shame to incinerate her.*

The fierce warrior glint in her eye was at odds with the freckles sprinkled across the bridge of her nose and flushed cheeks.

*Impatient. Passionate. Loyal.*

*Tempting.*

The word washed over him, dousing him before the tinder sparked.

"Well?"

He smiled. "Just information. I was told that he has a collection of regional maps. I'm in need of directions."

Tense, her gaze flicked from his smile to his eyes.

He met her stare.

Erevan remained patient. Controlled. Determined.

She waited another heartbeat before she made her decision. "If you harm him, I will deal with you myself, before any of the others have the chance to get to you."

"Understood."

She nodded toward the path. "Welcome to Kemberlan Keep, home of the Kindred."

He glanced up the narrow path that disappeared into the thick forest.

*Underwhelming.*

"Not many visitors?"

Her serious expression broke with a wide grin. "People come and go all the time. This is one of the back-end shortcuts. The main gates are a quarter hour ride from the village." Her eyes twinkled.

Erevan ground his teeth.

He'd let her distract him, right past that familiar landmark of the crooked tree that screamed she'd led him in circles.

"You could have asked anyone in that tavern where we are, and they would have happily pointed you in the right direction for a pint of Arlyss' finest. Still, you owe me a guide fee. You can put it in the Domini's hand when you meet him." Her gaze flicked over his features, lingering on the visible markings along his hairline and throat, stopping at ear level. "My warning stands. And you'll have to give your name at the gatehouse before they let you in."

He nodded.

"Mind your scowl, elf, else the guardsmen decide you're trouble. Their bolts don't miss."

As he followed her through the woods, invisible wards ghosted along his skin, making it prickle, testing him.

*Not as sophisticated as the wards around Myst Innys, but reliable.*

Bypassing more felled trees, the forest opened to a sloping cleared space littered with storm debris, dominated by a keep atop a hill, and enclosed by a curved wall. Even at this distance, worn sections of the keep's roof were visible. Parts of the curtain wall had new pointing between the stones.

*The architecture here lacks elegance.*

He sniffed, doubting the structure even had running water.

Overall, the place was quiet, aside from the dull ring of a smith's hammer and nearby wildlife and livestock.

His guide stopped below a gatehouse with a reinforced door large enough for a horse and rider to pass through.

"You're late."

Siobhann McLeighan shrugged up at the guard who barked down at her. "I'm here."

"Two days late. The Domini left orders for Master Egrimmbe to find you if you weren't back by tomorrow."

"Well, I'm back now. Grimms doesn't need to leave his cozy forge. I found a visitor for Donnen at Arlyss' place."

"Pies?" The hope in the guardsman's voice was undeniable.

She reached back and patted the box tied beside her gear. "You all owe me for this."

The man snorted. "You didn't make 'em."

"I delivered 'em."

His head tilted to address Erevan. "Name?"

"Erevan ap Brodin y Draighdoine."

The guard whistled. "You're a long way from home, Your Highness." He waved to someone beyond the wall.

A thunk signalled admittance as someone beyond the door unbarred and opened it.

A young man stared wide-eyed at Erevan.

"Close your mouth, Roan." McLeighan snapped as she passed him.

"Yes, ma'am." He hurried to secure the heavy door once both newcomers were inside. "Master Egrimmbe will want to see you."

McLeighan grunted. "See that our guest's horse is stabled and find him a clean room since the Domini isn't here."

The young man nodded and gestured across the bailey. "This way, sir."

"You'll want my payment, mistress?" Erevan said to the woman as they both dismounted their horses, handing the reins to the young man.

She waved a hand as she rounded the horse to retrieve the box of pies. "As I said before, give it to Domini Kember when you see him."

Erevan ground his teeth at her dismissal.

*Rude human.*

The boy's eyes widened even further, darting between Mistress McLeighan and himself.

"Roan, please ensure Odyn receives extra care, and I'll give you a few extra silvers. He really earned it this trip." She patted his shoulder on her way past him.

"Yes, ma'am." Roan beamed at her before leading Erevan in the opposite direction.

Erevan couldn't resist watching her stride away.

"Mistress McLeighan has a sharp bark, but she only bites when she needs to."

Erevan turned his attention down to the young man, watching *him* with a too keen eye.

"This way, sir."

Siobhann brought the pies straight to the kitchen to leave them in Alda's care.

She dropped the box on the heavy wooden table harder than she meant to and gave it a shove.

"I hope ye haven't ruined Arlyss' lovely creations now." Alda eyed Siobhann warily.

"Apologies." She sighed, rubbing her hands over her face, trying to shunt her frustrations.

"Tough assignment, was it?" Alda untied the twine and sorted through the wooden crate, inspecting each pastry as she freed it, murmuring, "Ah good, good, just a little crumble here and there."

"Assignment? Oh yes. Challenging, but successful." She hefted her pack, having forgotten about the little bastards that had caused the injury which forced the delay in her return home. Which, in turn, gave that elf plenty of time to take over her favourite spot to relax in, before going home.

And, because of said elf, she hadn't even had time to ease her frustrations through a solid tumble with a handsome man.

And the only one that had time to approach her was louse -ridden... though he was very attractive, with nice thick arms... she shuddered.

*No. Not even an option.*

*I could go back...*

"Siobhann?"

"Hmm?"

"You alright, dear?"

"Yes, I'm fine. Long journey." She smiled at Alda and rubbed a hand on the older woman's shoulder. "It's good to be home."

Alda's concern faded, easing the wrinkles as she smiled back. "I'm always pleased to see ye make it home safe and sound."

"Make sure you let everyone know I brought those pies from Arlyss. I have to go see Grimms."

"I will do." Alda chuckled, returning to her chore of unpacking and sorting the pies.

Siobhann made it as far as the door before she leaned back into the arch. "Oh, and we have a guest here to see the Domini."

"A guest?" Alda glanced up from her task. "Anyone important?"

"No, just some Elven prince. Roan is seeing to him."

A pie plate smacked the table. "What? A prince? And you left him with Roan? Siobhann McLeighan, you can't drop information like that on me and... Siobhann!"

Siobhann escaped out of the side door through the kitchen gardens, rushing for Grimms' forge. She heard the wheeze of the bellows long before she rounded the final turn to his domain within Kemberlan.

From the open door, she watched Kindred's weapon master and smith, Master Jelani Egrimmbe, work for some time so as not to disrupt his concentration.

The thick grey ropes of his hair were bound in a knot at his nape. The meticulous rows from hairline to nape to keep them safe from the forge's flame, told Siobhann that his daughter had visited recently.

She smiled.

*Good.*

He glanced over his shoulder at her, then turned to take up a heavy mallet. "You're not dead."

"I'm not, so there's no need to leave your *beloved* this week." She nodded toward Bella, the massive flaming hearth.

"She keeps me warm at night better than any woman ever did."

Siobhann snorted. "Well, at least one did well enough to give you a daughter. I see Kwayssi fixed your hair."

"She did." He raised a thick arm and brought the heavy hammer down on the glowing ingot pinched at the end of his tongs.

She watched him shape the mass, quiet until he plunged it in the nearby barrel.

"You wanted to see me?"

"I did."

She lifted a brow as she stared down into his handsome, weathered face. Kwayssi had even trimmed his thick beard and moustache. Like his hair, his facial hair and his brows were two-tone black and silver, framing his dark face.

"Are you ever going to tell me how old you really are? Two hundred? Three?"

He started at the sudden change of topic, scowled and set the cooling ingot and tools aside.

"Three-fifty." She nodded, sure.

"No."

"There's a pie for you if you do."

Indecision flickered across his features. Mild amusement eased the perma-scowl as he locked his powerful arms across his chest. "There's a pie for me even if I don't."

She poked a tattoo-covered forearm, the colour of roasted walnut shells. "You're going to tell me some day."

Looking up into her face, his expression softened. "Kwayssi brought me letters for you. From Darya."

Siobhann stiffened. The movement twinged her back, reminding her of the real reason for her extensive detour.

"She's concerned."

"Darya is always *concerned*. Concerned enough to interfere where she has no business interfering."

"She's your sister and—," He held up a massive open-palm to stop Siobhann's protests when she opened her mouth. "I know Kindred is your family. But she is your *sister*. And she loves you. That means something too, Siobhann. Don't throw it away over some petty disagreement."

"Petty? Disagreement?" Siobhann spluttered, words sticking in her throat, making her growl in her frustration.

*What a shitty,* shitty *day.*

Hands balled into fists, she glared at her mentor, who stared patiently back.

Jelani Egrimmbe knew her better than anyone. *Anyone.*

And she hadn't told him the truth about their petty disagreement. And she never would.

He reached into the hard leather case fastened to his belt and withdrew several squares of folded parchment.

She swallowed. How much had that cost, Darya? With the rising costs of parchment, along with everything else...

He reached for her hand, placing the letters in them.

*It doesn't matter.*

"I'll read those when you tell me how old you are." She lifted her chin as she glared down at Grimms.

He grunted.

She shrugged, stepping toward Bella's glowing embers.

"Four hundred and seventy-five," he barked before she could flick her wrist and feed the parchment to the hearth.

Siobhann stilled, heart pounding.

*Shit.*

"You're not."

"I am. Now read the damned things and get this ridiculous rift over with."

Tears filled her vision. "All these years and you refused to tell me. And now? Over this?" She fisted the letters, holding them up to his face. "She sent them to you because everyone knows you're the only damned person that can persuade me to do anything I don't want to."

He nodded, lips pressed. "I know it. And?" He challenged her, as he'd always done. "What was it you used to call me when you were young, and you didn't want to train anymore? A 'heaping pile of goat dung'? Go on, say it."

Siobhann didn't want to laugh. She growled instead, crushing the letters further, resisting the urge to throw them into the forge anyway. But she couldn't. Not with that kind of an exchange. Instead, she jammed them into her own belt satchel and headed for the nearest curtain wall door.

"Read them, Siobhann."

"Tomorrow, Grimms. I'm too damned tired today."

"And crankier than a cornered wildcat."

# FOUR

SIOBHANN SAT BY THE quiet river, listening as sparrows chirped, playfully tagging the armour piled neatly beside her stool.

A wistful smiled teased her lips as she absently slid the whetstone along the edge of the ax laid across her thighs. The sun played over the shining, feather light steel, illuminating the intricate etchings along the side of the blade. She pulled up its mate to compare the sharpness of each, certain they met her standards.

'Assailant' and 'Attrition'. Sally and Trish.

Satisfied with her work, she fastened each ax to a hip, and took up her maple bow for inspection. With the quiver depleted, she'd have to visit the aerie to collect more feathers for fletching.

Smiling to herself, remembering the first weapons she had acquired. Stolen, really. A rusty wood ax and a cracked hunting bow.

These were much nicer.

Her fingers trailed over the freshly oiled, sun-warmed chain mail hauberk before gathering it up to replace it in her pack. It was time to head back to the keep. She'd indulged in her riverside rest long enough.

As Siobhann picked up her pack, she noted the letters Grimms had given her. They peeked out of the side pocket where she'd shoved them, thinking to deal with them later.

Her throat tightened.

*Not yet.*

Easing her pack onto her back, she turned toward the path that would lead her back to Kemberlan, and let her mind fall back into her nostalgia. Her gaze followed the weathered lines of the keep's splintering roof above the distant treeline and down to the crumbled stone that wasn't covered in ivy.

*Home.*

Kemberlan, ancient seat of the Kember family, and Kemberton's market and temple had established the nearby village.

Current home of the Kindred. Her *chosen* family.

Siobhann's thoughts flicked back to her sister's unopened letters.

*It could be something important...*

*... they're probably just more words of justification.*

The path narrowed through the forest leading away from the river when she heard a male voice.

Roan?

"What do you mean, she likes to hide? The Domini said she'd be by the river and the nearest point of the river to Kemberlan is that way."

*Yes, Roan.*

Siobhann didn't hear a second voice.

"If you say so," Roan said.

Siobhann continued moving forward, calling out. "Who are looking for?"

Roan and Dea stood at the tree line where the path opened to the rolling meadow.

Dea beamed, hand out, palm up in Siobhann's direction. She had an 'I told you so' expression as she looked at Roan.

Using her hands, Dea signed, 'We were looking for you, mistress. Domini Kember wishes to see you.'

"He's been in his library with His Highness all morning," Roan supplied.

"The elf still with him?"

Dea nodded.

Curiosity and caution rolled through Siobhann.

She sighed and nodded. "Message delivered. You both did well on the training field this morning. You make great sparring partners."

Dea's cheeks flushed as she glanced at Roan.

Roan beamed. "We've been practicing."

Siobhann's gaze flickered between the two. A grin tugged at the corner of her mouth. *I'll bet you have.*

"Keep up the good work, and Dea, thank you for keeping Boru off the field. You know I adore him, but the others are too distracted by the presence of a wolf—especially one of his size."

Dea's expression faltered. She signed, 'I wanted to train with him.'

"I know, and you will. Soon."

Dea nodded.

Siobhann moved past the young squires when she paused, looking at Dea. "And I don't hide."

The young woman's left brow rose as she smirked at her mistress, arms crossing over her chest.

"It's called 'enjoying a little quiet time'. Alone."

Dea grinned and shrugged.

"Crack of dawn," eyes narrowed, Siobhann barked. "Training field. Warmed up."

Dea's arms dropped along with her smug expression. Roan scowled at both of them.

Siobhann resumed her journey home, chuckling.

"Great, Dea. We were supposed to have tomorrow off for the fair," Roan grumbled.

Once inside the keep, Siobhann quickly ran her gear up to her quarters.

About to leave her room, she glanced in the polished silver mirror affixed to the white-washed plaster.

She scowled at her dishevelled reflection. After a morning of training, she wasn't presentable for *His Highness.*

Siobhann snorted.

*Why should I care what he thinks of how I look?*

His handsome face, long, perfect hair and impeccable clothing loomed in her mind's eye.

*And what is it about him has me behaving rudely to Donnen's royal guests?*

Taking two extra minutes, she quickly washed her face, changed into fresh clothes, and combed her hair.

Apparently, she *did* care.

One last glance over her clean tunic, trousers, and boots.

*Should I wear my dress?*

*I don't want to embarrass Donnen. This meeting could be political.*

She bit her lip, worrying it between her teeth. She hadn't exactly been polite to the Elven prince the previous day.

*But I also don't want the elf to think I care what* he *thinks.*

She growled at her blurred reflection before stripping down again and snatching her 'good' dress from the armoire.

She pulled it on, struggling with the lacing on the back while trying to ensure her bits were tucked into place, while also not straining the healing wound on her back.

Ignoring the polished boots, she grabbed the matching slippers to her dress and shoved her feet into them.

She almost made it to the door this time, when she paused one last time to retrieve her dagger, strapping it to her thigh beneath the bell of her dress.

*Just in case.*

*Elves are crafty and dangerously unpredictable.*

Smoothing the skirt down, she finally exited her room, ignoring the looks of surprise she met along the way.

*I need to dress up more often just so I'm not shocking everyone when I do.*

She paused before the heavily carved door to Donnen's office.

Resisting the urge to check her dress and ensure she was presentable, she gritted her teeth and knocked on the door.

"Enter." Donnen's muffled voice sounded through the thick oak.

Siobhann gripped the over-sized latch and pushed, scanning the room in a glance.

Her gaze rested on Donnen's smiling, bearded face. "Hiding in the forest again?"

"I don't hide, Donnen. I revel in quiet time."

"Because you don't get enough of that when you're on the road," he said as he glanced at her dress, with a curious expression that he didn't voice.

The elf stood in a darkened corner of the room, perusing Donnen's collection of thick tomes.

Ignoring him, as he ignored her arrival, she approached Donnen's heavy oak war table with its maps spread across its surface.

The builder designs for the keep's repairs lay haphazardly beneath the crisp scrolls.

"The front?"

"Only a month old." Donnen confirmed. "I was at the capital while you were gone, helping Ghalen reinforce our permits to operate independently."

She turned to Donnen. "And?"

He nodded. "We're good."

She breathed a sigh of relief.

"Though the Emperor is making it harder, forcing us to renegotiate on already promised terms, and quarterly instead of annually."

"Wasn't it just every five years, not so long ago?" Siobhann scowled, but kept the rest of her thoughts to herself in present company.

Donnen's lips compressed. "It was. Enough politics. Our guest has a request." He gestured toward the elf, who finally turned his attention in their direction.

But not to Siobhann. He leaned over the table, studying Donnen's maps.

She glanced between him and Donnen. "Since I just returned, I have a week's respite owed," she said for the elf's sake, since it was Donnen's rule.

"I mentioned it."

When she looked up at Donnen, her heart sank at his uneasy expression.

Had the elf threatened him?

Her palm grazed the dagger strapped to her thigh.

Donnen must have read her intent and stopped her with a hand on her shoulder. "Everyone else is gone on assignments."

She glanced at the elf's ears. "And Grimms won't budge."

"Not on this."

"What does *His Highness* need?" she asked Donnen, unable to neutralize her tone.

"I require guidance north through the Shield, and it seems even the most up-to-date maps are vague on the best routes." The elf finally looked at her. He placed a soft leather pouch on the peaked drawings of the Shield on the map spread before him.

Her eyes darted around the room as the sensation of a claw gripped her throat, trapping her breath.

"No."

"Siobhann—," Donnen tried.

"Find someone else."

"I'll pay well," the elf said.

"There isn't enough titanium on the continent that would motivate me to take you through that region," Siobhann hissed, heart pounding, skin alternately flaming and icing over.

"Because I'm Elvenkind?" the prince snarled.

"Sure, I'll start with that."

"McLeighan," Donnen barked, whipping her attention back to his stony face.

She straightened, lifting her chin as she stared at her superior, daring him to force her to accept the request. "Sir."

Steel glinted in his eyes as he held her stare.

She dropped her voice. "Do you remember what I told you? When you took me in?"

His scowl eased, and he glanced away.

"I may have been a child when I said I would never go back, but I meant it. Still do."

"I'd hoped you'd change your mind." His voice was gruff.

She looked at the elf.

He stood with his hands behind his back on the far side of the war table, observing the exchange with mild curiosity.

The leather pouch remained where he'd placed it.

She swallowed. Judging by its size and the sound it made when he put it down, there was a fortune encased in that little bundle.

She didn't need it.

But Kemberlan did.

*And I need Kemberlan. The Kindred.*

Even the small percentage owed to the guildhall would be enough to finish the roof work and stop the leak ruining the stonework down to the foundation.

"This journey is supremely important. I have been assured by many other travelers along my way here that the Kindred are the best suited to my needs." He rounded the table.

Siobhann walked over to the table next to the elf.

The hairs rose on her arms when she stopped, inches from him.

Her heart beat faster. Her skin no longer felt iced. It scorched in his proximity, which inflamed her temper, now that her initial shock and fear had subsided.

She leaned over the table to upend the pouch.

A mixture of titanium ingots and substantially sized gemstones rested amid a small mountain of gold Elven coin.

She gestured to the coinage. "Those are useless here." Unable to resist, she picked one up, inspecting its beautifully crafted sides. "They'd have to be melted and recast."

Her gaze flicked from the image imprinted on the coin to the elf.

*A relation? His father, maybe?*

He shrugged. "Whatever suits your needs."

Siobhann tossed the coin onto its mates. Stepping away from the table with its fortune, and the elf with his disturbing impact on her, she turned for the door. "Nirran will be back in a week or two. He's the best scout we have."

"You don't understand how important this is."

Hand on the latch, she turned. "Apparently not. And you don't understand how important a respite is." She turned her gaze back to Donnen. She waited a heartbeat to see if he'd reprimand her and order her to stay.

He didn't, so she opened the door.

"Master Kember—,"

"Give her time, Your Highness."

"I don't have time to give her."

Those last words followed her out of the room as the heavy door eased closed on well-oiled hinges.

Her peace and nostalgia long gone, quashed under the weight of that fortune sitting atop the drawings of the Shield.

*I can't. Not even for the Kindred.*

She shivered, seeking a place of sanctuary to ease her thoughts, her cowardice firmly lodged in her throat.

EREVAN'S GAZE FOLLOWED THE woman as she disappeared beyond the closing door.

Her appearance, dressed as a maiden and not as the warrior he'd expected, had taken him off-guard. The fabric of the dress softened her appearance, hugging her shapely contours. And the open lacing of the back revealed the fresh, angry scar that arced down from one shoulder blade, disappearing below the edge of the bodice.

He drew a slow, deep breath to ease the rise of his own temper.

She'd blanched and frozen in place like an arctic fawn at the mention of the Shield.

"My apologies, Your Highness." Domini Kember said wearily.

Erevan returned his attention to his host. "No need. You did warn me."

Kember nodded. "So I did. I'd just hoped enough time had passed that she could set it aside." He approached the table with its unrolled scrolls and maps. He pulled one from under the map.

Erevan glanced over the structural drawing of the keep.

"Whatever your reasons are for needing to go into that dangerous region, she has her own reasons for refusing to go. And I won't order her to." He set aside the building plan and gently swept the payment of precious metals and gems aside to look over the new map. There were many blank spots as Aelozia seeped up into the Shield, where the boundary was still heavily disputed. "All of my people choose to accept their assignments or not. Siobhann McLeighan has never turned one down before. She's one of my best and knows that area. I'm afraid if you can't give her time, you'll have to go elsewhere for guidance, Your Highness."

*Perhaps I should.*

"What do you propose, Domini Kember?"

Kember looked down at the payment on the table. He pointed at the capital city, Osteri, drawn in bold strokes at the centre of the map as though it were the centre of the world. "There are other guilds there you could query."

Kemberlan lay between Osteri and the Shield.

"Lose a few weeks travelling back and forth with querying in between. Or wait here for a few days for her to decide, and hope she agrees."

"Yes."

"And you think she might change her mind?"

"I do. Maybe." Kember pointed at the building plan. "She loves this place more than anything."

"Kemberlan is crumbling around you."

Domini Kember cleared his throat, his skin flushed above the graying beard. "I wouldn't have put it that way, but yes, that description is appropriate." His gaze dropped to the plan as he slid his ink-stained fingers tips over the drawing. "Most of us here do. Love this place more than anything."

Erevan nodded. "It's your home."

Kember straightened from his position over the map-strewn table. "It's more than that. This keep is the ancient seat of the Kember family. My brother Ghalen and I care for it until the next generation steps in to do the same. Ghalen and I share a vision for this place."

"Ashiel's vision? I noticed several paintings and statues dedicated to her as I passed through the keep."

The corners of Donnen Kember's eyes crinkled as he smiled. "Precisely."

"Not true mercenaries, then. I encountered one of her temples. Goddess of the lost—One of the three deities of travelers?"

Kember laughed, shaking a finger at Erevan. "Don't let any of *them* hear you say that. Kindred are definitely sell-swords and we have economical agreements. Would you care to sample a glass of Kemberlan wine?"

"I would, thank you. I am curious, Domini Kember—,"

"Donnen, please, Your Highness."

"Donnen. Then I insist you use my given name as well." Erevan accepted the glass of wine. He swirled the glass, inhaled, and sipped a moment later. "Very nice."

The older man raised his glass and sipped his own with a grin. "Another revenue stream to support our vision."

"Which is to repair a decaying roof."

"To repair our decaying roof and crumbling walls so that war-made orphans have somewhere to go to learn how to defend themselves in a world that leaves them with nothing. We're not an orphanage, per se—with a few exceptions. Just Ghalen and I are Ashiel's followers. Everyone else follows their own path."

*Mistress McLeighan?*

*'... When you took me in...'*

*Yes.*

His gaze drifted to the door.

An orphan with a sister, if he recalled the innkeeper's words correctly.

*None of my business.*

He returned his attention to Donnen as he continued on about the guild's history for a few moments longer before returning to the maps, and Erevan's options.

His payment remained on the table as their conversation danced around it.

His jaw clenched over the delays. He inhaled through his nose and sipped more of Kemberlan's wine.

*Nolgan.*

Erevan's fingers tightened on the glass. He drained it and set it aside.

*It's been years. What's a few more days? And if she still refuses, then it's a few more weeks.*

Donnen's voice faded out as he stared at the jagged lines of the Shield.

*What are you doing* there, *of all places? Surely you don't think* it's *there?*

"... Whatever your purpose is, know that the Shield *is* dangerous."

Erevan blinked, returning his focus to his host. "I've been told that your empire is waging war with the Torgolis that live in those mountains."

The lord of Kemberlan sighed, his expression as weary as when he'd put Erevan's request to Mistress McLeighan.

"Our empire is at war with, or has subdued, every bordering neighbour we've had over the last few decades. There are key strongholds in those mountains that we lost some time ago."

"And your emperor can't *reason* with them to join in peacefully?" Erevan's lips twisted.

Donnen cast him a pained expression before he finished off his own wine, making his opinion on the matter clear without stating the words. He shook his head. "And they're more dangerous than arctic dire bears after hibernation." He sighed. "I will bid you good night, Your Highness; my journey home was long, and my aging bones require rest. Would you like me to escort you to your room before I retire for the evening? I'm sorry your request wasn't met favourably."

Erevan shook his head. "Your squire gave me a fair tour, and I remember the way. If you're agreeable, I would stay here awhile longer."

Donnen inclined his head. "Of course."

As soon as the master of Kemberlan was gone, Erevan returned his attention to the tomes he'd been inspecting when his guide had arrived and refused him.

Striding forward, he retrieved the volume he sought and pulled it from the shelf.

*An Illustrated Gazetteer and History of the Aelozian Empire.*

Flipping through the first few pages, he found it had been published in the decade before the current emperor rose to power. Still, it was enough to give Erevan a basic education in the realm he meant to travel through.

There was nothing else more than a couple of centuries old. Certainly nothing about previous cycles or the fact that the Shield had been in the dominion of Dwarves and Elves during that time.

*Does anyone even know what's there? It should never have been left to the humans and the Torgolis.*

A guide would be more expedient, but if he had to, he would go alone. As he had much of the rest of this goddess-forsaken journey he'd already wasted years on.

If he had a few more days to wait, he may as well arm his arsenal of knowledge while he had access to the master's library.

He glanced at the heavy sideboard where Donnen had retrieved the wine. The bottle remained on its surface.

Erevan retrieved the bottle, leaving a silver coin in its place, and settled in for an extended evening of quiet reading.

# FIVE

As soon as Siobhann left the library, she went back to Grimms' forge.

"I'm sure as hells not going anywhere with an elf," the gruff dwarf had grumbled as he struck the red metal of his newest project. "But you should."

"What?" Siobhann's body jerked. "I'm not going back into the Shield. Why would you even suggest that?"

Grimms glanced up at her pointedly, but didn't answer as he continued his work.

*Because I'm like that hot metal, and every beat of the hammer finds its weaknesses and strengths, shaping it to perfection.*

He'd long ago used that analogy on her. Shortly after she'd been introduced to his forge, and she'd thrown question after question at him.

His forge was his altar.

She'd grumbled that it would do *him* some good to spend time with an elf. Maybe he'd grow and perfect himself in some mystical, unknown ways.

Grimms stared at her, impassive.

As he'd always done when she behaved like a child; as he had done since he became very much her adoptive parent and mentor, when she had nothing but a rusty knife with a frayed handle and a chipped ax that dragged through the dirt as she walked the streets looking for pockets to pick.

That look always brought her back to that moment—a mixture of fond memories that cradled the shame of innocence and survival, and the elusive potential to belong somewhere.

Donnen had let her pick his pocket. It was his way.

Grimms had stepped in front of her with that same stalwart stare until she gave back the silvers she'd pilfered.

Nothing had changed. They were her constants in her chaotic world.

Siobhann scowled at her ancient mentor.

She left the heat of Grimms' forge to cool her frustrations by returning to her room.

The door was barely closed when she kicked off the slippers and reached behind her to untie the lace that fastened the back of her gown.

Pain arced down her back, following the path of that little flayer-bastard's blade. The flayers, blue underground dwellers, dipped all of their weapons into poison. At least she'd been able to retrieve the stolen temple goods that Donnen would return in her stead.

The muscles, stiff and unhealed, worked against her ability to catch the strings with her fingertips.

She quickly realized she was so tense because she'd missed her customary bed play before returning home after an assignment.

Tense, for a lack of physical release.

That damned elf had interrupted her homecoming ritual.

And still very sore despite the healer's efforts.

Tired due to interrupted sleep; the damned elf invaded her dreams, too.

Tall, so that he towered over her. Silky hair, black as soot. Eyes that sparked with intelligence and lips that... lips that she *knew* could whisper passion without a word.

*Are his golden markings textured?*

She imagined tracing them with her fingertips.

The thought of touching his skin sent a ripple of desire through her, so strong it left her breathless.

She huffed, returning her attention to the dress, determined not to shred it with her dagger.

She'd made a promise to Ghalen to preserve at least one of the dresses he brought her from the Capital, and this was the last one.

Deciding to give up before she broke her promise, her gaze darted around the room, seeking *something* to deter her thoughts from the elf.

Darya's letters still poked from her pack pocket.

Guilt swept through her.

*Don't go soft, Siobhann.*

Stomping across the room, she snatched the offensive parchments up and paused, frozen on tip toe.

Her gaze slid to the fireplace.

*No, I can't break that bargain either.*

She growled to the empty room, recalling Grimms' upheld side.

*'Four hundred and seventy-five'.*

*Fuck.*

The folded letters landed haphazardly on her narrow cot where she flung them, before reaching for her stash of Grimms' Dwarven whiskey.

*Not much left.*

She sighed, uncorked the thick glass bottle and let it scald its way down her throat, around her heart to pool in her belly like lava. Moments later, the liquor flared its way through the rest of her body, making her limbs tingle.

*That's better.*

She finally smiled.

*Still an inch left...*

Shrugging, she tipped the rest down, corked the empty bottle and left it on the small table under the window.

After several moments of staring at the letters, she rolled her shoulders, limbering herself up for...

What? More of Darya's truths that Siobhann didn't want to know?

Truths that should have been left in the past. Scabbed and scarred over.

Ridged and ugly around her heart.

*Like the Shield.*

"Who needs the truth? After all this time? What's the point *now*?" She shrugged, squinting at the paper as the alcohol continued to do its job.

She gave one last try for the dress fastening. Limber, but still unable to coordinate her movement, she huffed and dropped onto the bed.

She'd been able to tie it. Why couldn't she get it undone?

Four letters.

*How long was I gone? Couldn't be more than a few weeks...*

Months since she last saw Darya. Half a year, maybe?

She broke the wax seal on the first letter, unfolding it with shaking fingers, not wanting to read about Darya's apologies and excuses.

There were none—at least not in the first letter.

Siobhann's jaw clenched as her eyes blurred.

*Sendi.*

She sniffled as she smiled at her niece's drawing.

Charcoal stick figures resembling two female adults with a child between them. A circle sun with spokes took up most of the top corner while stick flowers lined the entire bottom of the parchment and trailed up the sides, reaching for the sun.

Darya, Sendi and herself.

Her heart ached despite the whiskey's efforts.

She sniffled again, snapping the wax seals of the other letters, unfolding and glancing over them. She set aside the one in Darya's neat hand in favour of Sendi's drawings.

One of Sendi and Siobhann and the other with everyone, including Sendi's father.

Siobhann squinted, noting the large lump over Darya's midsection.

She lifted a brow at that detail. "Oh."

Delight for her sister dug its way through the frustration and anger.

She set aside the drawing, staring at Darya's letter.

Snatching it up, she steeled herself.

Just a few lines confirming what Sendi's picture already told her.

*She's with child again.*

*'…We've had some trouble hereabouts and Nate is still missing. I'm sorry for the way things turned out, but despite all of that and your feelings and opinions about him, I hope you could find the time to visit us. I think he's in trouble that I can't get him out of.'*

Siobhann snorted, tossing the letter aside as she stood after a couple of tries. "That's what you get for marrying a pacifist."

*... trouble...*

*... still missing...*

*... visit us...*

Heart pounding, Siobhann checked her empty bottle.

Still empty.

*Can't deal with this tonight.*

*Not tonight.*

She tried the dress again.

And failed again.

"Fuck it."

The door banged against the wall as she ripped it open and went in search of someone to help her with the damned lacing on her dress so that she wouldn't break her promise to Ghalen, now that she had ensured she hadn't broken her promise to Grimms.

How had she managed to tie it in the first place?

"Goddess-damn them all," she snarled, stalking along the darkened stone corridors.

She descended the spiralling steps, hand brushing the rough wall for balance. By the time she reached the bottom, her head spun.

"Where in the hells is everyone?"

Her bare feet moved across the smooth tiled floor.

Alda's kitchen was dark, save for the embers for the morning fires.

*I'm not going to Grimms' place with no shoes. Maybe someone else is around.*

She shuddered at the thought of stepping barefoot in a dung pile between the keep and the forge, if the stable lads were lax in their duties this late in the evening.

Siobhann rounded the corner toward Donnen's library. The door stood ajar, bathed in the golden glow from the fireplace.

Rushing forward on silent feet, she eased the door open enough to slip inside.

"Donnen? Sorry to disturb you, but I need a little help."

Her shoulders dropped as she scanned the empty room.

The grill across the fireplace allowed the last logs to burn down without threatening the treasure trove of the library.

Her gaze found the war table.

Donnen's maps remained strewn across its surface. The elf's payment glinted against the flickering firelight. Two empty glasses and three-quarters of a bottle of Donnen's wine lay abandoned at the end of the table.

Eyes suddenly glued to the bottle, so as to avoid the maps, she bit her lip.

"It's been a shit week, Siobhann. Donnen won't mind."

Seconds later, she gripped the bottle by the neck, uncorked it, and drank several mouthfuls.

The flavours rushed over her tongue in a very different way from Grimms' whiskey.

Belatedly, she recalled Donnen's warning not to mix the drinks.

She shrugged and drank a bit more.

"It'll be fine."

Fortified, she turned her attention back to the table to study Donnen's new maps. Setting aside the bottle, she pulled the sheaves toward her and turned them around. A bound atlas lay open at the other end of the table. Bringing it over, she compared the differences in borders. There were many place names she didn't recognize in the old tome.

Including her original home, nestled in the folds of the Shield.

Her fingertip ghosted over the lost name.

*Freylin.*

"Freylin," she whispered.

Nothing but snow and ice-covered ash by now.

A glance at the new map confirmed it.

No label marking the community where she was born.

She swallowed.

*For the best.*

The new map included the Shield as Aelozian territory, but the roads leading to it were fewer, some only dotted sketches. Just one road of significance connected the capital city to the route through the base of the mountains, which she knew was heavily fortified to ensure the safety of the trade caravans.

Beyond it, the map was washed out.

In the atlas, Torgolia was printed in bold letters along the curving stretch of the mountain range. Other names dotted the expanse beyond.

Torgolia.

The Torgolis.

Siobhann shivered and took another long swig from the bottle.

Her vision blurred. Unable to focus on the script, she turned her attention to the elf's guide fee, still piled where she'd left it.

She poked at the precious metals and gems until they created a meandering line from Kemberlan to the Shield's foothills.

Her eyes drooped.

*Sleepy.*

She set the bottle aside, leaning on the table.

Her knees buckled. Catching herself on the edge of the war table, she leaned over until she could roll onto it, curling up on her side.

*Just a little nap.*

UNABLE TO SLEEP, EREVAN returned to the library.

Memorizing the newer maps as well as the older tomes would be useful.

Would the Domini sell them to him?

*Copies would be better. Just a few pages.*

He paused in the shadowed hall.

A woman's melodic voice drifted along the plaster-covered walls.

He followed it to the library.

His keen hearing picked out the low words in the melody.

Old words.

An ancient melody that reminded him of home, but different.

The hairs on his body rose at the sound as he entered the room, bathed in flickering golden light.

Across the top of the war table lay a woman, one leg bent at the knee, while the other leg stretched a foot toward the warmth of the fireplace, toes wriggling.

Her red hair shone a burnished copper.

Her bare legs, below the pooled skirt at her upper thighs, looked like silken gold in the firelight. Her body was a softened mountain range of light and dark mysterious hills and valleys.

Donnen's bottle dangled from her fingertips as she hummed, rising to a mumble until the words became decipherable again.

*Where have I heard that before?*

*Home?*

Somewhere in his distant past.

She hummed and sighed, bending the knee with the warmed foot and stretching out the other.

Basking in the warmth of the hearth like a contented cat, lost in her song, she didn't hear him approach.

Below her, the maps remained strewn.

His gaze followed the line of titanium ingots, gold coins and gemstones from the tiny dot marking Kemberlan Keep toward the mountainous landscape where he wished to go.

Polished dark amber and cut orange diamonds marked a meandering line from the foothills toward the rising peaks, where one section in particular was littered with rubies and garnets.

He frowned at the imagery, invoking splashed blood on white snow.

"Mistress McLeighan?" He kept his voice low so as not to startle her.

Her head rolled in his direction. A grin spread across her flushed face. "Ah, there you are, you lovely man. I—I need a bit of help, if you would." She struggled to sit up.

Fearing she'd fall off the other side of the table, he quickly rounded it, hand extended to balance her.

Once she was upright, seated on the edge of the table, she poked him with a finger extended from the fist gripping the bottle.

"You're a gentleman."

"You're inebriated." He couldn't help the smile that tugged at the corner of his mouth.

She looked at the bottle as though he'd imparted some fascinating bit of knowledge. But then she shrugged. "'Cause of the Dwarven whiskey I had before this. They warned me." She sighed, swaying. "But I was having sush a shit week. You know how it is?"

Erevan wasn't sure how to respond.

She went on, arms sweeping out to either side of her. "Like a massive pile of steaming Torgolis shit. Massive, because those fuckers are big and eat *anything*."

He lifted a brow.

She scowled at him, giving him another poke. "Don't scowl at me like that. I get enough of that from Grimms."

"I'm not scowling."

"You, sir, are scowling. But that doesn't matter. What matters is my need to get out of this dress. I'm trapped."

"Trapped?"

"Yes," she said, as though it was obvious.

She blinked. Her free hand drifted up toward his face, fingers outstretched.

He didn't move.

His mouth went dry at the sudden change in the expression writ across her features.

Breath held, he waited to see what she would do as he studied her face. The freckles seemed even more endearing in present circumstances. There were faint scars slashed through one auburn brow and along the cheekbone below it, which he hadn't noticed before. The tightness of her mouth was gone. Her lips were soft and lush and inviting.

*She is beautiful.*

The surrounding air turned charged as they suddenly focused on one another, like when he gathered power to release an incantation.

Charged in a way he'd never experienced with any other person he'd met in his life.

Her fingertips didn't touch his ears, as he'd expected. Instead, they grazed along his markings, eliciting shivers of pleasure at the contact.

His magic flared, awakening, reacting to her magic.

Whatever that was.

Erevan closed his eyes against the onslaught of tempestuous emotions that ripped through him. He grasped for control of his emotions, so that he could control the magic.

She traced the permanent marks denoting a royal rank he no longer held, changing their meaning in some way, just by the act of touching them.

Touching him.

When no one had touched him in a long, long time.

This human woman he'd met just one day ago.

In a tavern, looking for a man to bed.

He opened his eyes as her thumb stroked over the corner of his mouth. His gaze found hers, then dropped to the low neckline of the gown which she remained trapped in, and lower still, to her bare legs dangling to either side of his hips.

Desire surged through him from her fingertips straight downward so fast it left him reeling.

*Too easy.*

Erevan returned his focus to her face.

"What magic do you have?" he whispered.

She shook her head. "I don't have magic." Her eyes searched his face. "You're so beautiful," she whispered, eyes trained on his lips. Her face tilted upward.

He hadn't realized he leaned over her until her fingers curled around his nape. Her inner thighs grazed his hips as she perched on the edge of the table.

Her tongue slid across her plump lower lip before she caught it between her teeth.

Magic and desire flared through and around him in a way he'd never experienced before.

He reached for her, fingers trembling as they slid along her cheek so that his thumb stroked over the silvered scar. His other hand slipped around her waist, dragging her forward so that there were no questions between them.

Strangers.

The heat of their bodies ignited something else. Something his desire and magic reacted to. And something more he couldn't yet name as his lips brushed across hers.

She met him, kiss for kiss.

Her lips parted, and he didn't hesitate at the invitation.

She moaned.

Fire raged through him.

He needed to stop before he lay her back on the table and claimed her completely, but he wasn't ready to give up the feel and taste of her mouth just yet.

His hand slid up over the open back of her dress. His fingertips grazed the bare flesh behind the laces securing the dress.

*Trapped.*

He released her face so that he could untie the back of the dress, hands splayed across the warm flesh. The other, newer scar he'd seen glimpses of before was raised and noticeable against his palms.

He distantly recalled the exchange between her and the innkeeper about a skirmish and a visit to a healer.

And her custom of finding a man for her bed before going home.

*So easy.*

The desire to embed himself in her warm body was so overwhelming, he shook with it.

Confusing him.

*'You're inebriated.'*

The first few cool drips of reason gathered in a thin stream, enough to displace the heat of his rising passion.

Not here. Not in his host's library.

*If I'm going to bed this woman, I'm going to bed her properly.*

He opened his eyes, easing away from her.

Her own eyes fluttered open, hand falling from his nape to her thigh.

He held her unfocused gaze for a moment. "You are no longer trapped, mistress. The knot is undone."

She blinked as though trying to clear her mind from a thick spell.

He stepped back, away from the heat of her bare thighs.

She looked down at the sagging bodice of her gown.

The fabric lay loosely draped over the tops of her generous breasts. Her skirt remained puddled over the tops of her creamy thighs.

Recalling that she still clutched the coloured wine bottle, she set it on the table, pushing it away. Her fingers drifted to her head as she teetered on the edge of the table.

"I'm so tired." She turned as though to lie back on the table.

"Let me help you to bed." Erevan swept her up into his arms, revelling in the few extra minutes of closeness as he carried her through the hall and up to the sleeping chambers.

She lay her head on his shoulder, relaxing into him.

With a few words, she directed him to her quarters.

His gaze flicked over the sparse room.

A simple cot, a small table with the empty whiskey bottle and several letters, a washbasin and jug in the corner, and an armoire next to the fireplace.

He left the door open as he moved through the room.

"Dress," she murmured as he set her on her feet. She wriggled so that it fell from her shoulders, caught on her hips before dropping to the floor.

Beneath it, she wore a thin silk shift that covered just enough.

As soon as he had her tucked under the coverlet, he retrieved the dress from the floor and stowed it away in the armoire, then added the abandoned slippers.

With a hand on the door latch, he paused for a last glimpse of her face.

"Thank you for freeing me," she mumbled before rolling over toward the wall.

"My pleasure," he murmured, closing the door behind him.

Alone in the corridor, he dragged a deep breath into his lungs, staring at his shaking hands.

His palms tingled, along with much of the rest of his body, magic far too close to the surface.

"Holy mother of goddesses, what in the hells was that?"

# SIX

SIOBHANN'S DREAMS WERE CHARGED with heated images of the elf, sensations of his body against hers and infused with the impression of being consumed by an inferno.

It was erotic and terrifying all at once.

She woke to a knock at her door and a muffled voice. "Mistress?"

Roan?

Her eyes snapped open, and she rolled to a seated position, quickly taking stock of where she was and when.

*My room. Alone. Undressed. Empty whiskey bottle.*

Head spinning.

A shadow beneath her door danced back and forth.

She closed her eyes and drew several slow, deep breaths.

"Yes?"

"You're needed downstairs."

"I'll be down shortly."

The shadow disappeared.

Siobhann moved toward the washbasin. In the armoire, her dress hung with the matching shoes set beneath it.

She stared at it for a long moment, turned back to glance at the empty bottle, then back to the dress.

The dreams.

The kiss, the heat, the raging desire.

*The elf.*

"Oh no."

Her fingertips drifted over her lips.

How much was a dream, and how much was reality?

She turned to look at her bed.

The linens weren't terribly disturbed so nothing much happened there... unless the event was *that* mundane...

No.

The library? She vaguely recalled... Donnen's wine.

*Shit.*

No time for that now.

Ignoring the discomfort in her skull, she dressed in her usual trousers, tunic, and boots, forgoing the rest of her gear, except for her favourite dagger.

She spared Sally and Trish a glance.

*Not today, ladies. I'm still on respite.*

At least not until she knew why she was needed downstairs.

Siobhann left her room, combing her fingers through her hair as she moved through the keep, braiding it as she descended the stairs to the main hall. Wrapping the bottom of the braid in a small strip of leather, she glanced around for the servant, who waited near the library where Donnen saw most of his visitors.

*This had better not be round two of why I have to guide that damned elf into the Shield.*

She entered the room, scowling.

"Rough morning?" Donnen stood, brow raised. His empty wine bottle stood on the corner of his desk.

She cleared her throat. "I'll pay you for that."

He waved a hand. "No matter, you earned it with that last assignment. In fact, you're probably going to need another one."

"Domini," she started, using his formal title. "I already said I wasn't going to the Shield."

They both glanced at the maps.

She frowned, moving toward the table. The ingots and gems glinted in the morning sun, detailing the route that she made the night before. The edges were creased over the far edge of the table.

Memories slammed through her, causing her skin to flush. She dry swallowed, staring at the table.

He *had* kissed her.

And she'd kissed him back and would have done so much more.

*Ashiel's toes, Siobhann!*

She suppressed a groan, praying Donnen didn't know she'd nearly bedded his royal guest on his war table.

"It's not about the Shield. Darya Kirin is here. She arrived just after dawn."

Siobhann spun around.

"Shit. Why?"

"Didn't say. Just asked for you. She's in the garden. I offered her a room to rest, but she refused until she speaks with you. Given her delicate condition, you may want to do that sooner rather than later."

Siobhann blinked.

Sendi's drawings and Darya's short message.

"She sent me a letter stating that her husband was missing."

Donnen's black and grey brows rose. "If General Kirin is missing, then this is a serious matter. I can send out ravens within the hour to call the others back."

"No. Let me talk to her first. Something about her letter makes me think she wants to handle this quietly, whatever is going on."

Donnen nodded. "Whatever she needs."

She nodded. "Thank you, sir."

His lips quirked. "Would you like me to help with your hangover before you go out there?"

Siobhann blew her breath out. "I deserve it. I finished off Grimms' whiskey before I started on your bottle."

Donnen winced, shaking his head at her. "You were warned."

"I was."

He waved her over, and she moved forward, grateful. He rubbed his palms together several times, murmuring before he placed one on her forehead and the other at her nape.

The heaviness and pounding and stabbing dissipated.

She sighed, smiling up at him.

Head clear, she went to meet her sister.

Her smile disappeared as she turned, and heaviness returned to her heart instead of her head this time as she passed through the library to the adjacent garden.

The morning sun shone brilliantly over the green space with its climbing aromatic flowers and clusters of varying rose bushes. The honeysuckle next to the door calmed her senses as she watched her sister watching Sendi as she chased a butterfly.

Several moments later, the little girl turned, her entire face lighting up. "Auntie Shebi!" She ran toward Siobhann, arms extended.

Siobhann barely registered the twinge in her back as she scooped her niece up into arms.

Sendi's arms gripped her hard, making her laugh.

Once she released her, she kissed her cheek. "Siobhann. Sendi, can you say 'She-von'? That's my name."

"Yes, auntie Shebi. She-bi." She grinned.

"You're a little button." Siobhann tweaked her nose as she set her down, walking toward the bench Darya sat on.

Sendi moved on to a peony bush.

Siobhann settled next to her sister, glancing at her rounded belly. "How long?"

Darya's hand swept over her belly. Her face was tight, lips compressed. "Just a few weeks."

"And we're hoping Papa will be home soon to help. He knows what to do with babies, which is good because I don't." Sendi put up her hands. "I like babies, but I like flowers better."

Siobhann chuckled as Sendi reached over to touch a shrivelled bud in the nearby bush.

Its brown edges uncurled, changing colour to match the rest of the petals. It plumped, turning its face toward the morning sun.

Siobhann gasped, turning wide eyes on Darya.

Darya didn't look proud or even pleased. Tears filled her eyes as she studied her daughter.

Siobhann glanced around the garden again, realizing that many of the blooming flowers were opened out of season. She'd been too distracted to realize something wasn't right. The garden was designed to bloom in cadence throughout the year. Every plant was at its peak. Even the honeysuckle wasn't supposed to be open. Or the roses.

*Sendi is a healer too.*

Like Darya.

Like their mother had been.

Siobhann swallowed a lump as she looked at her niece.

*The Empire will take her.*

"What happened?"

Darya's eyes lingered on Sendi until she moved to the far end of the enclosed garden.

"She was making everything grow, and I couldn't contain it. People were noticing. I didn't know what to do." She swallowed a sob.

Siobhann resisted the urge to comfort Darya as her heart pounded, waiting to hear the rest.

"I couldn't do it, Siobhann." Darya struggled with the words. "I couldn't do what Mama and I did to you. I saw what it did to you, and I couldn't do it again."

"Not to your daughter," Siobhann whispered, fighting against the memories that roared to the surface. She shook them from her head, controlling her emotions and thoughts the same way she did before going into battle.

The words hung between them.

Birds chirped from the overhead tree. Sendi laughed as she chased a frog hopping for the safety of a dewy herb bed.

Siobhann hadn't remembered much of 'that day' until Darya had unburied it during their last visit. Her sister's need to apologize for her part. She'd always had the night terrors, but in the months since they briefly spoke of it, they'd been more insistent. More frequent.

Darya went on. "Nate's been working with our neighbour, Elder Holtmann, learning how to carve. He'd been working on small projects that left a lot of surplus pieces."

"And?" Siobhann wasn't sure where this was going.

"So, we thought Sendi could channel her power into talismans. It's much subtler than sprouting flowers in the wrong season." Darya drew another breath. "You can't leave too many of them clustered together. They... react."

"I see."

"So, I gave them to the villagers who came to see me for poultices, tinctures, and teas." She turned to Siobhann with torment clear in her eyes. "I'm very careful about how and when I use my magic. Though it's never spoken of, they know what I do and they're very protective of me and of Nate. I know none of them gave us away. They wouldn't. Not on purpose."

"But?"

Darya wiped an escaped tear from her cheek. "Somehow, the new local reeve found one or two of the amulets and went on the hunt."

"Tracing them back to you?"

Darya nodded. "He's been... a little too interested in me since he arrived to take over from the old reeve."

"He threatened to report you?" Siobhann blew out her breath. "I told you to just get a permit, Darya."

"That would require a public admission to my ability and my identity."

Siobhann rubbed her hands over her face. "I know. I know you don't want to go back out into the field." She looked at Sendi. A public declaration for Darya would be an automatic investigation into any and all of her children.

"We both knew the threat was to separate us—Nate and me. When the reeve came to arrest me, Nate stepped in saying that he bought them elsewhere and was selling them."

"Which is also illegal without a permit." Siobhann ground out.

Darya nodded. "I don't know if the reeve believed it. I don't think he cared. It was the excuse he wanted to pull us apart. If it wasn't for the threat to Sendi, Nate would never have left me alone."

"If he wasn't such a fucking pacifist, he could have put a knife in the man's throat and got rid of him. You know I'd have come to help with that."

Darya's stare turned flinty as she stared at her sister. Very calmly, too calmly, she said, "He's had more than enough violence on the battlefield. We both have."

"So the Emperor's famous general lets some asshole get away with threatening his pregnant wife because he's gone soft? Coward."

Darya lifted her chin, holding Siobhann's angry stare. "It was a mistake coming to you." She gripped the edge of the bench to push herself to her feet.

All Siobhann could see was her sister's distended belly blocking her view of anything else.

This is about the children.

"What do you need me to do, Darya?"

"Nothing, I'll find someone else."

"I have every right to be fucking angry. But you *know* I will do what you need, otherwise you wouldn't have travelled through the night to be here at dawn. Now sit down and tell me the rest."

Darya clasped her hands over her belly, refusing to look at Siobhann. "He isn't a coward. He nearly died for this empire."

Siobhann didn't respond.

"He was taken away with other offenders. He should have been charged a fine for operating without a permit. Most of the others eventually returned to the village. The last accused that returned said that Nate had been moved from their holding cells two days before his own turn before the magistrate. That was weeks ago. He should have come back long before that."

"Let me guess. The doting reeve has been to visit your cottage nearly every day since your husband left?"

Darya nodded. She blew out a breath, rubbing her hands over her face. "I'd have gone after him myself if..."

"If you didn't have a child to care for with another, soon to come." Siobhann leaned back on the bench, looking up into the overhanging tree branches. "I'm on respite right now. I have a week that's my own, so I can leave today."

"Siobhann, I—,"

"No need. Donnen will be delighted to host you. I'll go ask a few quiet questions, find your husband, knock a few heads and bring him back before that baby comes." She was about to stand when she felt a light tap on her shoulder.

Behind her, Sendi reached a flower over her should. "I brought you a flower, Auntie Shebi."

Siobhann twisted to accept the gift. She grunted as pain arced down her back.

Sendi's small hand drifted across Siobhann's back as she moved.

Sendi frowned, looking at Darya. "Mama, Auntie Shebi has a bo-bo on her back."

Siobhann leaned forward. "I'm fine, just a scratch during a recent assignment," she said at Darya's look of concern.

"I make auntie Shebi feel better," Sendi splayed her hand, stretching it toward Siobhann's back.

Darya twisted on the bench, a look of horror etched across her face as she reached for her daughter. "No!"

Sendi side-stepped Darya, as Siobhann twisted away.

Neither woman was fast enough.

Sendi's little hand impacted Siobhann right between the shoulder blades like a thunderbolt.

Her lungs squeezed shut against the flare of pain that ricocheted between her back and chest bone, around her heart.

Darya's hands shoved her to the ground, breaking the connection too late, as Siobhann fell into the terrors.

"Mama?"

Siobhann dimly heard Sendi's terrified voice... or was it Darya's from her memories long ago?

EREVAN PACED HIS GUEST room above the library, overlooking the idyllic garden.

Chest bare, dressed in loose trousers, he centred himself in the small room to work through the meditative movements.

Again.

Confusion over his intense reaction to the human woman meant he'd had less sleep than his usual few hours.

His muscles bunched and stretched through the controlled motions.

He'd gone back to the library to review the maps and atlas, thinking he'd go on his own if he had to, even though he was reluctant to waste more time than necessary.

*I'm so close.*

*Then I can just go home.*

All he needed was the best path to the temple that he was sure Nolgan was bound for.

There had to be one in the Shield.

This was the last part of his long journey to finish things. For good.

*How many times have I told myself that over the years?*

*I can't waste weeks wandering through ice-locked mountains.*

*And my closest opportunity is a rude mercenary that seems to have an intense dislike for me.*

It had been a surprise to find the irate woman splayed out on the war table like a festival feast, bathed in the warm glow of the hearth fire.

Singing that song that tickled his long memory, drawing him closer like a siren, igniting his magic.

*'I have no magic.'*

Which didn't make sense.

*I felt it.*

He'd felt it that first moment when she'd entered the tavern and sat next to him.

The intense draw and press of energy surrounding him—both of them.

*Especially last night.*

His hands tingled at the memory.

The sensual feel of her mixed with the sensation of the raw power moving through him.

Her soft and supple body. The smooth lines of her bare legs, the exposed tops of her creamy breasts.

He growled as his own body responded to the memories.

This wouldn't do, especially if he still had any hope of convincing her to guide him into the Shield.

*It isn't like she's Elvenkind. It wouldn't mean anything to her.*

He closed his eyes against the recollection of his need to claim her in those heated moments.

*None of this makes any sense.*

Without the alcohol, she was all sharp words and coiled muscle, especially toward him.

*'You're so beautiful,'* she'd said to him in her drunken state.

He smirked. The smirk quickly faded, also recalling he'd thought the same of her.

Without the inebriation.

He sighed, turning back to the window.

*So?*

There was some attraction between them.

A pretty face. And a lovely posterior.

*It doesn't matter. What matters is finally ending things with this journey.*

Finished, though unsuccessful in balancing his thoughts, he leaned a hip on the window ledge, watching the little girl spiralling about the garden while Mistress McLeighan spoke to another woman who bore her a strong resemblance.

Maybe someday he could go home and look down on his own garden, with his own red-haired, freckled children.

He blinked, spinning away from the window.

*Ridiculous.*

"The sooner I commission copies of both the key atlas pages and the maps, the sooner to be on my way. Alone. If necessary."

*Better alone...*

He returned to the window, frowning. Every flower was in bloom.

That couldn't be right.

It hadn't been so the previous day when he looked out over the garden.

He studied the child more closely as she touched a peony bush.

*Ah.*

He nodded.

*She has the power.*

He continued to watch with some curiosity. The interaction between the women was tense. The pregnant woman stood, clearly angry as the exchange continued. She sat next to Mistress McLeighan when the child rounded the bench, offering up a bloom.

The woman's wince was clearly visible as she turned to accept the gift.

*The wound on her back.*

Erevan's breath caught as the child moved to place her tiny hand on Siobhann's back. The child's mother shoved Siobhann away, but it was too late.

Power, intense and raw and fierce, blasted through the air like an incendiary, washing over him with a frizzling effect, igniting him.

His entire body went rigid against the single pulse that ripped through the air before the contact was broken.

Every one of his markings burned along his taut body. His vision flared infrared as it did during an incantation.

He shook, overwhelmed with power that needed to be diffused before he blew Kemberlan apart.

Sweat slicked his body from head to toe as his heart raced.

He recited the words of dissipation over and over until the inferno that threatened to consume him abated enough to approach the unlit hearth. He dropped to his knees, pressing his hands to the stack of dry logs, easing the fire through him, containing it, controlling it until the logs shrivelled to white ash.

With a soft puff of powdered cloud, he dispelled the rest harmlessly into the ether around him.

Chest still heaving from the effort, he rolled from his knees onto the floor, allowing the smooth stone to cool his body as his vision returned to normal.

Lifting a trembling arm, he confirmed his markings had also returned to normal.

"What the fuck just happened?"

# SEVEN

Erevan rolled to his feet, pulled on his tunic and ran down to the garden.

Donnen Kember was already there, kneeling over Mistress McLeighan's inert form.

The other woman knelt next to him while the child clutched her mother's arm, crying.

"She needs a dreamwalk," Donnen growled.

"No! You can't, it's too dangerous."

Donnen's face was thunderous as he glared at the woman.

"Just ease her pain. She'll come out of the terrors. She always does," she said, voice tight.

There was no denying the resemblance between the women. And the child.

"I'll work around her crown. You tend her solar plexus. Just do not apply energy to where her heart is."

"I recall your warnings, Mistress Kirin. And I'm telling you she can't continue like this. She needs a dreamwalker."

"I know she does, but we can't let that happen."

Erevan stepped forward. "What's happening?"

Mistress Kirin looked up at him, startled, taking in his appearance with a glance. "Nothing, sir. My sister fainted. No need for alarm."

His eyes narrowed at her lie.

The instinct to protect the unconscious woman snarled through him.

"At least let me help you move her somewhere more comfortable until she awakens." He moved in beside Donnen before either of them began working to heal Siobhann. He picked her up with ease, cradling her in his arms as he strode into the library, bypassing the table.

His heart quickened in his chest as he felt every minute spasm of her muscles and hitch of her breath. With his arm across her back, every rapid beat of her heart pulsed against his forearm.

"Here, there is a settee in my office," Donnen led them through a panelled door in the library that opened to a smaller room.

Erevan lay Siobhann down as gently as he might with a shattered sculpture.

Donnen's face remained pale and focused as he moved back into place, while Mistress Kirin did the same at Siobhann's head.

The softest touch drew Erevan's attention downward.

The child slid one tiny hand into his. Thumb in mouth, eyes wide as she watched.

Mistress Kirin and Domini Kember murmured to one another as they worked.

"The wound on her back was severe. I feel the healer's work still trying to knit the muscle where the poison damaged the flesh," Donnen said.

"Why didn't she come to one of us?"

"I think she's had enough of both of us harping at her. Besides, didn't you two have some sort of falling out a while back?"

"That doesn't matter," Kirin snapped.

"Clearly it does," Donnen countered.

"You shouldn't be letting her take dangerous assignments so often."

The child gripping Erevan's hand sobbed, pressing her face to his sleeve. He picked her up to offer better comfort.

"She's an adult, Darya. She does as she pleases."

"You don't need to keep enabling her to destroy herself."

"If you hadn't—,"

"Enough." Erevan's unraised voice cut across the room.

Both healers snapped their attention in his direction and equally noticed the upset child clinging to him.

Darya Kirin's face flushed. She blinked away tears but didn't dare remove her hands from her sister.

Donnen cleared his throat. "We will continue this discussion later, Darya." His voice brooked no argument.

Erevan moved around the room, looking for some object to distract the little girl. Across the room, he found a collection of spheres and stars suspended from several interconnected dowels and strings. "Look," he whispered. "A model of the heavens."

Sniffling, the child turned her face to see what he was talking about. Removing her thumb from her mouth, she poked a finger at the largest one at the centre, painted gold and red. It had a twin at the model's furthest reach.

"The sun?"

"It is. And this one too." He pointed at the far away twin, which was actually much smaller than the closer one. It, too, had many spheres dangling around it. "They can't see each other right now, but sometimes they get closer and visit."

"Like Mama and Auntie Shebi?" she gasped, "Do they argue too?"

He considered the question, darting a glance toward the settee. He whispered, "Sometimes they do make one another rumble. And sometimes they get along well and make new things that bring joy to everyone."

The child nodded. "I like to make new things too."

"I saw that from my window. You made the flowers bloom, and that's very special." He studied her little face and considered some of the local customs he'd seen since his arrival in the Aelozian Dominion. "It's so special, I think it's just a special secret for you and your mama."

"And Auntie Shebi and Papa. And the new baby."

"Right."

"She's sleeping now." Donnen said, as he rose from his kneeling position on the floor, then helped Darya to her feet, and to a padded chair to sit.

"She can't go on like this."

"I agree," Donnen said, solemn.

"Mama, the sun has a sister too!"

"Is that right, Sendi?"

Sendi wriggled to get down.

Erevan obliged.

"According to the Dwarven texts, it is." Donnen confirmed.

"According to Elven custom, it is, too," Erevan said.

Donnen nodded. "Grimms was the first to tell me about the partnership one night when he was reciting ancient Dwarven war stories.

Siobhann groaned as her eyes fluttered open. "What happened?"

"You fainted," Sendi said cheerfully.

Darya and Donnen exchanged glances that Siobhann didn't miss.

She frowned at them, then noticed Erevan's presence when she sat up. Her cheeks turned a deep shade of peach as she flicked her gaze away from him. "Well, that is most inconvenient, isn't it?" she said to the little girl. "You're all in here doting over me when you should be outside playing in the sunshine."

"Both of them!" Sendi said hopping.

"Both?" Siobhann turned confused eyes to Donnen.

"The sun's sister. Grimms' story; apparently, it's Elven too."

"And they visit and argue and make nice things, just like you and Mama!" Sendi held out her hands, palms up, excited about her newfound knowledge.

"That's... good to know." Siobhann struggled to stand. "Well, I'm going to ask Roan to get Odyn ready while I gather my things."

"Ashiel's toes, Siobhann, where are you going?" Donnen thundered.

*Ashiel's toes?*

Siobhann spared a glance in Darya's direction. "Seems The General was arrested and his wife would like him back. Don't worry, I'm just going to ask a few questions."

"At least wait until morning, Siobhann," Darya pleaded. "Please."

"No..." she paused a long moment as the sisters exchanged stares. "I think now is a good time to start on the trail."

Erevan didn't think. "I'll go with you."

Siobhann gaped at him. "You're not serious? Why?"

"You could run into trouble." He ignored the sting of her rejection.

"Always do. And?" Her familiar scowl slammed back into place.

"And it's better than going alone," Donnen said. "Lorne, Nirran and Veira are still on a scouting mission for the emperor and won't be back for weeks. Ghalen is still stuck in the Capitol and everyone else is scattered on other assignments. I can't leave your sister here alone, and Grimms... well, we both know Grimms doesn't leave his forge anymore."

"Again, why?" Siobhann demanded, stubbornly.

"Consider it fair payment for information about the Shield before I go. Without a guide, I'll need to know all I can."

"You can't go into the Shield alone," Darya blurted, "That's insanity."

"Madam, I will do as I must."

"If the Torgolis don't eat you before you accomplish your goal. They'll eat anything and anyone."

"So I've been told," his lips quirked.

"They eat people?" Sendi shifted closer to her mother.

"You musn't worry, Button." Siobhann tapped her niece's nose with a smile. "They live far, far away and prefer their side of the mountains."

"You aren't going too, are you?"

"Flowers don't grow there. I much prefer to stay here with you, where they do."

Sendi's face lit up, dispelling the worry.

"Domini?" A new voice pulled their attention to the open door between the study and the library.

"Yes, Alda?"

"Lunch is ready in the dining hall."

Donnen nodded, reaching out a hand toward Sendi. "Shall we go fill our bellies?"

She giggled, taking his hand.

Once they were through the door, Darya turned to her sister. "Are you well enough to travel so soon after..."

"Fainting?" She quirked an auburn brow as her voice turned acidic. "I feel fine. And apparently I might have a chaperon, so you have no need to worry about me."

Anguish twisted Darya's face.

Siobhann blew out a breath. "You can't go. And the past is the past. Go eat."

She waited while Darya struggled to her feet.

About to follow her sister out of the room, she turned to Erevan as though just recalling he was still there. Casting her sister a quick glance, she dropped her voice. "If you help me get my brother-in-law back to his wife and child in one piece, I promise I will find you the best guide to take you into the Shield. I still know a few who are crazy enough to go. And I'll throw in a bit of payment of my own. I have a few titanium ingots stashed away."

Erevan raised a brow as he stared down into her determined face. "Are you trying to turn me into a mercenary, too?"

She shrugged. "Call it what you want. The pay is fair. I'm assuming you're capable with a weapon of some kind, if you made it all the way here from wherever you came from in one piece."

"Myst Innys. And I am capable."

"Then you'll be paid for your services. I'm famished," she said, turning to go.

His stomach chose that moment to grumble, so he followed, noting how her fingers shook as she reached out to touch the door frame on her way through it.

# EIGHT

SIOBHANN SAID LITTLE TO her new travelling companion throughout lunch and afterward.

After their meal, Donnen attempted to dissuade her just once, mumbling about leaving Grimms alone again so soon and so on.

She brushed his arm affectionately. "I'll be fine, Domini. I'll bring my ravens along for communication, as I always do, and I'll check in on Grimms. Besides, with Darya here, I expect Kwayssi will remain nearby too."

The older man nodded, tugging on the edge of his short beard. "I will admit, Darya isn't wrong about her concerns, Siobhann. You take far too many unnecessary risks."

Siobhann snorted. "Just yesterday, you asked me to guide your Elven friend into the Shield, and now you're concerned about a quick jaunt to Darya's place?"

Donnen's face flushed. "Yes, well, that was before, your uhm—,"

"Fainting spell?" She lifted a brow. "From what Darya explained to me about the circumstances, it isn't likely to happen again."

"You can't be sure of that."

Siobhann shrugged. "I can't be sure of anything in life, can I? You and Grimms ingrained that into me from the moment you took me in."

He sighed, caught in his own weave again.

She smiled, voice lighter, she said, "Except for you and Grimms and the Kindred of Kemberlan."

Domini Donnen Kember chuckled. "Well played. As always, ensure you're well supplied. And His Highness, too. I've given him back his guide fee. Make sure he isn't robbed."

Siobhann rolled her eyes. "Yes sir. Though he said he was capable."

"You believe him?"

She nodded, though she wasn't sure why.


Hours later, she spared her companion's dark form a glance.

It was late. The trees blocked out the moonlight, creating a black tunnel in the darkness of the road.

The way was quiet in the hours before dawn, though she was vigilant for trouble hidden amongst the forest. The Elven prince had enough metals and gems to build a village and stock it with everything a soul could want or need.

Although she could barely see his outline, her body was hyper-aware of his presence.

That odd sensation continued, making her extremities tingle when they got too near.

She analyzed that, to keep her thoughts away from that morning's unexpected black out.

*You're fine, Siobhann. It won't happen again...*

And yet, it had taken hours for the trembling to dissipate from her body.

"Why are you here?" Her voice sounded especially loud after travelling so long in silence.

The prince's voice returned, soft in the darkness. "I told you, mistress. I need a guide to the mountains and I was told Domini Kember had a reliable collection of maps and guides."

In the blackness of the night and the closeness of the forest, the slight roll of his speech sent a shiver through her.

*Best not talk any more than necessary.*

Instead, she turned her thoughts to the task at hand.

A skeezy reeve manipulating the situation, forcing his attention on her pregnant sister and doing away with her husband.

Should be easy enough to scare information out of him, find the man in question, and trot him home to his doting wife.

They arrived at a split in the road. "This way. Darya's cottage isn't far. We can rest there for a few hours."


The moon rode the treetops when Siobhann guided Odyn around the lilac bush that marked the path to the quaint stone cottage that Darya had bought with her service medal. The new slate, which had replaced the thatched roof since her last visit, had weathered the recent storm well.

The same storm that had ravaged Kemberlan had swept right across the region, leaving many homeless. These high velocity storms were becoming more frequent in the last few years. It seemed as though they were constantly repairing one part of the keep or another due to storm damage.

She dismounted Odyn and led him to the shelter behind the cottage. The Elven prince followed her, tending his stallion in silence, murmuring to him as he worked. Much like she did with Odyn.

Neither horse complained about being hobbled together as their people unloaded their supplies and equipment.

Bags slung over her shoulders and saddle in hand, Siobhann surveyed the property before heading toward the back door.

Always alert, nothing appeared out of order.

The forest thrived around the cottage, held back by the simplest of wooden fences to safeguard the vegetable and herb patches sectioned off at ground level and bordered by raised boxes.

Darya's livelihood.

Pushing the door open, she stepped inside and paused, to listen and scan the space for intruders. Anyone could have observed Darya's departure and come in to take what they wanted, not that she kept much of value. Not that that would stop anyone, anyway.

The house was silent save for the cricket song drifting in from outside. She set her equipment by the door and moved further inward to light a lantern.

That done, she swept the room again, then moved into the bedroom. Nothing was visibly out of place.

She smiled when her gaze landed on Sendi's little trundle bed set next to the crib that Elder Holtmann had made before she was born, now ready for the new baby.

More stick-figure drawings lay stacked on a table beside her bed.

No matter how strained her relationship with her sister was, Darya's children were precious to Siobhann.

Perhaps more so, knowing she would never have her own and she doubted their brother, Garioch, would ever make room for fatherhood. Even if the McLeighan name died out, at least their bloodline—the right branch of their bloodline—would continue on with Darya's babies.

Not a privilege that Siobhann could risk.

Siobhann dismissed the turn of her thoughts. "You can sleep in Darya's bed tonight."

"Where will you bed down?" The elf approached, glancing over her head into the simple room.

His personal scent mingled with those of the forest, drifted toward her at his proximity.

She leaned against the edge of the door frame, mindful of her healing wound. "I'll be fine by the hearth for a few hours. I'll visit the neighbours once the sun is a decent height for socializing." She gestured toward a set of heavy chairs padded with thick cushions, paired with carved footstools, which were also new since her last visit.

The carved patterns were distinctly different from that of the crib.

*Nate's getting better.*

"You take the bed. I'll rest here." Erevan's rich voice curled around Siobhann.

They faced each other within the arch of the open door.

"You can't believe that Darya wouldn't flay me alive if I didn't insist that a royal Elven guest sleep comfortably in her home. No, I will sleep here and preserve my peace of mind and my hide."

The golden lamp glow flickered over the tanned planes of his face as one corner of his lips lifted. A brow flicked upward.

With her gaze trained on his sensuous mouth, desire ripped through her. Her breath hitched as she swayed toward him.

All day and throughout the night's ride, she hadn't been sure she hadn't dreamed about the kiss in the library.

She blinked.

Of course it was a drunken dream.

*Why in any of the hells would an Elven prince dare to pay any attention to a scarred and angry base-born human nobody such as me?*

And yet, his presence enveloped her, drawing her inevitably toward him, like no other ever had.

*Not like this.*

Was it that Elven woo-woo she'd heard of? Some form of mesmer? A glamour to entice unwary humans?

*You don't like elves, remember? They're untrustworthy.*

*Do I care?*

Her gaze lingered on his perfectly sculpted lips, desperate to make last night's dream real.

*I don't need to trust him to bed him.*

His warm fingers drifted to her face, ghosting over the old scars on her brow and cheekbone.

Breath held, she remained still under his scrutiny.

Erevan's thumb slid across the ridge of her lower lip. "Last night you said I was beautiful."

His touch ignited a spark through her.

Siobhann swallowed a breath and murmured, "Did I?"

The space between them narrowed, making her skin come alive as it did when too close to a heat source.

A warning?

Or an invitation?

Her gaze flicked up over his features as the space between them continued to diminish.

At the intensity of his gaze on her face, her breath locked in her chest.

Her heart pounded as her anticipation soared.

He didn't close the distance.

"Care to remind me of what else I may have expressed?"

The corner of his mouth curled as his warm fingers slid along her jaw, tilting her head to the perfect angle as his lips grazed hers.

The earlier spark flared as their breaths mingled during the contact.

That was all it took to ignite her entire body, leaving her breathless as he savoured her.

She wanted him to consume her in a way she'd never wanted anyone to consume her before.

The notion thrilled and terrified her at once.

*It's just a kiss, Siobhann.*

But it wasn't, not really.

Somewhere deep in the back of her consciousness, some buried part of her took notice.

Ignoring it, she gave in to the physical sensations, shutting out any emotional triggers or logical interferences.

He was a man—an Elven man.

She pressed her body to his, confirming all she needed to know.

His hand slid around her waist and splayed across the small of her back, pressing her ever closer, his desire obvious against her belly.

His warm tongue teased along her lip.

She opened to him, losing herself.

Unable to get enough, she pushed at his coat, then the vest. The buttons of his shirt gave way under her nimble fingers to reveal the expanse of his hard planed chest.

As she reached for the buttons of his trousers, his fingers caught hers, linking them together, and he pinned their hands above her head as his mouth descended along the column of her throat to her collarbone, eliciting a moan.

Releasing her hands, his fingers slipped through the knots to release the lacing of her bodice, giving way for his palms to slide up under the fabric of her shift to cover her breasts.

Her head fell back against the door frame, her hands dropped to his shoulders as he nuzzled and nipped the sensitive flesh below her ear.

Her hands slid through his silky black hair until her fingers grazed the edge of his ears.

He growled against her throat.

His hands returned to her face, cradling her jaw and throat.

He lifted his head, pinning her with his heated gaze.

The desire glittered, masking something else she couldn't decipher.

The gold markings denoting his Elven station seemed brighter than she recalled.

*Danger.*

The warning prickled along her nape and down her body.

She ignored it as he glanced toward the bed.

His low voice rolled through her. "I nearly accepted your invitation last night. Were it not for the circumstances..."

Her face still cradled in his grasp, she turned so that she could place a kiss on the pad of his thumb, then drew it between her lips, suckling. She swirled her tongue around the calloused ridge and released him.

His throat worked as he swallowed before claiming her mouth again and pressing her back into the door frame.

She gasped as pain twinged along her wound. She dismissed it with a grunt. Instead, she took control of the kiss and slid her knee up to his hip.

Erevan slid his hands under her bottom, pulling her up against him, supporting her weight.

He carried her to the bed as though she weren't a full-grown woman made of bone, solid muscle and a few soft curves.

Clearly stronger than most human men she'd known, he handled her with the utmost care, despite the urgency rising between them.

In moments they divested each other of their clothing with deft hands and sweeping glances, admiring one another's bodies.

Siobhann's fingers slid around Erevan's nape, pulling him down atop her, tongues entwined.

Supporting himself on his elbows, he broke the kiss and held her gaze, reading her. His hands slid under her back, curled around her shoulders.

The intensity in his expression sent another surge of desire through her body. She was more than ready for him.

Her fingers brushed the silky hair from his face, tucking it back behind his ears. She studied his face as she caressed the tips and outer shell. He closed his eyes as a shudder wracked his powerful body.

"You shouldn't do that," he said, voice strained.

It was her turn to smirk, brow quirked.

She slid one hand down between them to grasp his erection while the other stroked his ear.

He murmured words she couldn't understand.

Everything about him was intoxicating.

His beauty, his scent, the sound of his voice, the taste of his kiss, the gentle way he touched her, the heated atmosphere that drew them closer.

She stroked him as she drew him closer to her entrance.

He didn't enter her with a frenzy of need, though his body remained rigid with self-control.

With his hot tip at her moist entrance, he held her gaze.

Her fingers caressed his ear.

He closed his eyes and turned to press a kiss to her palm.

The gentleness of the gesture tugged at the distant part of her.

Ignoring it, she rolled her hips against his, pulling him into her.

He allowed it, sinking, filling.

She gasped as her world went white, struggling against a surge so raw and blinding and terrifying her eyes flew open into his strained face.

His eyes opened into hers, his irises ringed with brilliant gold, like his markings. Flecks, like embers, glittered in the blackest part of his eyes.

She had the sensation that he really could consume her, as he struggled against himself.

Or that she could consume him.

'What magic do you have?' he'd asked her.

The atmosphere of the room crackled.

Fear sliced through the overwhelming desire, urging her to take control, shoving the beast away.

But whose? Her beast or his?

She didn't care as she gave into her body's needs.

Siobhann should have been terrified by what she'd seen, but she wasn't.

She shoved him over onto his back but held him firmly encased inside of her.

His hands scalded down her back to her hips.

She shuddered against the sensation, then grasped his fingers with her own.

Palm to heated palm, it was her turn to pin his hands above his head. Her breasts pressed to his chest. She reclaimed his mouth as she rolled her hips.

His fingers grasped hers so hard she thought the bones might shatter. Still, she rode him as he rose to meet her, colliding, ascending ever higher.

She crested, gripping him so hard that when he followed seconds later, she savoured every spasm within her.

The haze of desire and power dissipated.

The heat of Erevan's palms against hers returned to normal.

The buried beast within her returned to sleep with a sigh.

When she released his grasp, he pulled her into his embrace, whispering more words she didn't understand but in some way soothed that deeply buried part of her. Her head nestled against the muscle of his shoulder as they caught their breaths and their bodies cooled.

Her fingertip drifted over his chest.

His fingers slid through her hair, toying with the strands.

Despite being deeply sated, the ether surrounding them remained charged.

Whatever had just happened, as glorious as it was, could never, ever happen again.

The last time she'd bedded a magic handler, he'd nearly lost control of his power, but she never had.

Something about the Elven prince threatened the spell binding her.

*A tomorrow problem.*

For now, she let sleep overtake her.

# NINE

ErEVAN watched Siobhann's face, deep in sleep.

The single window in the room allowed the early dawn light to filter in.

Surely by now, he'd memorized every freckle and scar on her creamy skin. In sleep, her features were so relaxed, her lips enticed him with their softness.

Her rest was sound, bearing none of the struggles he'd witnessed in her before.

She appeared... vulnerable.

*Be careful, Erevan. You have your own path to follow, which diverges with the Shield.*

*Does it?*

He suppressed the whisper. The instinct telling him otherwise. Teasing him with chivalric notions from a lost time.

*I cannot take a human woman as a mate. No matter that I'm no longer heir to my clan's throne. It isn't done.*

The whirlwind of desire and power in those last moments after their arrival at the cottage had taken him off guard.

Such a sudden flare of desire.

Every encounter with her set him off balance in a way that he regained it with a new footing.

*What is it about her that claims some hold over his magic like that?*

Each time, the fuse shortens.

Her eyes fluttered behind her closed lids before opening to his gaze.

*It's just curiosity. It will burn itself out soon enough.*

She shifted, resting her chin on her hand atop his chest so she could study his face. He noted the slight trembling of her fingers.

Erevan ignored the desire to address the cause of her discomfort and cast it out of her mind.

"So, *Your Majesty*, what magic do *you* have?" Her voice was light, but a frown marred her pretty brow as she turned his own question on him.

He slid his thumb over her brow, smoothing the worry lines.

*She didn't panic.*

She hadn't recoiled in horror from him when his magic had come to the surface.

Aside from the mages at the academy, nearly everyone else that had witnessed the slightest display of his power had.

But then, she had deeply held secrets of her own.

Secrets he meant to learn.

The power that she denied having whispered to his.

"Seems my power may not be so different from your own?"

She withdrew from him with deliberate movements. The air between them cooled immediately.

"I have no magic," she repeated, tone low and strained.

"Hmm." He propped his arm behind his head, watching as she found her shift and pulled it over her head, covering her lush body from his view. The stirrings of desire returned. He ignored it.

"Get some sleep, Your Highness." She stooped to grab the rest of her clothing and boots before moving into the common area of the cottage.

He closed his eyes. He still had a few days yet to figure her out.

SIOBHANN HADN'T GONE BACK to sleep on the chair, though they were comfortable enough when she sat on one to lace up her boots. Instead, she perused the small collection of carved artifacts adorning the few surfaces and free spaces on the walls.

Nate's projects mingled with Sendi's drawings and Darya's drying herbs. There were many pieces that bore similarities between Nate's work and those pieces that Elder Holtmann had paid Darya with for her healing services. The evolution between Holtmann's teachings and Nate's style was obvious.

She picked up a game piece from the table set between the two chairs.

She grudgingly admitted to herself that Nate was good at carving and could see the usefulness of turning cast offs into gaming pieces and talismans.

Though talismans were illegal without permits, it made sense to try to find a way to help Sendi channel her talents in the most discreet way that her mother knew of.

As children, Darya had been taken to the sisterhood while their brother, Garioch, was sent to the imperial military academy. Female and magic-absent, Siobhann was shoved over the threshold of a regional orphanage.

At the sisterhood, there'd been no need for discretion. Darya's training involved a high level of prestige and respect, which had accompanied her all throughout her commendable career as a military medic at the front.

Now, discretion meant the difference between Sendi's freedom and a forced induction into the sisterhood, like her mother.

Siobhann replaced the game piece on the table. Elder Holtmann was Darya's fiercest ally in town. She'd patched him up often enough. No doubt the old man would have been dead years ago, were it not for Darya's gifts with herbs and poultices—and magical encouragements to stave away infection.

She smiled, spirits lifting at the thought of a visit with the rough old woodsman. Busier than a town gossip, Holtmann knew everything that went on in the district.

'My woods, my business,' he'd said.

She picked up several of the small bundles that Darya always had set aside for the old man.

Retrieving her weapon belts from where she'd set them with her pack, she fastened and straightened them in place.

There hadn't been any reports of raiders in the district for a few years—not since Nate had rallied the militia into fortifying their defenses properly. But that didn't mean there couldn't be some other threat during the quarter hour walk required to reach Holtmann's house.

She quickly pulled a small pouch of oats from her saddlebags, leaving the riding equipment behind. A quick peek into the bedroom confirmed her Elven bedmate slept soundly. Her gaze swept his relaxed form, still naked atop the bed, arm slung behind his head.

Her heart rate sped up and tripped at the thought of bedding him again.

*No.*

She turned away and silently made her way out to the hobbled horses. Offering each a few handfuls of oats, she whispered to them. "You two behave. I'm just going next door for a little bit. His Majesty is still inside."

Kelstorm huffed while Odyn nuzzled her. "I'll be careful," she promised, pressing her forehead to his.

While still early, she could see well enough to find and follow the worn path that connected the Kirin homestead to their elderly neighbour's. The sky above the treetops still had a rosy hue when she walked out of the wood toward the old man, smoking his morning pipe and rocking in the sturdy chair he'd made himself.

"Mistress McLeighan. Come to look after the reeve problem, are ye? Mistress Kirin made it safe with the wee one?"

"They did and I am. Darya gave me the basics. Care to fill me in?" She placed the herb bundles on his palm.

The old man squinted at her from beneath bushy brows as his gnarled fingers curled over the linen satchels. "You two still quarreling?" His voice held more than a measure of disgust. "Ye're sisters. Whatever happened or who said what, get over it before you're both too old and too full of regrets, or too dead to do anything about it."

"It's not that simple—," she bristled.

"Nothing's simpler. Ye care about each other, ye fix it." He pointed the stem of his pipe at her, eyes glittering.

Siobhann drew a breath and counted before she sniped at the elderly man who loved Darya dearly and only meant well for the both of them. "I suppose you're speaking from experience."

"I am," he growled, replacing the stem of his pipe between his lips.

"How is your nephew?" she asked as she settled on the low step, looking out over the scrubby yard before them.

"Still missing,"

Siobhann jerked her gaze up to the old man's. "Missing? How long?"

"Since before The General was arrested. He'd gone to visit his parents beyond the village as he does every couple of months, to appease his mother's worries that he's hale and healthy."

"Until he isn't." Siobhann said.

The old man grunted.

Noting the tightness of his mouth, rubbing her hands over her face, she said, "My apologies, Elder. When was Kit last seen?"

He nodded, accepting her apology. "He passed a neighbour between his mother's house and the village."

"I've come to inquire after my brother-in-law's predicament, but clearly you have your own concerns. I will help if I can." She drummed her fingers on her knee. "As I recall, he's a capable young man. Can handle himself in the wood?" She'd met him a couple of times. Kit Bower was a tall, strong, curly-haired young man, not yet twenty. She ran through the possibilities that could result in his disappearance. He hadn't seemed disgruntled to be living and apprenticing with the old woodsman. Just the opposite. His easy-going manner, respect for his elderly uncle and enthusiasm to share his newfound knowledge had stuck with her when he visited Nate.

"He can. Taught him all that I know, and he knows the distance between here and his mother's farm better than anyone." His pride in the young man made his voice gruff. "Like my own boy, he is. But you're here for The General."

"I'll see what I can find out about Kit all the same."

"I appreciate it." He pursed his lips. "The reeve and his men came here asking questions about Master Kirin and his family and their strange habits. '*Habits?*' I asked them what they were meaning by that. Wanted to know if he was peddling illegal trinkets. Said he'd heard complaints from registered vendors." The old man grumbled. "Ain't no legal magic trinket vendors in this area. No one bothers with that around here, not really. And besides, I told him Master Kirin is a respected merchant, carrying wares for his aunt. And I know she has permits for anything one can think of selling. But Nate," the old man shrugged. "He's a good man, sees to his family, keeps to himself, uses his talents where he can."

"Like the fortifications before the frontier was pushed back."

"Aye, just like. It's that new reeve causing trouble."

Siobhann lifted a brow and leaned closer. "What kind of trouble?"

"Strutting through town like he owns the place. Well, sure, he handles business for the magistrate since he was appointed, but he ain't no elected official. He hasn't earned the respect of the locals, he's too busy poking his nose in places it don't belong. And Mistress Kirin? He's been hounding our poor Darya, with a babe coming! And that little girl needs her father. Everyone knows the reeve's the one that had Master Kirin arrested on ridiculous charges of magic peddling. There isn't a soul hereabouts that would sling such accusations at Nate Kirin."

The wrinkled skin of the old man's cheeks flushed, eyes wide as his voice rose with his indignation. But the way his throat worked, and his fingers played over the bowl of his pipe, told Siobhann what she'd suspected.

He knew about Sendi. How many others did as well?

"Anyone you ask would have nothing but respectable things to say about the Kirin family. But that new reeve? He ain't right."

Siobhann blinked.

"You'll see what I mean when you go talk to him." Leaning forward, he pointed the stem of his pipe at her. "And I wouldn't be surprised if he had something to do with my nephew's disappearance, too."

She straightened at that, studying him closely.

A conspiracy?

Perhaps the old man had been alone in the woods a little too long. "I'm sure there's a reasonable explanation for Kit's absence. Maybe he met a young lady."

Elder Holtmann eyed Siobhann for a long moment, then slowly settled back into his rocking chair. His open demeanour turned guarded.

"No reason to hide such a thing, or runaway without a word to his family, or to me."

"Maybe so. Perhaps he had some other reason."

"Not Kit," he barked, eyes glittering. "No one else around here will tell you any different than what I just said about Master Kirin. Pay the reeve a visit."

At his dismissal, Siobhann rose to her feet. "Thank you for your time. I'll ask after Kit."

"Appreciate it," he ground out around the stem of his pipe.

She hadn't walked half a dozen paces when he called, "Ye said our Darya and Sendi are safe?"

She turned back to the old man. He'd returned to the edge of his rocker. "Yes, sir. She's at Kemberlan with the Domini, and Kwayssi is on her way."

He nodded. "Good. That is good." He slid back into his chair, returning the pipe to his lips.

Siobhann returned to Darya's cottage, and went back into the house to find her unexpected travel companion.

Elder Holtmann's words didn't sit right. There was something more going on. But what?

# TEN

 E<small>REVAN LAY STILL, LISTENING</small> to Siobhann's movements through the cottage. She was all but silent, was it not for his naturally acute hearing.

She didn't take her saddle or bags. She wasn't going far.

The morning chill circled through the open doors and slid over his exposed skin.

Her scent surrounded him. She was part of him now.

As he would forever be a part of her, though she didn't know it. Not yet.

He rose from the bed, straightened the quilt, then went out to the property's stone well to wash.

The power she encapsulated, barely beneath the surface, wanted out, much like his own did.

It was no wonder she denied having magic. It felt like chaos burning beneath her flesh, pushing at its bonds.

She'd been spellbound. Willing or not, he couldn't determine.

Alive, reaching, seeking.

The child had nearly set her free.

And had nearly destroyed them all when Erevan's own power had answered its call.

Curious.

He should not be playing at intimacy with the human woman.

But he couldn't help himself.

Beautiful, fierce, loyal.

Powerful. Intoxicating.

In the few days since they'd met, each time their magics brushed, they seemed to catch and hold a little longer, a little stronger each time.

*Danger.*

*You will jeopardize everything you've worked for if you do not alter your course.*

Forcing his thoughts to the present course, regardless of the warnings slithering up his nape, he considered the little cottage and its grounds as he continued his morning habit.

The frigid ground water ensured he was awake as he pulled on his trousers. In the cottage's small common room, he moved through his morning routine, stretching, flexing, and honing his focus. As he worked through the movements, the subtle residue of magic teased his attention, tugging at him until he finished.

The lingering traces resembled the surges he'd felt emitting from the child in the garden, and from her mother, in Domini Kember's study.

Searching, he moved through the small cottage, seeking where it was strongest, until he stood before a cupboard that appeared to be as old as the house. Inside, the shelves were stocked with neat rows of clay pots, jars and bottles, carefully corked and labelled. On the bottom shelf lay a carved wooden box.

Crouching, Erevan's hand hovered over the receptacle, gauging whether the magic was safe or not, even though it felt the same as the child's.

Not trapped, he lifted the lid. Empty.

Replacing it as he'd found it, he continued to scan the contents of the cupboard, sensing that this wasn't what he was feeling. A narrow gap below the foot of the cabinet's decorative trim drew his attention.

He slid his finger into the space.

A gust of wind preceded Siobhann's voice. "What are you doing?"

His fingertip brushed an object. Working at it, he slid the carved token out from under the cabinet.

It tingled in his palm as he stood. "This belongs to your niece?"

The scents of trees and wind and horses clung to her as she stepped closer, hand outstretched for the token.

He slid it onto her outstretched hand, careful not to touch her. The urge to caress her fingers and hair and face taunted him.

Desire sparked through him at her proximity. He drew a deep breath. The subtle scents that were hers infiltrated him. The need to taste her again drove through him.

Erevan ignored it. All of it; reclaiming control over his focus.

Her distant demeanour told him she had no such inclinations.

*This distraction will pass.*

As he watched her inspect the token, he wasn't so sure. His gaze studied every subtle change in her expression in the same way she studied the object.

Her fingertips hesitated before smoothing over the lines of the carved flower.

"Do you sense the magic infusion?"

She glanced up at his question, eyes tightening at the corners. "No."

Erevan's body tensed at her lie.

"It's just a lost game token." She dropped it into the small pouch tied at her waist. "I'm going to speak to the reeve."

"Did the neighbour tell you anything more?"

"Nothing more about Nate than what Darya told me. He has his own worries, with his nephew missing." She went into the bedroom, paused before the bed for a long moment, then looked around its perimeter.

He crossed his arms over his chest. "You've left nothing in that room."

She glanced up at him. "You tidied the bed."

He nodded.

Her expression softened before she turned back into the room.

Erevan stepped into the door frame to observe as she picked up the child's drawings next to the little bed.

From his position, they appeared to contain images of the girl's life; people, flowers—many flowers—trees, animals and some other shapes he couldn't decipher. Not without closer study.

Siobhann shuffled through them, pausing on a few for several long moments. She seemed frozen, until she moved on to the next, as though she were memorizing them.

He didn't ask questions, just continued to observe her.

While she had seemed eager enough to engage him carnally, she showed no interest or appreciation for his help.

*No matter.*

He would simply shadow her until her mission was complete and he would learn what he could from her of the Shield as they travelled.

Though, surprisingly, he discovered he didn't like that thought.

She set the drawings aside and turned toward the door, expression troubled, intending to slide past him.

Without thought, his hand shot out to grasp the door frame, blocking her passage.

She paused, scowling at him. "It's time to go."

"This will go faster if you let me help you." His fingers reached for her cheek, despite his earlier thoughts to let things lie as they were.

On contact, her eyes closed, seeming to accept the touch, but as soon as the familiar surge of power rose, she jerked away from him.

She met his gaze. "It's best if we don't touch each other anymore." She searched his face, while her own seemed full of regret before it turned hungry. "Though it was very... enjoyable."

The corner of his lips curled at the memory her expression evoked. "Enjoyable."

He dropped his hand from the door frame and moved toward their gear. "You're right. We should focus on retrieving your kin so I can continue my quest." He stacked both saddles and picked them up, carrying them out to the horses.

Siobhann followed him out with their saddle bags before going back for the remaining gear while he secured the saddles.

Once everything was in place, she made a final check through the cottage, secured the door, then returned to her horse. Once mounted, she asked, "Why are you here, of all places? What's so important that you'd risk your life, and mine, to go into the Shield?"

Erevan stroked Kelstorm's neck before mounting.

At her question, he regarded her, brow raised. "I'll consider telling you about my business when you tell me what your power is."

"Fucking dwarves and elves," she muttered, then growled, "I told you I don't have any magic."

He shrugged, turning Kelstorm toward the road. "Then I don't have a story to share."

# ELEVEN

Siobhann glowered at Erevan's back as she secured Odyn's reins by the trough in the market square.

Odyn shouldered her with a huff, drawing her attention. He jerked his head back and stomped his foot, as was his habit when he was annoyed with her, which was usually when she was being obstinate with Grimms.

She glanced back at the elf and his steed as she stroked Odyn's neck. "Alright, alright. If you two can play nice, I can try too."

She closed her eyes, leaning against the horse to steady her thoughts.

Everything was happening so fast.

The Shield.

Darya and Sendi, and the shock of Sendi's magic against her bonds.

The elf, and most especially her reactions to him.

On multiple levels.

Despite having dismissed what had happened in bed, it had deeply rattled her.

*I have more important things to focus on right now.*

The problem was, he was making it so difficult, just by being around.

There was no doubt he had some sort of magic of his own. She'd seen it in his eyes, felt it surround her.

It called to her, and that confused and scared the hells out of her.

*What does it mean?*

*Anything?*

She couldn't risk finding out, in case someone else got hurt.

In case *she* hurt *him*.

Opening her eyes, she studied him as he tended to Kelstorm.

The thought of hurting him rended her heart as though she'd known him her entire life, overwhelming her.

At every turn, he'd treated her with respect and consideration.

He was there when she'd opened her eyes after the 'fainting' incident. Her memories were hazy, but she had the distinct sense that he'd treated her with genuine care and tenderness.

They had indeed kissed in Donnen's library. He'd confirmed it.

She hadn't dreamed it.

And she'd awaken in her own bed the following morning, her dress and shoes neatly stowed in her cupboard.

Nor had she dreamed of anything that had happened in Darya's house.

"Mistress McLeighan?" A woman's voice broke Siobhann's thoughts, drawing them from her travel companion to the present.

She turned to find Nate's elderly aunt standing several paces behind her, a heavy basket gripped in each hand. "Mistress Kirin, let me help you with those." Siobhann immediately stepped toward her.

"Only if you promise to come for a pot of tea." The older woman pulled the basket from Siobhann's reach with a determined twinkle in her eye.

Siobhann hesitated. "I meant to visit you after speaking to the town reeve."

"Ah, I guessed as much. Well, come for tea first. I insist."

A shadow cast over Siobhann's shoulder. She glanced back to see that her travel companion had joined her. "This is—,"

"Erevan ap Brodin." He extended his hands to take both baskets from Nate Kirin's aunt.

The woman's gaze flicked over Erevan's features, taking in his markings and his ears. She nodded, "Thank you sir, I'm Tilda Kirin. Everyone calls me Til. You'll join us as well."

Siobhann cast a look at the reeve's office across the market square before following the older woman back to her shop, and home above it.

Despite her age, the woman's stride was sure and brisk, waving to neighbours as they passed, but not stopping to engage.

Inside her shop, she closed and locked the door, ensuring the sign was set to 'closed' and the curtains drawn. Turning, she gestured for them to precede her toward the backroom stairs that led up to her private residence.

Til Kirin grabbed the iron poker to push the cast-iron kettle on its brace toward the glowing embers in the centre of the hearth. "Won't be long. Just set the baskets down." She waved her guests toward two chairs that matched those in Darya's house, before rummaging in her cupboard for cups.

Erevan set the baskets atop her table before reaching for a work stool, which he set beside the two chairs. He sat and waited for Siobhann and their host. As soon as Til stacked the teapot and cups on a tray, Siobhann carried it over.

"Right," Til began, checking the kettle before settling down on the remaining chair. "You'll be here for Nate, of course."

Reasonable assumption, though Siobhann could be in town for any number of reasons. "Of course."

"Well, that *reeve* will inform you that Nate was peddling unpermitted trinkets initially. Then he'll tell you that he's been selling all manner of black-market wares."

"Which carries a heavier judgment."

Til nodded. "Darya came into town every day to see him and plead his innocence, despite the strain with her current state. Right up until they charged him with the more serious offense, requiring transfer to the district magistrate. The *reeve* will tell you that too." She scowled and got up to check the kettle's progress. "What he won't tell you is that the transfer escort were barely across the town's border when he dressed himself up and headed straight to Darya's home to start harassing her with his attentions."

"She told me that he'd been to her home."

As soon as the water was hot enough, Erevan rose to retrieve the kettle, using the thick linen set aside to protect his hand from the hot handle. He poured the water into the teapot and replaced the kettle without a word.

"That's very kind of you, sir," Til said to her guest. To Siobhann, she said, "Exquisite manners, you should hold on to this one."

"He's not—,"

"We're just travelling together," Erevan said.

Til's eyes twinkled as she regarded the Elven prince. "You'll know this blend?"

Erevan leaned forward, inhaling the steam with a nod. "I do, and I've not had the pleasure for a very long time. Your trade links are impressive, madam."

The old woman beamed. "Takes years to cultivate a reputation like I have. My imports are top quality." She turned to Siobhann. "Black market dealers approach me all the time for my connections. I don't risk my business with such things. I may have done so a few times in the early days when I was getting started, but things have changed." She grinned at them as she poured the tea. "Besides, with this new reeve, the risk isn't worth it. And Nate would agree."

*The risk is worth it, if your daughter's life is at risk.*

"You don't like him." Siobhann picked up her cup, inhaling the exotic blend.

Til cackled. "Someone from the capital appointed him when the old reeve left office. This new one certainly doesn't fill the shoes of the old one."

"Do you stock magical wares?" Erevan asked, sipping the tea.

"Not so much anymore. Holding onto permits is harder than it used to be. The trade is there, but the costs...." Til shrugged.

Siobhann wasn't surprised. Donnen had mentioned the difficulties he'd had securing Kindred's operational permits. The emperor's grip was fierce when it came to the imperial coffers. His hunger for expansion was costing everyone.

She watched the tea leaves circling in her cup.

*At what point will everything just collapse?*

"You've been to see Holtmann?" Til asked.

Siobhann nodded. "His nephew hasn't come back from visiting his parents."

"Oh? Oh dear, not Kit too?"

"Too?"

Sadness filled Tilda Kirin's eyes. "There have been a few young lads gone missing in the last couple of years. None found. Not yet, anyhow."

"Surely the militia searched for them?"

"Aye, of course. Strong lads. And not a track left behind, so everyone has to assume that they've run away with a lover. Or some worry that the sadness took one or another of them and they've gone into the great river or into the Shield. But those theories don't make sense for any of these young men." She set her teacup down. "Take Lucas, for example. He's a lad from a farm out by Meiville. Middle child, hardworking, dedicated to his family, attends temple on the festival days and helps with local underprivileged. Sturdy too. He's taken home many of the festival wrestling competition ribbons. One day he came to town for supplies Meiville don't have access to and somewhere between here and there on his way home—gone. Cart too."

"No young lady in another town?"

Til shook her head. "His young lady lived next door. They were to be married the following spring. Promised since they were old enough to know what a promise was. He treated her like she was his empress and she adored him for it. Such a shy little thing."

"And there have been others? No young women?" Erevan asked.

Tilda gave Erevan a long look. "There are always young women that go missing. Always. Usually the vulnerable, as you would imagine. This is different."

"I'll bring it up with the reeve. I'll use Kemberlan's influence to put pressure on him."

Til snorted. "Any time anyone tries, he just sends a few men out to look for a couple of days. Probably gone to the next village for a few pints, then back again empty-handed. Then the militia go out as far as they can without jeopardizing their own families and homesteads with their absence."

"The district magistrate?"

"You don't think we've tried all we can?" Til's voice hardened, her eyes sparked.

"I'm sorry, of course you have," Siobhann said, voice soft.

"I don't know what's going on, but I fear for Nate. Everyone knows he served the Empire as a general, though he never talks about it. And why someone from the capital hasn't come to set things right, I don't know."

They wouldn't, if Nate didn't inform the new reeve about it. For Sendi, Darya wouldn't either because it would draw more attention to all of them.

*Til doesn't know about Sendi? Or she's keeping it to herself in present company.*

Siobhann couldn't be sure one way or the other.

All she'd learned here was that either Nate really was peddling on the black market, or his accusations were inflated so that the new reeve could pursue Darya unhindered by a husband.

And that multiple young men were missing.

She rubbed a hand over her face, considering these separate, yet equally important, issues.

*I'll have to send Aila to Donnen about these other goings on. Maybe he could find something out.*

"I'll ask about the young men at every opportunity while I'm working to bring Nate home."

*If I can bring him home.*

"I know you're doing it for your sister and little Sendi, but he's important to our whole community too."

The general who's no longer a general, still fighting weaponless battles—only from within, now.

*Goddess, I wish the conscription would just end. And the Emperor would cease his senseless wars and stop squeezing his empire for every silver and every drop of blood and flick of magic he can steal.*

She sighed.

*Real world, Siobhann.*

"Thank you for the tea, Elder Kirin."

"Elder." She puffed out her cheeks. "Til, *Mistress* Siobhann. Call me Til."

Siobhann smiled, "Yes, Til, though I'm sure Nate won't like it."

Til rolled her eyes and waved a hand as she got to her feet. "Before you go...just wait here."

She disappeared through a doorway tucked in the back corner of the room.

Siobhann turned her attention to Erevan. "Good tea?"

He finished the last of it and set the cup on the tray. "Very good. First time I've had this recipe since leaving home." He picked up the tray and moved it to Til's table next to her baskets.

"Where did you learn such manners?"

Erevan raised a brow at Siobhann's tone. "Common courtesy is universal, isn't it? Though I'll admit, it's somewhat lacking in more places than others." He held her gaze.

She flushed under his stare, recalling just how rude she'd been toward him on multiple occasions. She cleared her throat, "Perhaps."

"Took some digging, but I found it," Til said, holding up her hand.

Erevan looked at Siobhann in surprise when Til reached for his hand, placing the object on his palm.

"You'll recognize that, yes?" Til leaned back, smiling up at her guest.

Erevan's throat worked as the fingers from his other hand caressed whatever he held. He nodded. "How much would you like for it?"

"Nothing. It's a gift. It's not every day that I get to have tea with Elven royalty." Her grin widened. "I got that about the same time I bartered for the tea. I thought you might like to have it. And make sure you keep the tag with it in case anyone gives you trouble. It's fully registered, though I'm not sure how knowledgeable the dealer was that I got it from. I *am* sure you know more about it than I do."

Siobhann leaned closer to see what it was, but Erevan closed his hand, pulled his fist to his chest and bowed his head toward Til.

"Thank you, Til."

"You are most welcome, sir. I do hope you'll come back one day."

Siobhann's heart nearly melted at Erevan's unguarded gratitude.

"I hope so too," his soft voice tugged at Siobhann, though he spoke to his host.

"Well that's settled then. Siobhann, I trust you'll find Nate and bring him home, however you must. Even though he's not your favourite person."

"I—,"

Til held up her hand. "We all know that Darya and Sendi are, so that will do." She reached up to touch Siobhann's cheeks. "We're all family and we look out for one another, don't we?"

Siobhann nodded, grasping one of Til's soft hands.

*Damnit.*

Til had such a way with people. Probably why she was such a successful merchant.

"Take care and safe travels," Til said, allowing them to carry on with their journey.

# TWELVE

THE REEVE WAS MUCH as Darya and Til had described him.

Disinterested in Nate's fate. Obsequious where Darya was concerned.

Oily, pungent, eyes constantly resting where they shouldn't, upturned nose and persistently open-mouthed heavy breather.

Siobhann had to step back from him several times in order to keep him out of her personal space so she wouldn't be arrested and sent to prison alongside Nate for throat-punching the invasive, arrogant bureaucrat.

She considered it, then recalled that she would be sent to a women's gaol and not the men's prison that Nate was bound for.

Her fists tightened every time the reeve turned to Erevan to answer Siobhann's questions.

He said everything Til had said he would.

Nate was sent to the district magistrate where he would be judged and charged with black market peddling.

"There's nothing I can do, you understand." He spread his hands, appealing to Erevan's thorough understanding of political hierarchy. To Siobhann he said, "Please give my best to your sister and tell her that if there is anything—*anything*—I can do for her once her child is born, to come to me. I will do all in my power to see to her welfare."

*Except* not *send her husband to prison indefinitely.*

And as for the missing young men?

"Young people go missing all the time. Conscription dodgers, mostly," was all he said, eyes fixed on Siobhann's bodice lacings.

She pulled her cloak closed and fastened it with her Kindred insignia brooch.

The reeve blinked, blanched, and granted her the space she craved in the narrow meeting room with his retreat toward his office door. "I've invested valuable resources already. I'm afraid there's nothing more I can do on either matter. I have more meetings to prepare for, so I won't keep you any longer. Good day, sir." He bowed to Erevan and disappeared.

"Goddess, I hate politicians," she grumbled, stomping down the front steps toward Odyn.

It was late afternoon by the time they reached the district magistrate's building in the town of Millhaven, northwest of Harrowsmith where Darya lived.

The administrator tried to refuse her entrance, due to the late hour of the day and their impending early closing to celebrate the coming festivities.

Foot blocking the door and a barely concealed threat, Siobhann growled her way in.

She'd been here once, several years back on an errand with Grimms, before he stopped leaving Bella. She didn't have high hopes.

In fact, once she was given reluctant admission to the magistrate's ready room, she realized why they reeve seemed so familiar. The magistrate and the reeve were so alike she would have wagered an entire titanium ingot that they were related.

He spread his hands, imploring Erevan to understand the matter was beyond him now.

"Mr. Kirin was found guilty of black market dealing and peddling without a permit. He was too ill to send for conscription, so he has been assigned to the Ondaggan prison, where he will reside until he is recovered enough to serve the empire. The escort left yesterday and should arrive at the prison in two days' time."

*Ill?*

Too ill for conscription?

Why hasn't Nate told them he's a decorated general? Surely, that would warrant some respect if not a total drop of all accusations?

*Useless man. Why in all the hells does he have to make everything so damned difficult?*

First, he becomes a pacifist and now he refuses to use his rank to save himself and protect his wife and children.

"And what about the young men that have gone missing from various communities across this district?"

"Missing? No one has brought the topic to me before. I will have my people look into it. Good day, Mistress McLeighan. Sir." He bowed deeply to Erevan before escaping, much the same way the reeve had.

"You," she barked at a passing administrator who stopped, wide-eyed. "What route did yesterday's prison escort travel to the Ondaggan prison?" There were multiple roads that lead into that less populated area of the district. "I have a message to deliver to one of the prisoners. His wife was with child when he was arrested, and I've been paid to give him news before he's locked up."

The administrator's eyes flicked back and forth between Siobhann and Erevan, chin raised at Siobhann's tone.

Siobhann straightened, moving her cloak aside, giving the snootish woman a clear view of Trish's razor-sharp edges while she deepened her scowl.

"I'll check the schedule, mistress." She double-timed her step.

She caught Erevan's raised brow from the corner of her eye. "What?"

He shook his head without a word.

He hadn't said much since their visit to Til's early that morning and Siobhann hadn't given it much consideration, lost in her own tribulations.

Ensuring anyone else was out of earshot, she said, "I plan to track the escort as far as possible tonight. If you wish to stay at an inn here, I can meet you when I return with Nate."

His brow rose higher.

As did her irritation.

"You insult me to suggest I leave you to pursue a band of men through heavily forested roads. Alone."

"I'm more than capable of handling a small prison escort—"

"And if there's more than just a few armed prison guards?"

She turned toward him, full attention on his face. "You think there would be?"

He nodded but didn't say more as the administrator returned with several sheafs of rolled parchment. She spread them on the high counter that divided the public from the documents room. She quickly sorted through the pages, pulling three from the bundle.

She hesitated. "You say he has an expecting wife waiting for him?"

Siobhann nodded. From her pocket, she withdrew the drawing Sendi had given her of the whole family, depicting Darya with a large round belly, showing it to the woman.

The woman's expression softened. "The guards won't let you near the prisoners. You'll have to relay the news to them. They'll decide if they tell the prisoner or not. They're not generous men, so you may be wasting your time," she warned. "The prison guards scheduled for yesterday's escort take prisoners charged with fraud, smuggling, tax evasion and conscription dodgers to this facility," the woman pointed a perfectly trimmed and varnished fingernail at the ink sketch of a compound separate from the rest of the prison complex. There were two such smaller buildings set apart from the main section.

"What's that one?" Siobhann pointed to its twin.

"For the most dangerous prisoners. No one ever leaves there alive." She tapped the drawing of the roads leading from their current location toward the complex. "All Ondaggan prisoners follow the same route to this point, then diverge depending on which compound they're bound for." Her finger rested at a heavily wooded junction.

"Thank you." Siobhann said, tucking Sendi's picture back into her pocket.

"I hope you do get the message to him, not for his sake, really, not out of kindness. Just so he knows what's he's missing while he's locked away for his stupidity." The glare in her eyes was steely.

Siobhann's brows rose in surprise, wondering if the woman spoke from shared experience.

Her ever-looming shadow, Erevan, followed her out.

# THIRTEEN

Erevan guided Kelstorm alongside Siobhann up a narrow path that connected the main road to one of the routes indicated by the administrator at the magistrate's office.

She'd cursed the man's name while she called one of her ravens down from a nearby rooftop. Quickly scribbling a coded message onto a thin strip of paper, she tucked it into a tiny tube attached to the bird's leg and sent it off to Donnen at Kemberlan Keep.

They followed the shortcut through a dark forest, though his vision allowed him to see well enough. Not that he was concerned about his own safety, but he still didn't like surprises and he was beginning to suspect that his travel companion didn't have a plan as to how she was going to liberate her brother-in-law.

He decided to press. "Do you have a plan you care to tell me about, since I'm your accomplice?"

"You volunteered."

"I did, but that doesn't mean you should leave me blind."

She turned in her saddle to study him. "You're right," she said, surprising him. "I plan to approach the lead guard, as I insinuated to the administrator, deliver the message about Darya, and assess the group. Nate isn't a hardened criminal, but he may be travelling with those that are. And in my experience, prison guards and escorts are often little better than those they're over-seeing. I suggest you stay out of sight."

He nodded, intending as much. "I'll remain nearby."

Silence returned with nothing but cricket song and tree frog mating calls drifting through the brush.

So many times over the last few days, his thoughts turned to the woman he rode beside, trying to reconcile the different shimmering facets of her persona.

Acerbic, short-tempered, suspicious, vindictive, and rude.

Fierce warrior. Foolishly brave. Loyal Kindred. Stubbornly persistent, respected and undoubtedly loved. Steadfast.

And none of that had anything to do with her physical appeal.

Her unabashed sensuality.

The feel of her skin against his, her unique scent, the taste of her lips, the sound of her breathy passion.

His thoughts turned to that first night in Domini Kember's library.

The sweetness of her kiss when her inhibitions were replaced with expressive playfulness. The rose hue of her skin as she basked in the golden hearth fire, strewn across the table. The soft notes of her song that drew him to her like a siren.

"What was the melody you sang?" his voice pulled her attention toward him.

She turned her head in his direction, tilted as though considering.

"Melody?"

"You were singing when I found you in the library."

"Was I? Probably just a child's lullaby. I don't know any others that aren't bawdy Dwarven drinking songs. I assume it wasn't one of those?"

Erevan chuckled. "I'm sure I'd have recognized a bawdy Dwarven drinking song, as you say. It reminded me of a song I heard long ago."

"Just something my mother used to sing to us when we were small. I don't know what any of the words mean."

"Don't you?"

"No. She never told us."

"It sounded like an archaic branch of Elven tongue that is rarely heard in these times. A nearly dead language except for particular uses."

"But you know it."

"I do. We were forced to learn all the known Elven dialects."

"Whatever for?" She turned fully on her saddle to regard him in the darkness. "Surely there are much more important things to do with your time?"

"As princes of the realm, we are expected to communicate fluently with all cousins of Elvenkind."

"I forgot you were royalty for a little while." After a long silence, she asked, "What is it like?"

"Being a prince? I haven't been a true prince for several decades, but I imagine little has changed since I was removed from succession. Little ever changes in Myst Innys until it is forced upon them."

"Decades—how old *are* you? Removed?" Odyn stomped to a halt as Siobhann pulled his reins and tightened her knees against his sides.

She stared at him as he pulled up alongside her.

Kelstorm stopped next to Odyn.

Erevan met her stare. "Yes."

Her gaze fluttered over his face, and he felt it. He felt every turn of her expression as she processed those words stretching between them, drawing on her curiosity, reeling her toward him.

As he stared into her wide eyes in the darkness of the forest, he realized he wanted to tell someone something of himself. He'd been asked innumerable times with no desire to share his tale.

But now, as he stared into her lovely face, the proximity of this woman whom he wanted to bed again, regardless of the looming dangers, he wanted nothing more than to share it with *her*. He wanted her to know him.

She hadn't asked him about the brooch that Til Kirin had given him. He'd pinned the ancient royal insignia to his cloak. It was another one of the artifacts that Nolgan had stolen from his father's vault. Probably bartered for something else, though he couldn't imagine what would be so valuable that he would trade the invaluable clan artifact.

She licked her parted lips and swallowed. "Perhaps one day you'll tell me about your home?" She released the pressure to confide.

"Perhaps," he smiled, adoring the naked curiosity and disappointment tugging at her features.

She shook her head, "Never mind. It's none of my concern and very rude of me to ask."

He laughed again. She continued to surprise him. "Perhaps once we've finished this quest to rescue your sister's husband, we can exchange bawdy drinking songs and childhood stories."

She grunted, pressing her knee to Odyn's side so that he continued on. "We'll see."

The cricket song ceased, as did Odyn's movement, as a whistling missile raced toward them.

Erevan jerked backward while kicking Odyn's rump, forcing him to bolt forward as a second, aimed for Siobhann, hit the tree next to her at throat height.

He curled the fingers of his left hand as his palm heated. Shaping a globe of contained light which he flicked into the darkness, he drew his sword with his free hand. Within seconds multiple attackers were illuminated.

Already, Siobhann had turned Odyn around, bow in hand, arrow knocked. As soon as there was enough light for her to see by, she loosed it into the shoulder of an opposing archer aiming for Erevan.

The imbedded arrow broke the tension of the assailant's draw, forcing the arrow to flutter harmlessly into the dark underbrush.

Erevan formed another globe, this one full of fire, while urging Kelstorm toward the nearest enemy rushing toward him.

Mindful of not setting the forest ablaze, he focused on using the magic to blind the opponents while parrying their unskilled swords, hacking at his legs and horse.

He kicked one in the face, crunching bone, while he fire-blasted another's head, melting his hair and forehead. Kelstorm lunged back and forth, knocking attackers over and trampling them at will.

Erevan glanced up to see Odyn back-stepping between trees to give Siobhann more space to nock and loose her arrows as the distances closed down. She fluidly replaced the bow and snatched up Sally and Trish, swinging and blocking.

They fought amid a cacophony of battle clangs, screams, and grunts.

He alternated between slicing and melting anyone that got near enough to either his blade or his hand.

Siobhann cried out before slamming the heel of her foot into another attacker's face. She leaned to one side, pressing her arm inward as she continued to fight with the other.

Magic funnelled through his core and down his arms. He sheathed his sword to control the expulsion of power as it neared his hands. "Enough!" he roared, fingers curled around growing balls of flames.

What a sight he imagined he was.

His eyes would be aglow, as bright and fearsome as his hands, as he grimaced to control the sudden surge of rage ripping through him.

The power over fear was a warrior's greatest asset. To inspire it in the enemy was a significant advantage. The fire mages that trained him had instilled that as a fundamental tactic.

The remaining attackers spun toward the growing inferno atop the midnight steed. Eyes wide, they backed away from him as he urged Kelstorm forward.

One, not so afraid as his companions, took advantage of the situation to run at Erevan from his flank. Unfortunately for him, he crashed through the brush, drawing his attention and the full blast of power from one hand. He screamed as he burned, struggling to run away, but he couldn't.

He couldn't because Erevan held him prisoner, encased in fire, turning and manipulating it as a kinetic conjurer would with a buffet of air.

Several dropped their weapons, running in terror from the cruelty.

Erevan grimaced, clenching his teeth as he struggled for dominance and control over the element which wanted to burn through the forest. He gave it this man instead.

From the corner of his eye, Siobhann's arm flew out, releasing one of her throwing knives into the lower calf of one of the fleeing attackers. Dismounting, still clutching her side, she stomped through the brush toward the fallen man, sparing Erevan and his blazing man an uncertain glance.

Her downed quarry struggled and limped, dragging his injured leg as he tried to flee. Catching up to him, she grabbed him by the hair, wrenching him backward. "Who are you?" she screamed into his face.

Erevan increased the intensity of the fire, pushing air away from the man, forcing him to suffocate. He couldn't end him quickly with his sword without losing his dominance over the roiling, contained blaze that would consume the forest in a wild spread.

Kelstorm sidestepped and backed into another man creeping up on Erevan from behind, crushing him into a tree.

The man in Siobhann's grasp whimpered, the whites of his eyes showing as his gaze locked on the burning man. "I—we—" His words were cut short by an arrow to his larynx loosed from somewhere in the brush, outside of the lit area. She released him, ducking to retrieve her throwing knife, eyes scanning the darkness to locate the archer as she scurried for the cover of a nearby bush.

Erevan jerked sideways as another arrow whizzed toward him. As he did so, Siobhann stood and threw her dagger. It found its home in the man's chest.

Erevan kept an eye on her as he continued to focus his magic on the corpse, burning it down to ash. Siobhann retrieved her bow and arrows before scouting the area for more men. Staying low, she searched the bodies.

The only sounds were those of the fire consuming what remained of the man's bones.

Moments after the magic had spent itself, Siobhann returned to Odyn, cleaning and replacing her weapons. "If I'd had any appetite, it's most certainly gone now. Glad to see you weren't boasting about being capable of handling yourself."

Erevan grunted, dismounting Kelstorm to inspect the fallen attackers for himself. "Not just highwaymen."

"No, though they easily could have been. Or raiders, since we're getting closer to the border. These men likely thought we'd be easy prey, as they did little to disguise themselves. Their boots are sturdy militia issue. I didn't find any insignia to identify them, but given the timing of things, I'd guess they were sent by either the reeve or the magistrate." She retrieved her own arrows that were still salvageable and collected extra from the quivers of the dead. "The question is why?"

"A few escaped. They may send more."

She nodded at his words before mounting Odyn.

Erevan extinguished the harmless light spheres, throwing the forest back into darkness. "We should find somewhere to rest for a few hours before you go out to meet the prisoner escort."

"Come. Somewhere away from here, before forest predators catch the scent of blood."

He noted how her fingers trembled as she clenched and unclenched her hands on Odyn's reins, and how she leaned to one side. "You're injured?"

"It'll wait till we make camp," she said, leading him off trail, deeper into the forest.

# FOURTEEN

THERE WAS NO FIRE when they finally stopped to rest.

On checking the wound, Erevan opted to magically heat a blade to seal the flesh, rather than stitch the edges to stop the blood flow. "I don't sew."

Siobhann laughed, marvelling at the control he exhibited as he worked. "Skin is one of the few things that I do. Prerequisite to joining a mercenary guild. Stitch each other up well enough to get to a proper healer."

"You could use your niece's token to help speed up the healing process."

"It's superficial. I'll be fine with this." She nodded toward his knife as it slowly changed colour. "How do you do that? It takes Grimms a lot of effort to get Bella up to temperature for smithing."

"The fire mages taught me how to harness my power and focus it for battle."

"And for making bodies disappear."

He glanced up at her, then down at her hands. "You were upset by that."

"Yes, and no." She clasped her hands together to still the intermittent trembling.

"You needn't be afraid of me." He turned his attention back to heating the knife. "I won't hurt you."

"I'm not," she blurted, maybe a little too quickly. If she was, she'd never admit it. "And I know it was necessary, though I prefer not to take a man's life in that way."

"I prefer not to as well. I can teach you."

"Teach me what?" Her fingers tightened around each other, as she pretended not to know what he was talking about.

"How to control your power."

Her heart pounded in her ears, "I told you—,"

"You do have power. There's no sense in lying to me. I know what that power feels like, Siobhann." He stopped heating the knife to meet her gaze, his expression stern. His gaze dropped to her hands pressed to her thighs, then returned to heating the knife. "I felt your power the moment you sat next to my table at the inn."

"Sat next to *my* table. You were in my spot." She lifted a brow.

"Explains your rudeness. Anyway, the connection between us is growing. Our magics react to one another." He met her gaze again. "When you fainted, that power burst hit me right through the stone floors and walls of Kemberlan. I've never experienced anything like that before. It was so unexpected that I almost lost control of my magic."

Horror slid from Siobhann's pounding heart down into her gut. She dropped her gaze from his, staring at her hands.

And the reaction during their bed play, when she decided she would never bed him again, though she'd come to regret that decision, the more time she spent with him.

Wearily, she drew a deep breath, which disturbed the wound that had yet to be sealed.

She tried one last time. "There's no magic. Battle fever makes my hands shake. Same reason I go looking for a bedmate after jobs. I just need a little release and I'm back to normal."

"Battle fever?" He gaped at her. "I've seen battle fever, and those are two very different things."

"My father was a Baerskyr warrior." Seeing that the blade glowed, she lifted her shirt to expose the seeping wound.

He nodded, as though accepting this explanation before he challenged her, leaning closer. "If you really believe that's all it is, then let's take care of it. Tonight."

The look in his eyes when he issued the challenge made her mouth go dry. She couldn't help herself as desire, sudden and hot, flared through her. She swallowed; decisions forgotten.

Her fingers clutched the fabric of her shirt. Despite herself, she leaned toward him, eyes on his lovely lips.

If she were being honest with herself, she wanted nothing more than to spend hours and hours revelling in the feel of his mouth, and his hands, and every other part of his body.

That one night hadn't been enough. It was only a sample to entice her to want more.

"Elven woo-woo," she whispered as his lips met hers.

His tongue swiped hers, eliciting a moan. Lost, she gave into him.

Pain seared into her side as the blade met the open wound, firm and unforgiving.

She tore her mouth from his in a deep gasp, refusing to cry out. Her free fist pounded the craggy bark of the log she sat on until her breath returned.

"Ashiel's fucking toes, Erevan!" she finally said.

He removed the knife, then set about cleaning the skin around the burn and applied salves from her pack before bandaging it. Then he cleaned the blade and returned it to its sheath on her thigh.

Still, her fingers shook. A little more now.

Her chest heaved through the throbbing pain as she glared at his unconcerned expression.

"Your hands still tremble, Siobhann."

*Fuck.*

His brow raised, as though her thoughts were writ on her face.

She desperately wanted to knock the cocky expression off of his—his lovely, lovely face.

Instead, she decided to take control of the situation. She may crave him, but she wasn't going to let him see it. "Fine. If you're so in need, then why not?" She pulled her damaged and stained shirt up over her head and dropped it to the ground where her leather bodice already lay.

The late-night air swirled around her naked torso, forcing her nipples to tighten.

She reached for him, watching his face as she unbuttoned his vest. Slowly.

His gaze swept over her face and down her chest as his palms lifted to caress her breasts.

Outwardly, she didn't react to the sensation of his hands on her so intimately, though she instantly wanted more.

So much more.

She gently pushed him back toward the log until he sat again. Unfastening her trousers, she lifted the fabric tucked into the tops of her boots, then let them slide off. She didn't bother removing the boots, but stepped toward Erevan, to unfasten his trousers as well.

Reaching into the folds, she grasped him, strong and hard and ready for her.

She didn't waste time. Straddling him, she claimed his lips as she settled onto his erection.

She gasped, shuddering against the overwhelming pleasure of having him inside of her again.

His strong arms encircled her, supporting her as he deepened the kiss, drawing her closer and closer so that they were chest to chest.

She registered the care in which he held her, careful not to strain the fresh wound as she moved atop him.

Gripping her hips, he rolled his pelvis to meet her, striking that sweet spot deep within her.

Her need for release intensified. It wasn't just her hands that trembled now.

The magic vibrated through her, seeking, as it had before, but stronger now.

"Look at me, Siobhann."

Her desire spiked at his words. The way her name rolled off his tongue.

She opened her eyes to his.

As before, his irises were ringed with gold. His markings were aglow, as they were when he drew on his fire magic.

Her heart hammered in her chest with desire and fear.

There was no fear that he would hurt her.

The terror rose with the desire for what he was making her feel.

He had control over his power.

She didn't.

Siobhann craved that.

She longed to know what that kind of control over herself would feel like.

"Don't hide from me. Let me see who you are. Who you really are."

The fear lodged in her throat as emotion suddenly surfaced, encasing her heart. Heat swept through her entire body.

"I can't," she whispered, closing her eyes. "It's too terrible."

Erevan's hands slid up her waist and ribs, caressing his way up to her breasts.

She moved faster, seeking release despite the discomfort surrounding the fresh wound.

"Look at me," he commanded again, ever gentle but firm.

She did.

His desire and magic were at the surface, as were hers.

Erevan's arm encircled her hips again, holding her down against him. His free hand wandered back up along the valley between her breasts and up her throat, fingers warm on her face as he held her gaze.

The raw desire for her in his eyes, struck her.

She was consumed with the power of his desire at her core, but it also moved up into her solar plexus and threatened to split her heart wide open where her fear resided.

"Let me in." His voice resonated through her as she looked into his striking face with his glowing eyes.

It was too much as she arched against him, buried so deep within her. He gave in at the same time, swelling against the grip of her inner muscles.

The desire, the sensation of his magic seeking hers and hers seeking his as he held her face, their expressions raw and passion filled.

All of it ripped through her.

His hand slid from her face down her chest to rest on her heart so that not just their bodies collided, but now something more did, too. Ever so briefly. The barriers between them thinned all the more.

The raw exposure of their magics actually brushing one another deepened the intimacy as her orgasm rose and crashed into another.

Everything went white, and then red-orange, as together they were launched into another plane.

It lasted only seconds, but it was enough for her to register the thin translucent barrier that separated them.

Their naked bodies shrouded in fiery beasts. Different but of like value.

His resembled a massive reptilian creature, while the reflection of hers in the barrier resembled a great bird of prey.

*No!*

Her voice echoed through their consciousnesses, reverberating off of the barrier and through their bodies, breaking the connection.

Returning to her physical self, she shifted to move away from him, but he held her fast against her fear. Their chests rose and fell, their bodies glistened in the dull light of dawn.

"Now we've truly seen each other, Siobhann."

WITHOUT ANY MORE WORDS between them, they settled down to rest for a short while.

Clothing back in place, he stretched out his bedroll, and opened his arms for her to join him for warmth against the cooling night air.

Cradled with her back to his chest, she slept while Erevan considered all that had just happened.

The glimpses were forming into a larger picture. One that disturbed him deeply, but not for any of the reasons she would have thought.

The power.

The melody.

Their beasts.

*Does she know?*

Perhaps not? She and her siblings had been orphaned. How long ago?

Surely Domini Kember and her sister Darya knew something—but how much?

Even Erevan wasn't certain. Not yet.

*Too soon.*

But there were too many similarities to the old tales, derived from that very ancient melody in the long-dead Elven language that she claimed to not understand.

*It can't be.*

*She can't be.*

His fingers trailed through the loose strands of her copper hair as she sighed in her sleep. She burrowed into him.

As he looked down at her profile, he knew he'd never walk away from her willingly.

Even without his suspicions and concerns, he had known.

But more so now.

Since their previous bedding, he'd known their fates were entwined.

He just hadn't known how deeply or why.

And now? He thought he knew.

There was no untangling them.

Even if he hadn't been pursuing Nolgan and Kossa for all these years, perhaps the gods would have found some other reason to put them in each other's paths?

But what are the odds?

From different cultures, different empires. Half a world between them.

And he was brought here.

To her.

*How long before she accepts that?*

*Will she?*

A smile tugged at his lips.

"So stubborn," he whispered. "I will just have to keep showing you so that there is nothing left to deny."

He would see that they found and rescued this Nate Kirin, former imperial general turned pacifist; who'd sacrificed himself so that his child could grow up in peace.

In Myst Innys, such a child as Sendi would have been honoured and allowed all that she needed.

A healer like her mother, but more.


By the time he woke Siobhann to resume their journey, he had his thoughts in order. And though he didn't have all of the pieces to the story unfolding before him, his instinct gave him the direction he needed.

Until then, they had a prison escort to meet and assess.

# FIFTEEN

Siobhann guided Odyn back onto the trail.

She hadn't realized just how used to the atmospheric changes Erevan's proximity caused she had become, until he left her side to guard her flank.

He'd awoken her with the gentlest of kisses on her brow, his low voice beckoning her from the sweetest dreams she'd had in years.

It had taken her a full minute to come to her senses, recalling she was in the middle of the forest and in the arms of the Elven prince she'd once labelled arrogant and sly.

He was neither of those things.

She tapped Odyn with her knee, urging him forward.

Cocky, maybe. What prince wouldn't be, at least a little? Prince.

A disinherited prince with an urgent personal mission that was on hold so he could help her retrieve her sister's husband from a long prison sentence.

One last glance into the forest to gauge his position. Her instinct reassured her he was nearby.

Even if he wasn't, she still had a mission to accomplish.

For free, during her respite.

Normally, for a job like this, she wouldn't have been alone. There would have been at least one other Kindred, if not two or three.

The path widened. Odyn sped into a trot.

Perhaps the coin raised by her guildsmen would see Kemberlan's roof finished.

The job she'd just completed would buy another cartload of slate for the southern tower.

Erevan's purse alone could have rebuilt the whole damned keep.

But the idea of going into the Shield...

*Home.*

She'd never wanted to go there again.

Kemberlan was her home now.

The Shield meant too many memories; trying to crash down on her like its many life-threatening avalanches.

And perhaps facing the truth that she was the one responsible for what had happened.

Which, deep, deep down, she knew she was.

Giving Odyn his lead, she checked her weapons one last time, mindful of the newest healing wound to her person that still ached and stung when she twisted the wrong way.

She whispered her thanks to the goddess that this arrow wasn't poisoned.

And that her back was nearly mended. The healer's anti-poison spell saw to that.

Or was it that brief contact with Sendi's magic?

The one that almost cracked the binding of her mother's magic.

Magic that Erevan was doing his best to fracture.

*Focus, Siobhann! You can't afford to be distracted.*

But no matter how much she tried to ignore it, she could feel it.

Not just when Erevan was around. Not just during the healing session that plunged her into the nightmare.

Something was changing. Each time she went into battle, the fever was harder to dispel. Each wound also seemed to chip away at the magic caging the beast within.

It was getting stronger.

And she was terrified.

Terrified that she would destroy her new family too.

A sound drew her attention.

The path widened further as the woods thinned. Siobhann eased Odyn's reins so that he would slow, and she could listen.

Voices and chains.

She and Odyn continued forward, finally reaching the head of the path where it connected to the main road toward the prison compound.

They approached from her right.

Odyn stopped, she waited.

The sounds of many feet trudging along the forest road. Murmurs and curses and thuds as someone tripped over upturned roots or unearthed stones. The constant rattle of chain underlay every other sound.

She inhaled the heavy scents of pine, oak and maple. And unwashed men.

No birds or forest rodents added to the sounds.

Just men.

Prisoners.

Any of which could use her as a distraction to escape. It would be violent. With shackles, there was no other way.

*How the fuck am I going to free Nate and get him home?*

*Darya asks the impossible.*

*She also wouldn't ask you if she didn't believe you could do it.*

Siobhann didn't bother trying to guess how many guards and prisoners there were. No matter her skill, there would be too many to allow her success on her own, should it come to a fight.

No matter. Not right now.

First, find Nate.

The rest will come.

*Breathe.*

Two guards, side by side, appeared first. One watched his feet as he walked, the other scanned the road and forest around them. He seemed surprised when his gaze landed on Siobhann atop her horse nearly in the middle of the road.

He scowled, reaching for his weapon, glancing in all directions, ready for an ambush. "State your purpose here. This be an Empire road, for prison business only," he shouted.

The second guard looked up to see that the road was no longer empty and signalled for the line of prisoners to halt. Twelve in all, shackled in pairs. Two more guards were to either side at their midst and a final pair at the rear.

"Peace, sir. I'm paid to deliver a message. That is all." Her eyes scanned the faces. Nate wasn't among the fore group who obscured her view of the rest.

The guard assessed her, his growing suspicion obvious. "State your message then."

"It's a missive." She reached for her purse tied to her waist.

"Hold!" The guard barked, drawing his weapon. The others tensed, prepared for an attack. "The administrators don't send written instructions."

"It isn't from them. It's for one of your prisoners." She raised her voice, craning to better see the shackled men.

"Prisoners don't get the privilege of letters or news until visiting days at the compound. Once a month and heavily guarded. Strict rules."

"It's just a drawing from his child, sir. You may see for yourself. His wife paid me to come all this way to give it to him when she approached her delivery date to remind him of what he's missing for his irresponsible folly. It's no kindness." Her hand swept toward her brooch, clasped at her shoulder, denoting the emblem that marked her as a paid service.

A couple of the guards chuckled.

"Aye, wouldn't be the first," the lead guard murmured, reaching forward, sword drawn and ready. His eyes flicked between Odyn, Siobhann's feet and her hands hovering by her waist. "Give it here."

She spread her fingers and moved cautiously to ease his suspicions. With deliberation, she removed Sendi's drawing of the whole family. Holding it up at chest height, she unfolded the parchment to expose the charcoal lines and smudged pigments.

He took it from her and backed away, scanning the image. His lips quirked as he chuckled, looking up at her. "Shame to leave such a family. Who's is it?"

"Kirin. Nate Kirin." She leaned, scanning the faces.

"Kirin? Isn't there a general by that name? Some kinsmen?"

Siobhann shrugged. "There is and could be. Black sheep cousin, maybe?" She grinned when Nate stepped aside, as far as his ankle shackles would allow, and met her gaze.

He scowled at her.

Her grin widened.

*Shit.*

Even as her stomach tightened seeing the sight of him, her smile didn't falter as she took in the battered state he was in.

Filthy, hunched as though favouring injured ribs, face bruised and one eye was swollen shut. Some of his knuckles were split and scabbed.

He may have turned pacifist, but he still gave as good as he got with his fists and bare feet.

His trousers and shirt were stained and torn in various places. No boots or shoes. He was barely dressed.

*Had he been dragged from his bed?*

She swallowed, thinking of Darya and Sendi. They must have seen him arrested and taken away.

"Anyhow, if you'll see it delivered to the man, I'll have completed my job so I can report back to the wife and collect my payment. I can tell her how miserable he is and how sorry he'll be to miss the arrival of his new child."

"If she's anything like my own wife, she'll be appeased by that news," he nodded. "Kirin," he barked.

"Aye," Nate rasped.

The guard approached him, gave him the once over, "Ye kinsman to the general?"

"Distant."

The guard grunted and shoved the parchment into his chest.

Nate's throat worked as he visibly resisted the urge to look at the drawing. Instead, he carefully refolded it and tucked it into his shirt, then glared at Siobhann.

"Message delivered," the guard chuckled and turned back to the head of the prisoner column.

"Thank you, good sir. I have another job before I return to my guildhall. A delivery. Might you know the fastest way to Harlau?"

Siobhann held Nate's angry gaze. She lifted a hand toward her Kindred brooch, signalling to him she wasn't done yet.

He gave his head a nearly perceptible shake, tilting his head over his shoulder toward the men behind him.

Her gaze went first to the armed men, swords at their hips, bows in hand. The left rearguard glared at her. Her skin prickled as she dropped her gaze to his hands, holding his knocked bow pointed at her. His hands had been hastily bound in wrappings, the fingers reddened and swollen.

Burned? Or some other injury?

Her attention slid to the rest of the prisoners.

A few looked like simple farm boys, young men beaten and terrified.

*Something isn't right.*

"Straight back along this road," the lead guard, drew her attention back to himself, pointing back the way they'd come.

She nodded her thanks. Odyn gave the group a wide berth as they headed in the direction suggested, before the guard thought to ask how she'd come to be where she was in the first place.

They were barely past the group when she set Odyn to a trot and let him build to canter, taking them away as fast as her mind raced.

At a safe distance, they left the road, cutting back through the forest.

Ashiel's fucking toes!

Why was nothing ever simple with Darya and Nate?

Erevan waited in the dense forest, out of sight but close enough to hear the exchange between Siobhann and the escort guard.

With Kirin's presence confirmed, he considered their options to extract the man without bloodshed before they reached the security of the prison.

He was always up for a challenge.

Prisons.

Myst Innys didn't waste their resources with such structures. Instead, resources went into ensuring every member of the Elven community had a home and enough food for their families.

Criminals were executed or exiled.

Everyone knew the rules. They abided by them, or they didn't.

He wasn't sure the prison system was less harsh, better or lesser than their own system. Just different.

Kirin was charged with selling spelled tokens, which wouldn't have been illegal in his own kingdom. It was little different from selling most anything else.

Different realms, different customs.

He scanned the forest for sounds of Odyn's hooves on the forest floor, or glimpses of Siobhann's coppery hair amid the greenery.

He let his thoughts turn to the magic between them.

With each moment he spent with her, she drew him deeper.

The mystery she posed created a new sense of urgency to his original quest to find Nolgan and Kossa.

Was there something to the ancient prophecies as they'd said? He'd seen the tomes and scrolls, the astrological maps and calendars.

*It was nearly time.*

He knew it even before, deep down, long before he'd read the scripts.

He could feel it.

His mentors felt it and spoke of it.

"The Sisters will reunite soon, dance their dance and then spin away back into darkness."

He was just trying to figure out what that meant for Nolgan's interest in the mountains.

The ancient Dragon Temple that the dwarves had buried by engineered landslide centuries ago, which resulted in the great rift between them and the Elves? Was it even real? He hadn't seen mention of it in the Aelozian texts. No one he met ever mentioned its existence.

And the Elven texts were unclear.

Most of the ancient tablets had been buried or sundered.

Just the oral stories remained of the dragon and the phoenix and the coming of a new cycle that peaked with the reunion of the sisters and would decline with their parting.

Each telling he'd read or heard was different.

Kelstorm's ears twitched.

Erevan returned his focus to the surrounding forest.

Hooves. Odyn. Siobhann.

Her copper hair glinted in a shaft of sunlight that found a gap in the tree canopy.

The branches shifted and for a second, she appeared to have a crown of flames.

He blinked, and she met his gaze.

"We've got a problem."

He lifted a brow. "Of course, we do, you're determined to break a man out of prison before he gets there. Care to elaborate?"

She scowled at him. "There are young men in that gang that don't strike me as the criminal type."

"And you wish to extend your contract?"

"One of the guards had fresh burn marks on his hands. If those boys aren't prisoners, I can't just leave them there."

"Doesn't help your mercenary bottom line."

"Since when are you funny?"

"You know I'm expensive and generally don't to two for the price of one deals."

Siobhann snorted and rolled her eyes. "Who's the mercenary now? Besides, we have two horses."

"Kelstorm doesn't like humans."

Siobhann lifted a brow, mimicking Erevan's signature expression. "Odyn doesn't like elves, you don't hear him complaining."

Erevan laughed, Siobhann grinned.

"Come on, it's going to be a long night and we have yet to figure out just how we're going to get Nate back to Darya before the baby comes."

NOLGAN STARED AT THE old massacre site. Nearly two decades of snow and ice, scavenging animals and mountain debris had covered it before their workers excavated it.

"This is it. I know it. This is it."

"You've said that before." His sister, Kossa, scowled at him. "And I'm tired of these mountains." Though it was spring in the valleys and foothills, the mountains clutched at winter, holding fast to its jagged and peaked spine.

Nolgan had painstakingly pieced together the legends, far and wide, using the liberated codex as the skeletal telling. He'd spent decades fleshing it out until they'd finally reached this place.

The codex that his cousin hunted him for.

Nolgan knew Erevan would never see them executed, nor would he ever leave the Codex alone. His stalwart cousin would return it to his father himself, though he didn't deserve it.

"We can't leave until it's finished."

"*You* won't leave. There's no reason I can't," she snapped.

"You'd abandon me? After all I've done for you?"

Kossa's lips compressed, eyes glittering as she turned away from him to survey the ruined farm.

Nolgan stared at the preserved remnants of the lost scouting party he'd sent out all those years ago. Slaughtered. He surveyed what was left of a human homestead. No human remains had been found, only those of his Torgolis soldiers. The locals would have claimed their dead and seen to their death rituals.

This place had been abandoned.

Were it not for the clear evidence scorched into the earth, timber remains and petrified corpses, he'd have dismissed it as another dead end.

The magic resonating from the char hummed through him.

He adjusted the ring that allowed him to detect elemental magics.

This was fire magic, pure and chaotic and concentrated.

Raw power had exploded in all directions here, its fierceness trapped in the mountain rock, it changed the soil and tainted the very ether so that it slid across his tongue when he breathed.

He inhaled deeply of the old destruction; eyes closed.

He'd nearly had it then, had his scouting party survived.

Yes, a storm had wailed through the mountains, the reason for the party losing their way.

Not lost quite yet.

He removed his fur-lined leather mittens.

He crouched, lowering a trembling hand, fingers splayed, palm flat against the burnt rock with reverence.

"Don't you feel it, Kossa? The magic? I've never been closer than this in all these years," he said to his sister as he stood and replaced his mittens.

"Whatever happened here was years ago. Everyone and everything is long, long gone." Her acerbic tone drew his attention.

Nolgan smiled, gripping her fur-covered shoulder. "Yes. And mountain people have long memories. This tale will have been preserved as these remnants are. They will know. And then we will know."

# SIXTEEN

SIOBHANN EXTRACTED HERSELF FROM Erevan's warm arms.

She studied him in the darkness, resisting the desire to trail her fingertips over his skin or press her lips to his.

They'd followed the prison gang until they made camp for the last night before reaching the compound.

There were still a few hours before nightfall, so they found a discreet clearing in the forest to rest. Though they had no fire to cook with, Erevan warmed the biscuits and hard tack with his hands before giving it to Siobhann.

The gesture had been unnecessary but thoughtful and she'd kissed him for it, which had inevitably deepened and become something more.

She couldn't help herself, and she no longer wanted to.

Once they reached the foothills to the Shield, she would find him a guide and they would part ways.

Her heart twisted.

Ignoring it, her gaze lingered on Erevan's profile as he slept.

Her time with him was running out, and she was surprised by her regret.

She straightened.

She'd needed a bedmate, he'd obliged.

The quality of his lovemaking had been like nothing she'd experienced before.

Elven woo-woo.

Whatever it was, she was all for it and would enjoy it while it lasted.

She allowed herself one more moment to absorb the way the forest light highlighted and sculpted the bones and planes of his handsome face. The arched jet brows, deep dark eyes with thick black lashes, the straight nose and beautifully sculpted lips that did indeed know how to show a woman pleasure.

Her fingers itched to slide through his long silken black hair and trace the tips of his ears and along the golden lines of his markings once more.

Curling her fingers into her palms, she mentally dispelled the urge.

*There is work to do.*

Retrieving her pack, she settled on a log to choose her gear. Though her fingers drifted over her hauberk, she bypassed it for her lighter, reinforced leather gear.

She would be on foot and silence was paramount.

All of the leather pieces were dyed green and black for Kindred guild colours, but they would also serve her well while skulking through the forest after dark.

Kindred often served as imperial scouts before important campaigns. Their success was a combination of skill and practical application, such as the simplicity of their gear, helping them blend into the landscape.

She ensured all the buckles were the right tension, then pulled on her bracers as Erevan stepped toward her. He reached for her hand, lifting it so he could fasten the bindings for her.

She allowed it, using the moment to steal more glimpses of his face.

If events were unfavourable for them, she might never see him again.

"Thank you."

He held her fingers as she stood. His hands slid up her arms and leather-encased shoulders to her neck and nape, pulling her toward him.

The look in his eyes made her throat and her heart pound.

No one had ever looked at her that way.

There were no words between them now.

Just touch.

She lost herself in the sensation of his lips, just once more.

The tenor of his kiss was different than every one that preceded it.

His lips lingered on hers before he released her. His cheek caressed hers as he inhaled her scent.

She shivered, her fingers clasping his shirt.

He pressed his forehead to hers a moment before he moved back enough to look into her eyes.

*Be careful.*

*I will.*

*I'll be nearby.*

*I know.*

His thumb brushed her cheek before stepping away.

She forced herself not to reach for him. Instead, she ensured her knives and axes were secure before she slung her quiver over her head and checked her bow.

She met his gaze once more.

His brows furrowed, lips tight.

They'd gone back and forth and in the end, she'd convinced him that he needed to get Nate back to Darya and the children, no matter what happened to her.

This wasn't a Kindred assignment for coin, and she was trusting him to see it through.

She'd used one of Sendi's drawings—the one of just the two of them and the sunshine and flowers, to write the name of the best Shield guide she knew, along with their address and instruction to find them and their fees. He was crotchety and generally didn't deal with anyone without her presence as a recommendation, but Erevan might be able to convince him. She'd tucked the parchment into Kelstorm's feed bag.

She searched the trees for her shadows. Omi and Moa perched nearby.

Raising her arm, she called for Omi, who swooped down to land on her extended fist.

Extracting a small treat from her belt pouch, she fed it to the raven and rubbed its feathered head, whispering compliments and endearments.

Finally, she said, "Follow." Omi flew up to Moa where they exchanged a few croaks and Siobhann turned her attention to the task at hand.

With only a lingering glance and no more words, Siobhann turned her back on Erevan and ran through the forest toward Nate, and his iron shackles, and six armed guards, and eleven desperate inmates.

NATE KIRIN SHOULDN'T HAVE been surprised to see his sister-in-law in the middle of nowhere on the road to the empire's most secure prison compound in the district.

Of course his wife would seek her sister's aid.

But he was surprised.

Siobhann had no love for him.

She thought he was a coward.

Sometimes he did too, since he'd made the decision not to kill if it could be helped.

*A pacifist.*

Siobhann's voice, laced with acid and disgust, clung to his consciousness because a buried part of him rejected the decision too.

In the end, all that mattered was that Darya understood his decision and supported him as he supported her endeavour to continue healing and somehow keep her activities and Sendi's growing power hidden from the authorities.

There were risks with those decisions, and they'd made it work until the day came that they no longer could.

And here he was. On his way to prison, tired, hungry and battered. But he'd been through worse, on the front and on the battlefields where he'd nearly died.

The last time, he had for a little while.

Thank the gods it had been only for a little while.

It had given him the chance to come back. Back to find Darya and make her his. They'd been gifted with Sendi for his efforts. And another soon to come. Gods willing, he would see them all and his children would know him.

If not, then he would do his best to ensure his actions could find some meaning.

So, yes, he knew how to endure. And he was doing his best to help the other young men endure, as he had with his troops before battles.

Lead by example.

And when the young men struggled and the guards decided to beat them, Nate didn't stand by and allow it, he helped them fight back, though in the end they all suffered for it, but the goal had been to keep them alive, not unharmed.

Some of these young men were arrested for stealing food or firewood for their families. Families without fathers because they'd been conscripted for the emperor's wars in a place they'd never heard of.

Now, the eighteen men travelling to Ondaggan prison were camped and preparing to bed down for the night.

Except, he suspected, not all of them were headed for one of the two prisons.

He'd seen the exchanges between a couple of the guards, heard their whispers. One of the guards had snuck off in the night for a few hours, while his companion covered for him and later returned from some excursion that had failed, with his hands burned.

When Siobhann had appeared in the road, they resumed their whispers behind him.

The woman from the forest attack.

And she hadn't been alone. A fire mage had burned half their crew alive.

He questioned whether he heard right.

Fire mages were rare, and he hadn't heard of one joining Kindred's ranks.

Tomorrow they'd reach the gates. Once through them, there was no escape.

Even if he couldn't get away, he could at least warn her of the northern threat.

He scanned the tree line, listening for sounds outside of the noise the guards and prisoners made. Any telltale signs that she was there.

The posted guards would be too, but there were only six.

For now.

KELSTORM GRUMBLED AT EREVAN'S tightening of the reins. He released his grip and rubbed the stallion's long neck.

Erevan's unease affected his old friend. He couldn't remember the last time he was this out of sorts, tightly strung and ready to leap to action.

Still, he did his best to maintain his composure.

"She'll be fine," he told Kelstorm.

Kelstorm rolled his eye at him.

"She'll bring your new friend back soon. It's been some time since you had a companion."

He considered all of the things that could go wrong. She was alone in the forest in the middle of the night, except for all of the hardened men in the camp she spied on.

*Everything could go wrong.*

His hands tingled as the magic stirred, sensing his desire to unleash it. To feed it.

He fisted his hands and flexed them wide, dispelling the desire to cast. The itch to free the magic.

*She's a skilled fighter.*

She'd held her own against multiple attackers the night before.

One of which was among the encamped men.

He had to trust that she knew what she was doing.

He closed his eyes, drawing long, deep breaths, seeking his centre.

She was a Kindred mercenary, respected for their ability.

The waiting was endless, yet when he sighted the moon, it hadn't moved much.

He blew out his breath.

*Goddess, I hate waiting.*

Siobhann crept through the forest, circling the encampment. There were a lot more guards and prisoners now than there were that morning on the road.

*Fuck.*

The second escort group had arrived. She kept her distance, straining to see Nate.

There? She couldn't be sure.

With so many more added to the camp, he was harder to spot. They were all dirty and haggard. Long days of forest travel did that, especially when you had to be on full alert for opportunities to escape, prisoner and guard alike.

She spotted the guard with the burnt hands glaring in her direction. She ducked further back into the brush, heart pounding.

Surely he hadn't seen her. She altered her course, senses wide open.

Instinctively, she ducked again as an inky shadow swooped overhead, drawing her attention for a split second.

*Omi.*

Drawing comfort from the friendly observer, she continued. Eyes darting from light to shadow, from man to man to picketed horses. Ears trained for snapping branches or shouts of alert. The odour of unwashed bodies seeped through the foliage. The stench of the open latrine assaulted her approach, forcing her stomach to flip.

Painstakingly, she made it around to the far side of the encampment before she finally spotted her target, set away from the main prisoner column, still chained to one another.

He huddled next to another, smaller man curled up on his side, outside of the light of the campfire, where the air was chilled. Nate whispered to him, gaze darting toward the guards. Blood seeped from Nate's nose, while one eye was swollen shut.

Moving closer, she gave the horses a wide berth, eyes flicking from guard to guard.

The one with the burnt hands from that morning reappeared within the camp, checking the prisoner's chains. Her fingers brushed the metal shivs concealed amongst her gear.

Had he recognized her on the road?

He wandered toward a cluster of chatting guards, exchanged a few words, laughed and continued on, away from where Nate was.

Where was the lead from that morning? None of them looked familiar, except that one.

*Something's not right.*

*Once he passes through the prison gates, he's lost forever. It's now or never, Siobhann.*

On nimble feet she made her way to the brush behind his position. Pressing closer, she made sounds mimicking scurrying animals to draw his attention, then moved just close enough to allow him to see her.

"Gods in the heavens, you and my wife have balls enough to lead the emperor's armies yourselves, Siobhann."

"Yeah, now get your soft ass over here so you can tell her so yourself."

"I'm not going, Siobhann. I can't leave. Not yet, I need to—,"

"What the fuck do you mean, you're not leaving?" It was all she could do to control her voice and maintain the whispered exchange.

"Holtmann's nephew. He won't survive the journey into the Shield. Get him home alive while I figure out what's going on in the north."

*The Shield—Holtmann's nephew?*

She squinted through the foliage at Nate's companion, curled up on his side in the dirt, shivering.

"This isn't the prison escort. We were transferred to slavers a few hours after you delivered your message. Some of these men are not convicts." He whispered, head turning as his gaze swung across the camp. "Get word to Kemberlan. These slavers are selling to the Torgolis that took over Carlane. The northern front is a weak point for the Empire. If the Torgolis attack—,"

"Carlane? Who in the hells cares about some abandoned fortress in the Shield?"

"Will you shut the fuck up and listen? I heard the guards talking, Aelozia is at risk of invasion."

"Fuck sake, Nate, why is nothing ever simple and straightforward with you and Darya? You're not making sense. Carlane's been abandoned for centuries, and why the hell would slavers deal with the Torgolis. Let's go, I have a horse nearby and—,"
cold steel pricked the tender flesh just below her ear.

Ice swept her body as a thick arm came around her throat. "And a fire mage hidden in the woods. Where is he then?"

Stinking breath assaulted her as she struggled for breath against the pressure to her windpipe as he dragged her backwards, away from the camp and into the darkness of the forest.

Bandages covered the hand that held the blade tip against her skin, leaving the swollen fingers exposed.

*Fucking hells.*

"Go on, call for him, luv. We have orders to execute everyone and disperse at the slightest threat," he goaded her as he pressed himself against her backside.

Her stomach flipped as rage ripped through her, clawing at the arm across her neck. She closed her eyes and drew a deep calming breath, reaching for her bandolier of sheathed blades with her free hand.

"He's not the one you need to worry about," she rasped as she plunged the small blade into the stained bandages.

His knife nicked her throat as he jerked away, but not enough to do serious damage as she continued her assault. Spinning around, she punched him in the throat, then brought her knee up between his spread legs, which forced him to the ground. She kicked him onto his back. Yanking her blade from his hand, she pressed it to his throat now, pinning the weight of her body behind it as he gasped.

"Since I've got your full attention," she growled, "who sent you to attack us? Was it the reeve or the magistrate?"

He wheezed and gurgled, shaking his head.

"No one knew we were out there, except the administ rator...." Who showed them exactly where to go with little hesitation.

*Fuck.*

She glanced toward Nate, as what he'd said before clicked into place.

"Let me guess. Prisoners come in, transients, young men looking for work, other vulnerable folks who wander through town, and some come through the magistrate's doors. The helpful administrator gives them some direction. Then passes word along that there might be some free labour, ripe for the picking, and where to find them?" She snarled in disgust, pressing the knife into the scraggy beard covering his jugular. "Is the magistrate involved or is he just so damned incompetent and self-serving that he's oblivious?"

"Siobhann!" Nate hissed, appearing through the bushes, supporting Kit Bower's weight, while trying to keep their chains quiet. "You're wasting time."

She glanced down into the man's face, tipped back as far as he could to avoid the blade.

*He's right.*

In a swift movement, she rolled away from him as her blade punctured his jugular that sliced across his exposed Adam's apple to cut off air supply to his lungs. He gasped and gurgled.

"Damnit, that's not what I meant," Nate glared at her, struggling to support the younger man's weight. "You didn't need to kill him."

Siobhann shot to her feet. "Yes, I did." She hissed back at him, jabbing a finger in his direction. "Your decision to become a life-loving pacifist puts the onus on the rest of us to do what we must. You know he would have alerted the whole camp, and we'd both be dead or chained. Let's go. Odyn is waiting a quarter mile south of here."

"I told you, I can't go. Kit won't last another day without a healer, let alone the journey into the Shield."

Fear iced through her as he mentioned the Shield again, prompting terrifying memories of raging Torgolis.

She sucked in a breath. "If you don't come with me, your children will be fatherless, and Darya would never forgive me."

"She will understand that I must do what I can to ensure the safety of Aelozia. If I infiltrate, I can uncover the slaver routes and their hubs. Send ravens to Kemberlan as soon as you can, and we can rescue those that have already been sold."

"If they're even still alive. The Torgolis aren't known for keeping slaves, Nate."

"I overheard the guards. They're terrified of the Torgolis, but they keep buying slaves for excavation work in the mountains near Carlane. For some reason, they're gathering there."

She studied him in the darkness, listening for disturbances from the camp. They hadn't yet noticed the absence of their guard and two prisoners. "You said the north isn't secure."

He shook his head. "The emperor has most of the armies expanding the other fronts. The Shield has been quiet for so long he decided it was a waste of his resources to secure Carlane, which is strategically important only for a conflict zone."

"If they're gathering, and decide to come south..."

"Then Aelozia is fucked," his voice tightened as he swallowed. "Darya—,"

"Is safe at Kemberlan with Sendi, and Kwayssi is with her. She loves you."

He grinned. "You're here, aren't you?"

She scowled at him as she backed away. "You look like shit, Nate. You better not die, you fucking pacifist. If someone tries to kill you, you kill them first."

She slid her shoulder under Kit's, helping him walk the distance to her horse.

Nate's lips twitched. "You're getting soft, little sister. Send that message about Carlane."

Siobhann snorted. "I'll send the ravens. Don't die."

He chuckled before disappearing back into the bushes.

It was a long, slow way back to Odyn, who was pleased to see that she was still alive.

# SEVENTEEN

Of all the scenarios Erevan could have imagined, this was not one of them.

"Kirin's neighbour's nephew?" He'd asked when Siobhann hastily pressed him to help her hoist the barely conscious man from her saddle to his so they could move faster.

"Nate said that he would hide the dead guard and tell the others that he last saw him taking Kit into the woods, if asked. Apparently, he did this often with some of the other prisoners. The guards ignored him."

She turned about, face tilted up to the trees as she called out for one of her beloved messengers.

Moments later, Moa, the King Raven, swept down from a nearby birch, answering her call. She cooed to him, rubbing his head with a fingertip before placing the large black bird on her shoulder so that she could extract what she needed from her hip pouch. She scribbled a message on a small strip of parchment, rolled it and tucked it into the tiny container attached to the bird's ankle.

Omi was to follow Nate.

She kissed Moa's head and he nibbled at her lips before sauntering to the end of her extended arm. "Ghalen," she whispered and tilted her wrist up for him to launch from.

Erevan shifted the young man's weight to a more comfortable position. "Elder Holtmann's instincts were right."

"I just hope we can get him to a healer in time."

They travelled non-stop, though at a pace that Kelstorm and Odyn could handle. The horses sensed the urgency to keep moving.

Erevan cast Siobhann a glance across the road, adjusting his grip on the nearly dead man sharing his saddle. The heat radiating from him indicated fever. His cheeks were flushed, and his face glistened with sweat.

Siobhann monitored the trees for her raven, Aila, from Donnen, who had not yet returned.

The golden glow of illuminated cottage windows provided a sense of relief from the constant darkness of the forest as it opened to the town of Millhaven.

"Hilda Bruner lives this way," Siobhann pointed to a narrow path from the main road. Odyn picked his way between the low, thatch roofed homes. She dismounted and knocked at the weather-worn door.

A face appeared, peeking from a slight gap in the curtain of the window set next to the door. The door swung wide. "Aye, you're back, and I see you brought your friends." The old woman grinned, her gaze sweeping Erevan, who was still supporting the young man atop his horse. "Come inside before the lad expires, then! Lay him out on the worktable. You know where it is, mistress."

Erevan dismounted and eased young Kit Bower down from the horse. Too weak to stand, Erevan lifted him up and followed Siobhann inside the old woman's cottage. It was laid out similarly to Darya Kirin's home.

The healer bustled behind her workbench, snatching at herbs suspended from the low ceiling and tinctures from the shelves lining the walls. "I've just boiled the kettle for tea. Be a dear and haul it over, would ye?"

Erevan wasn't sure to whom she spoke, but moved at her bidding as soon as Bower was stretched out on the table.

Siobhann sought a rolled blanket to prop his head on. "I don't know what is wrong with him. A friend asked that we find him a healer."

"Poor lad." The old woman peered at the young man's face, her fingers gently touching and prodding, tsking and humming. "Aye, good ye did. And timely too. Pour the water into the teacup, would ye, sir?" she said without looking up from her patient. She moved to a dry sink set before a curtain-less window. A pitcher of water occupied the moonlit sill. From it she poured water over her hands, washing and murmuring.

"The tea will boost his strength while I sort out the ailments. Good thing I didn't skip Temple this week. I'll be asking the Goddess' help, this night."

Erevan handed the steaming cup to Siobhann so that he could lift Holtmann's head and shoulders to drink.

Siobhann whispered to the young man. "Kit, drink this so we can return you to your uncle."

Bower's eyes cracked up, eyes rolling between Siobhann and Erevan as he gasped and sighed. His head jerked forward as he struggled to sip and swallow.

The old woman's murmurings continued as she moved her hands above her patient's body, hovering here and there, from forehead to chest to belly, pelvis, and down along his arms and legs. Her craggy face compressed as she scowled and clucked.

"He'll live?" Siobhann asked her once the teacup was done.

Erevan eased him back onto the blanket roll.

"If his spirit has the will to, I can work with him. It may knock me out of service for the next week, though. Whoever did this to him meant to break him. And that complicates things."

Siobhann looked up at Erevan. "I promised Darya I'd bring Nate home. And I left Nate behind with the promise that I'd get Kit to a healer so his family could have him back." She scrubbed her face with her hands, then leaned on the table. "I can't let him die. That would break Elder Holtmann's heart. I will pay for his mending and for the week ahead, in lieu of your lost income."

The healer placed a hand on Siobhann's. "Men of all ages die all the time, mistress. It is the will of their spirit and of the Goddess that determines their fates in the end."

"He drank the tea. He will do his part," Erevan said to the women.

The old woman picked up the empty teacup. "Aye, that is a good sign." She nodded, placing it on the counter next to the remainder of the herbs. "If you would help me undress him, sir, you and the mistress can take his clothing to the village inn for laundering and mending and rest there for the night while I tend to him."

"I could stay and help," Siobhann offered.

"Ye're not a healer, and ye'd be better served with rest, and to send for his family."

Siobhann nodded, then turned to Erevan. "I'll take Kelstorm and Odyn to settle in at the livery, then send messengers."

As she strode toward the door, the old woman called out, "Mistress, a moment." She glanced in Erevan's direction before following Siobhann out of the small house.

Erevan did as she requested, carefully undressing the young man, mindful of the many injuries and bruises revealed, including slash or whip marks along his back.

The women stepped outside, but the door remained open as they spoke.

Voice low, the old woman said to Siobhann, "Mind what I told you about a dreamwalk. Even if you don't come to me for it. Whatever the source of the dream terrors, they're keeping you small, locked—frozen in place. I don't know what yer story is, but I can feel the bigness in you. Ye've a mighty power in there." She poked a finger toward Siobhann but didn't touch her.

"I'm fine as I am."

"Better to learn to live free of it. The terrors, I mean, they reduce your spirit, mistress. It could mean the difference between life and death for you, too. I've seen it many times. On the battlefield, and well away from it, too." Though she kept her voice low, her tone was stern. "Now go and rest. I intend to have my ward stable by noon tomorrow."

She returned, closing the door, glancing at Erevan, and Bower stretched out on the table. "There's a linen there for modesty. Not that I mind, a body's a body, but the lad might."

Erevan found the cloth and covered young Bower from knee to belly button.

"Thank ye for staying back. I would normally work on my own, but young men can be... skittish when it comes to old crones such as myself when they rouse and are disoriented. Best to have another male around, especially a friendly face. And I appreciate your strength."

Erevan nodded. "The lad is a stranger to me, though I would help."

"Kin to your lady?"

"The lady is my travelling companion."

"Oh?" Her brows rose as she turned her attention back to Bower.

He chose to ignore her knowing grin as she held her hands over the young man. Her magic brushed against Erevan in a much different way than Siobhann's had. A completely different tenor. Its resonance reminded him of Darya Kirin and Donnen Kember's when they worked on stabilizing Siobhann after the child touched her.

"Will you tell me what a dreamwalk is?"

Her easy manner disappeared. "You overheard us?"

"I'm Elvenkind. My hearing is far more sensitive than human hearing. You needn't tell me anything about the lady. I merely wish to know if dreamwalking is similar to an Elven practice I know."

"To tell you of dreamwalking, would tell you something of the mistress," she levelled her gaze on him, studied his impassive expression, then sighed. "It's much what the words mean. Someone with the ability can go into a person's dream and help them walk through parts that need healing. Only specialized dreamwalker healers are certified to perform the ritual. Anyone working outside regulation is considered to be working under darkcraft and not to be trusted."

Erevan nodded. "Trust is strictly necessary."

"Aye. Please turn him so that I may mend the wounds on his back. After that, I can manage on my own."

Erevan stayed nearly an hour longer, as her work was slow and methodical.

She directed him toward the inn where he met with Siobhann, who was still in the livery with the horses.

Erevan stood at the open stable door, observing Siobhann as she fed and talked to their horses. His gaze traced her profile and the lines of her body as she moved. Her voice was soft and husky as she murmured to them. The seductive call of her low voice drew him closer, wanting nothing more than to take her into his arms and kiss her so that she would speak *his* name. To hear that breathlessness in her voice because of his touch on her skin.

He also didn't want to disturb the peace and ease of her moments, so he remained silent and observant.

He'd stopped questioning his unexpected desire for her. Now he only questioned how long it would take her to recognize the intertwining of their paths.

*Fate.*

The more time he spent with her, the deeper the enchantment burrowed.

And the more he learned about her, the more concerned he was about their destinies.

Had Nolgan been right about the prophecy?

Right about the prophecy, wrong about the individuals?

Erevan was beginning to suspect, gut sinking, that Siobhann was somehow connected to their dark quest for knowledge.

On the surface, he denied the nagging suspicions, when in the deepest part of him—his magic —*knew*.

There were no suspicions for Magic. There was only knowing.

And that kind of knowing was dangerous and terrifying.

The way their magics called to one another, reaching.

Their beasts within yearned to connect.

He didn't want to fall in love with a woman that was prophesied to be the bringer of the new era, whatever chaotic world changes that meant.

But was she? Was she the bringer? Or an integral part of the awakening?

As Nolgan and Kossa thought that Erevan might be.

He'd been removed from succession for a reason.

Erevan's magic was a threat to Elvenkind, combined with power to rule.

So, he'd been turned into a war mage. His destiny as a leader of his people ripped away so that he could be molded into a weapon at their behest instead, should they need him.

One of the versions of the prophecy spoke of the destruction of the world when the dragon and the phoenix reunited.

Nolgan had shown him the pages in the stolen book. He'd seen the drawings and the ancient text describing the last ascension.

And they were on the cusp of a new ascension.

Nolgan was convinced that Erevan *was* the Dragon, or had some connection to it.

And now, if he allowed himself to believe Nolgan's creative pairings even the tiniest bit, Erevan feared that Siobhann might be linked to the Phoenix.

But all of that was ridiculous. They were ancient fables and cautionary tales of doom and world-ending conclusions.

That would never happen.

He was just a rejected prince.

And she was just a lost orphan trying to do right by her family.

Neither were legendary world destroyers.

Kelstorm broke the spell he'd fallen into and gave him away with a grunt and a stomp, demanding he join in the nighttime ritual.

Siobhann glanced up, noting his presence, but continued to brush Odyn's coat down. "Aila returned. I've sent her back to Donnen, and a messenger to Elder Holtmann's cottage to notify him that his nephew has been recovered."

"What do you plan to do next?" he asked, taking up a spare brush in the stall to tend Kelstorm.

*Run away with me, far away from the Shield and this realm and mine. Somewhere far away and unknown to everyone but us.*

His gaze bounced back to Siobhann as the thoughts took him by surprise.

An uncomfortable tightening in his chest reminded him that would never happen.

*I have a duty to fulfil to my father, my clan and my people.*

*As does she—to her family and her guild and potentially her realm.*

Siobhann's hands stilled over her horse. "After I interview Kit Bower, I will send a testimony each to Ghalen and Donnen Kember. Then you and I will discuss our journey into the Shield."

He froze, trying to process what that meant.

To rescue her brother-in-law, or to guide him to his destination?

She put the brush down, but still hadn't turned to face him.

No, she would not abandon her sister's husband. Especially not while he was on a mission to rescue stolen men from slavers.

On the surface she was rough and earthy and fiery tempered. He saw through all of that to her inner grace, in brilliant glimpses so bright that she blinded him at times.

She turned, her expression guarded. "What is your destination in the Shield that is so important?"

"The Dragon temple of Aelieth."

Her complexion turned milky, and her jaw tightened. She blinked as her chest stilled, then rose and fell in quick succession.

Finally, she nodded. "That is not so far from Carlane."

"You know it?"

Her head jerked forward again. Her lips compressed. She gave Odyn a final pat, brushed her hand along Kelstorm's neck and strode toward the open livery door.

Erevan set the brush aside, grazed his palm along Kelstorm's shoulder, bidding him good night as he followed her out into the cool night air and into the stuffy atmosphere of the crowded inn. They were given a simple dinner and a key to the last available room. The bunking rooms were all full, and all that remained was their lord's suite available at no discount.

He decided that if they were to pay for a luxurious room for the night, he might as well hire a servant to port hot water for the tub, hoping it would be ready by the time they finished their meal, though he could have done it himself.

They managed a table barely large enough to support their wooden bowls and pewter cups. The inn was nothing like the one where they'd first crossed paths, yet he couldn't help but be reminded of it.

Even now, though they seemed to have become accustomed to the sensation of their magics mingling, he was fully aware of her.

*Does it affect her in the same way? Does the call pull at her or was he more sensitive to the magic being Elven? Perhaps her humanity muted her access to the power.*

He studied her as she ate, wanting to see her in all of her power. The tiniest exposure he'd experienced had dug into him, stolen his breath, his self-control and ultimately his heart.

He craved the vision of her essence. To see her raw power. To unleash it and let it know his.

No barriers.

His fingers shook as he imagined it.

"Are you unwell?" she glanced up into his face.

He clenched his fingers, staving off the thoughts that overtook his emotion. "No."

*Too much.*

Her expression turned doubtful as she studied his face.

She didn't say anything more, dropping her gaze to her bowl.

Obviously reluctant to engage in conversation of any kind while in public, Erevan held his questions and thoughts until they could speak freely.

The longer they sat in the dining hall, the more subdued and distracted she was.

"Perhaps I should be the one asking that of you?"

"I'm fine." She offered a half smile.

Erevan finished the fare, and on noting that she merely pushed her spoon through the unappetizing liquid, he stood. "Ready?"

As though returning from a journey, she slowly looked up and blinked, then pushed her chair back and joined him.

# EIGHTEEN

Siobhann followed Erevan up the steps to their rented room. Erevan unlocked it using the key the innkeeper had handed him in exchange for a bag of silvers. The servant had brought up their gear. Once inside, she relocked it, slipping the key onto the thick fireplace mantel. She stared down at the cozy fire the servant had lit to warm the room.

"Will you tell me what drags at your thoughts?" Erevan's warm fingers slid across her shoulder, startling her.

She turned toward his concerned expression with so many thoughts, but unsure of which to begin with.

"Siobhann?"

"Does your beast control you?" she finally blurted.

He frowned, straightening. "The magic?"

"Yes." She swallowed. "You saw the vision, didn't you?"

"I did." His hands slid up to cup her face. "We saw each other's essences."

"What are we?" she barely managed the words, her throat was so tight.

*Finally.*

His thumbs slid over her cheeks, so tender, her heart ached with it.

"You are Siobhann, and I am Erevan. And we have been gifted with a connection to the essence of fire."

She swallowed a second time, steadying the words she needed to say.

"My mother and Darya bound whatever this is inside of me because I destroyed everything. I lost control. I—I killed them—all of them. And I didn't even save my family. I—I should have saved them and instead I let them all die."

The pain of every word rising from her shame-filled heart rasped its way up her chest and throat, leaving behind a rawness that left her shaking.

She glanced up at his face, then squeezed her eyes shut at the deep sadness she saw there.

He held fast, ever gentle, as she tried to turn away. "I don't believe that was your intention."

She shook her bowed head. With her eyes shut, the memories slammed her. Her little brothers' bodies strewn near her invincible father's. Orlan falling as he defended her life.

*Orlan.*

Her beloved Orlan, whom she idolized. Eldest brother, who had nothing but patience and affection for her, taught her everything she thought was important at that age, including how to wield an ax.

The same wood ax she'd tried to engage their attackers with, screaming rage, but too small and weak to do more than slice a few tendons of the towering Torgolis warrior who'd sent her flying with a swipe.

She gasped, throwing herself out of the memory, opening her eyes into Erevan's.

"I can't be powerless like that again, nor can I lose control."

"Harming another with your magic requires intention, Siobhann." His voice was ever so soft. "Just like Darya's magic requires intention to heal."

"What do you mean? My mother bound my magic because I destroyed the farm and everyone there."

"Siobhann," his voice was firm as she stared at him through a shield of unshed tears. "She and Darya survived to bind your magic."

She nodded.

"And you have another brother that also survived."

Again, she nodded.

"Which tells me that there is more to what happened than the trauma would allow you to recall."

She knew where he was leading.

A dreamwalk. As the healer had said that she needed. And Donnen.

And what Darya said could never happen.

That it was too dangerous.

"I can't. I can't do what you're going to suggest, Erevan." She backed away as though to flee. But to where? Anywhere but the compassion in his face, his voice. His touch.

He held fast to her hand as she turned away from him.

"Do you trust me?"

The words immobilized her.

"I do," she said without any thought, as though someone else spoke them through her voice, without doubt.

It surprised her, yet it didn't.

"Then you will let me undress you and bathe you, and then we will begin."

Her eyes found the solid copper tub in the corner, though she hadn't noticed it before.

She licked her dry lips, watching the steam rising from the mass of water.

"You know how to dreamwalk?" She turned her gaze back to his.

"I know a comparable ritual. Elven."

Her head tilted.

*More Elven woo-woo.*

"But it won't work unless you trust me."

She drew a deep, steadying breath, easing it out through her nose as she held his dark gaze.

"You can teach me? To control it."

"If you will allow it, I can teach you how to work with it."

"I feel it trying to escape when you get too close."

His smile was gentle before he pressed his lips to her forehead. "It wants you to be free. Both of you."

The sudden pain that gripped her heart stole every breath, making her gasp.

Still, she refused to weep.

It wasn't time. She hadn't earned the right yet.

With shaking fingers, she began to undress before she could change her mind.

Erevan did likewise.

For several heartbeats, her ever-present desire for him eased the pain.

He stood still and quiet, allowing her to explore him as her fingertips trailed the lines and ridges of his torso. His warm flesh and the gold ink that marked him. Bound him to his clan.

"You'll tell me what this all means, one day."

It wasn't a request.

"I will."

She was about to give him access to her soul, she wanted to know his story. One day, even if it couldn't be this day.

Fingers linked, she led him to the tub, where he helped her step into it, before he joined her. The hot liquid rushed around her in gentle swirls, instantly easing her muscles. Eyes closed, she sighed, relishing the sensations.

When she opened her eyes, Erevan picked up the small cake of soap from the tub's ledge. Dipping it into the water, he rubbed it between his palms to make it froth.

She expected him to wash himself.

He proceeded to wash her instead.

The slide of his soaped hands over her arms and shoulders and legs and hips was both comforting and erotic.

He helped her wash her hair before returning to the rest of her body.

She dipped her head below the surface and when she re-emerged, he washed every inch of her, including her back, belly, breasts and the apex of her thighs, causing her body to react while she struggled to remain impassive.

He placed the soap in her palm, wherein she repeated the actions on his body and discovered beneath the soapy surface he wasn't anymore impassive than she was.

She grasped him, allowing mischief to take the moment.

His lips quirked as he moved to collect her wayward hands and lifted them from the water to kiss the backs of her knuckles. "Soon."

She lifted a brow at that. "Your ritual requires sex?"

"The ritual can be facilitated with it. Some use blood or some other means."

"But you do this with sex. How often have you performed this ritual?"

He glanced up at her teasing tone. "Only once, and blood was used. Do you prefer that?"

Questions tumbled through her mind. Leaving them unspoken, she shook her head. "I do not."

"Any other questions?"

Perhaps Aelozian healers had a different method.

And perhaps she didn't care for Aelozian methods.

Her gaze hungrily consumed his features. His skin had taken on a rosy hue from the heat of the bathwater and glistened in the low firelight.

Again, she was faced with the notion that this could be their last joining.

Each day presented new obstacles that left her questioning where her future lay. None more so than the day that he walked into her life. Before then, her life belonged wholly to the Kindred.

Such a short while ago.

His dark gaze held hers, unwaveringly.

Her heart sped up several beats. She recalled the vision of their beasts—their magics staring at one another through the barrier.

The recognition was profound.

*They* knew each other.

*For how long?*

These entities that were part of them, yet other.

How long have their souls, bound into human and Elven bodies, known each other?

She'd never met anyone like him.

Nor had she met anyone that could guide her through her partnership with her magic.

Not her family, none of her respected mentors.

Her mother could have, but she'd died, ensuring Siobhann never would have the opportunity.

"Nothing else. No other questions. For now."

His lips curled at the corners. "Good."

Through the water, his hands slid toward her hips, then gently pulled her toward him.

"Our bodies have already been joined and will forever know each other. Like a blood bond, we have mingled, exchanged and become part of one another."

His erection brushed her inner thigh as she moved closer. Silk-encased steel.

She licked her lips in anticipation.

"For you," he went on as he guided her onto him, filling her. "You open to me. You relinquish your barriers, allowing our essences to meet. This is just a way of knowing more deeply. Together, we can examine what binds you. It will not unbind you. You will always have that choice."

She gasped, revelling in the sensation of him within her. "I can break my own binding?"

"With your niece's token. She is your kin, carries the same blood and magics as your sister and mother. That can be your key. And I believe *you* can unlock it."

"But you're not sure."

"Not entirely, as I'm not a master mage. We can find you one, if you wish it."

"I will think on it later."

"Later." He nodded as his hands returned below the surface of the water to still the movement of her hips. "Not yet."

She gripped him tighter, unable to relax while he was within her.

He closed his eyes against her need, drawing a steadying breath. "Siobhann."

Erevan opened his eyes. The ring of fire was bright in them, his palms several degrees warmer than the water.

She gasped as his hands trailed up her body. Her head fell back, eyes closed.

His own need made him pulse against her sweet spot.

"We must focus, my love."

# NINETEEN

*'MY LOVE.'*

Siobhann's eyes flew open at his words, heart twisting.

Two words that no one had ever said to her.

Two words she hadn't known she longed to hear.

*Focus.*

They had a purpose.

The dreamwalk.

*'My Love.'*

Surely, he hadn't meant it that way.

Lover, maybe. Yes, that must be his meaning.

She rose from the building haze of desire enough to control her body and mind.

Still and silent, she held his gaze and waited.

Reaching for her hands again, he spread her fingers. He placed her left hand on his heart and her right so that her splayed hand cradled his head from behind his ear through his hair across the back of his skull.

He did the same to her, drawing her closer so that their foreheads touched.

Connected at the mind, heart and body points, his palms illuminated as he drew on his magic, murmuring words she could not fathom.

Their cadence, the sound of his voice, drew her ever forward.

Her heart burned. She squeezed her eyes shut against the sensation.

Her vision turned white behind her eyelids.

A roar deafened her inner hearing.

Another voice, not Erevan's.

She knew this voice.

The one that sounded like an ancient volcano. The one that challenged her every time she fell into the dream. The terrors from that day.

*Look.*

She forced her eyes open.

The mountain farm. The cold and whiteness of the snow struck her first. Then came the scents of burning and of blood. Then the howl of the wind swirling ice pellets and frozen flakes as the storm descended on her childhood home.

This part was always the same. She knew it well.

Now she was within her child-body, looking down at the small hands and spindly arms. Full of energy and excitement to return home from the endless boredom of being on her best behaviour until Darya finished.

She studied her siblings. They were all so young.

Now they were on the road. She and Darya and Garioch returned from a neighbouring farm. Darya had been tending their sick children, even at her young age. Their mother had allowed Darya to go and practice her healing skills, so long as Siobhann and Garioch accompanied her on the journey.

The coming storm had ushered them home. There would be much to do for their own family.

Jesting and throwing snow at one another, they rounded the bend to a scene of chaos.

Siobhann sucked in her breath, knowing what came next.

Erevan slid his hand into hers. She looked up at him from her child-body as he towered over her. Even taller than Orlan and her father.

She turned her gaze back to the scene. The shock reverberated through her small body, filling her with desperation.

She began to run.

Erevan squeezed Siobhann's hand, holding fast to her adult essence, bisecting her from her child body.

The cold, wind, smoke and blood no longer reached her senses.

There was only what she saw and heard and the anchoring of Erevan's hand grasping hers as they watched.

She fought against the urge to close her eyes.

Somehow, this felt even worse.

At least, from her child-body she had the sense that she was acting, even if she failed.

She struggled against the need to fly into battle, cutting down the enemies that shaped her path by their vicious, senseless actions.

She'd always assumed they'd been there to harvest her family for their winter stores.

She couldn't imagine how wrong she was.

Outside of her body, yet within range of her senses, she observed far more than the immediate threat of the Torgolis warrior that she and Orlan fought.

Across the yard, Darya fell to her knees next to their wounded mother, already dying. Darya's hands fluttering over her, desperate to stave off the bleeding as their mother held fast to stop her.

"It's too late. Get the others away. Go to the Temple."

"We won't leave you," Darya sobbed, wrenching her hands free.

"You must, Siobhann—hide her until another priestess can come for her. The Empire mustn't know." She gasped as Siobhann's child-self flew back several feet, striking the side of the well.

Her mother struggled toward her and Orlan, who continued to fight.

Siobhann staggered to her feet, picked up her ax, and ran forward to defend her eldest brother.

What she hadn't seen was the second Torgolis bearing down on them, that Orlan had.

Instead of turning to parry one enemy, he slid his body between Siobhann and another, taking the impact of the attack, before shoving her away.

From her vantage point, watching and listening, her ethereal self gripped Erevan's hand all the harder.

"No!" their mother screamed, dragging herself forward toward her children.

The child, Siobhann, screamed her fury as Orlan fell before her.

A sudden, raging inferno exploded from her in all directions.

Ethereal Siobhann stood in the centre of the yard. She knew well that the child saw nothing but the interior of the flames that twisted orange and red. Then white and blue before exploding outwards.

From this position, Siobhann looked on as her mother crawled toward the rising bird of flame, even as her other brother, Garioch, fought against more Torgolis incoming from the road. One of which looked on with an expression of awe on it's beastly face before it shouted its excitement in the same mountain language her community used. "That's the one. That is the human the Goddess of the Flame seeks."

Garioch brought down one of the smaller attackers, working his way toward their fallen mother. He clearly saw what was happening with his sister, but held fast to their father's training to defend the family.

The other Torgolis ran forward with the intention to contain the child. Perhaps they meant to capture her when her power was spent, but they didn't have the chance.

The child turned, seeing her other brother battling for his life, and threw her hands out. Fire consumed the Torgolis attackers. All of them. The magic swept out in torrents. They screamed, struggling to escape as their hairy bodies ignited.

Her power was far from spent.

It was unleashed, and raw and sought vengeance.

Ethereal Siobhann turned toward her mother and sister.

Her mother grabbed Darya's hand. "They can't find her. They mustn't know, Darya. Not until a High Priestess can train her to protect the Phoenix properly. Help me."

Garioch ran after the fleeing Torgolis, wounded and burning. He slashed the back of its leg, then ran his sword through its back.

Their mother's voice rang loud and clear through the destroyed courtyard.

The words—the ancient words pulled at Siobhann.

Both of them.

The struggling Phoenix raged against them as light struck it and surrounded it.

"Darya!" Their mother gasped then began the chanting again. Gripping Darya's hand, she forced her to participate in the binding spell.

Darya sobbed as their mother channeled her magic, directing it to imprison the beast within her sister.

"It's too dangerous."

Child Siobhann sagged to the ground, losing consciousness.

Darya's wide eyes darted from her sister's inert form to her mother's failing one. "Mother?"

"They can't know. They'll use her and destroy everything. There's no time to..." She swallowed as her weakened body gave out. "There's no time..."

Garioch dropped his sword, narrow shoulders heaving as he looked around him at the destruction, head turning from one sister to the other. He ran forward as their mother reached for him. There were no words as her spirit left her.

He stared down at her, then his gaze swept the rest of the homestead and their fallen family members.

"She said to hide at the temple."

"We have to bury them, Darya. We can't just leave them like this." His voice cracked under the sudden knowledge that he was now the head of the family.

The snow swirled harder.

Darya touched his shoulder. "The neighbours. They will help."

He nodded, swiped the back of his grimy hand across his eyes, and got to his feet. He struggled to pick Siobhann up from the dirt. "Darya, help me get her on my back."

She did. They stood several long moments, looking at the surrounding destruction.

Ethereal Siobhann stood next to them.

All still children.

Everything burned. The Torgolis, what was left of the house and barn and other outbuildings, everything.

Everything except their dead kin.

They remain untouched by the fire as the snow fell, coating them in a gathering crystalline blanket.

Erevan woke to the early sun shining on his face.

Siobhann's body was warm and supple against his between the soft mattress and the down filled blanket.

Opening his eyes, he noted she still slept.

Relieved, he eased out from beneath her, careful not to disrupt her slumber.

He retrieved his loose cotton trousers and pulled them on.

Passing the tub still full of its cold water, his mind returned to the previous night's vision.

He'd known it would be something terrible.

Yet, it still made his soul ache for her. For her losses.

There was no longer any doubt about her connection to the legends.

There couldn't be.

He'd witnessed it.

They'd completed the ritual and released the magic.

They did not complete the coupling. There was no need, and the desire had dissolved into exhausted heartache.

Instead, he'd helped her from the tub, dried her, then carried her to bed, where they remained the rest of the night in each other's arms.

She hadn't wept, as he thought she would.

He began his morning routine with a deep breath.

Slow, purposeful movement, reaching, holding, then releasing, before moving into the next pose.

With the soles of his bare feet firmly planted on the floor, lungs full of morning air and his face bathed in sunlight, his fire magic settled contentedly within his body, meandering through his veins.

The ritual had taken its toll on him as much as Siobhann. The link not only meant that he saw and heard everything in her memory, but he also experienced it as she did.

He felt it. All of it. Every heartbeat of rage and terror and grief.

There would be so much more to come.

He pressed his palms together, allowing the magic to flow from one to the other before releasing a small burst into the ether. An offering to the goddess.

Finished, he turned back toward the bed.

Siobhann lay with her face propped on a pillow, watching him.

"Is that part of your training?"

He nodded, reaching out a hand, palm up. "Come, I'll show you."

She slid from the bed, adjusting her shift so that it fell to her thighs, then joined him at the window, hand in his.

He stood with his chest pressed to her back, hands easing down her arms to lightly grasp her fingers.

She shivered against him, leaning into his warmth.

He moved, she moved with him, trusting his guidance.

The proximity of her magic brought his back to the surface. The movements, steady breaths, and calm mind eased the restlessness.

He could feel it swirling around them, swishing that way, swirling the other, dancing together.

Once she freed herself, what power they would have together.

*The power to consume, to destroy, to rule.*

He froze. Their easy movement jerking to a stop.

"Erevan?" Siobhann's voice was instantly concerned.

"It's nothing." He cleared the dark thoughts from his mind. He released her hands, stepping away from her. "You should see to the young man while I make preparations for the journey to the Shield."

She studied his face, seeking hints at the sudden change.

Pressing a forefinger and thumb to her chin, he leaned in to place a soft kiss, hoping to distract her.

She accepted and returned the gesture, but her expression sharpened. Finally, she nodded. "I don't want to delay your journey any longer than necessary. I must coordinate with Kember which may ultimately involve the Aelozian military if Nate is right about Carlane. If you wish to go straight away, I've a guide in mind that can get you into the region. But as we discussed, Nate's warnings about the Torgolis are to be heeded. They are dangerous."

Erevan picked up his shirt from the back of a nearby chair and pulled it on. "As I saw in your memory, Siobhann. I understand. I merely go to make inquiries about supplies while you fulfil your duties."

He finished dressing quickly, grabbed his pack and sword and left her watching his every move. Assessing his behaviour.

What he needed was distance.

He hadn't heard wayward thoughts such as those in a long, long time. Not since before his mage training. Before his family discovered his secret.

The reason he'd been removed from his birthright and shoved toward a new destiny.

Had he made a mistake by encouraging Siobhann to unlock her power?

*What have I done?*

# TWENTY

Siobhann's gaze followed Erevan as he left her standing by the window, struggling to understand what caused the abrupt change in his demeanour.

But he was right. She had a duty to fulfil to Kit Bower, and she needed to check if either of her ravens had returned from Donnen or Ghalen. Omi would remain Nate's shadow for now.

She dressed. As she donned her leather armour and weapons, her mind strayed, sliding from Erevan to the ritual the previous night.

Despite the exhaustion earned by the revisiting the memories hidden from her, her thoughts had spun and spun through to the wee hours.

The lack of sleep dragged at her body and weighed on her mind.

She should be relieved that she hadn't incinerated her family. Her magic had left them untouched.

But she had been the cause of Orlan's death. He'd died protecting her. And she was the reason her mother expelled the last of her magic. Magic she could have used to save her own life. Instead, she'd channeled the last of it through Darya to lock Siobhann's powers away.

Powers she was now on the cusp of unlocking.

She adjusted the last strap of her bracers, gaze falling to her pack. Erevan had given her Sendi's talisman, which Siobhann had tucked away with her drawings.

Could she unbind herself?

Should she?

The image of the phoenix rising from her body, lashing out at the Torgolis with flame to consume and destroy.

The sensation of the raw power surged through her body, easy to call to the surface now that the memory was near.

There'd been nothing left of the homestead.

The neighbours, other Wanderers, had returned for the bodies of her parents, Orlan, and younger brothers, to perform the death rituals, ashen and silent. They'd seen what she'd done. They knew the stories and been to the temple in the mountains.

Where her family lay entombed with their ancestors.

Grief and guilt, raw and overpowering, had blotted out those days following the incident.

There was no easy memory of the burial preparations or the deathsleep itself. She would have been part of it. All of them that remained, to observe and bear witness to the crossing from life to death.

She shivered again.

*Not now, Siobhann.*

*There are more immediate and pressing matters at hand.*

*Matters that might lead me right back there.*

Exactly where she never wanted to be again. Ever.

Snatching up her pack, she ripped the door open and grunted at the wide-eyed servant with a hand raised to knock on the door. "Tub," she barked and barged her way into the narrow hall, descended the dark stairs and emerged into the sun-shining morning.

She growled at the bird chirping too loudly as she made her way down the dirt road toward the healer's cottage.

"Oy, someone's musty this morning," Hilda Bruner snapped as Siobhann shoved the door open without knocking or announcing herself.

The sight of the young man still stretched out on the table halted her.

Her worries, her guilt and grief, her sleeplessness slid away in the face of his pale features turned toward her with large, grateful eyes.

"Mistress McLeighan." His voice was weak and full of heartfelt appreciation.

Another figure rose from a chair in the corner. "I be with the local militia. Master Bower insisted we wait for you," he grunted.

She acknowledged him and turned her attention back to young Bower. "Don't look at me like that. Nate Kirin is the one who risked himself and I've just delivered you as requested; else your uncle would never let me hear the end of it."

He chuckled, "Yes, mistress. I forgot how surly you can be."

She quirked a brow at him.

He swallowed and sighed, clearly still in pain. "I used to spy on you when you came to visit mistress Kirin."

"Ah," she said by way of answer.

A crush? Or just a curiosity for a female warrior?

It didn't matter.

"I am relieved to see that you are awake."

"Though I wish I weren't. I understand you need information."

She nodded, gaze flicking over his blanket-covered body, then to the militiaman waiting nearby.

"Ye'll ask yer Elven companion to help me move him to a proper bed?" The healer said as she worked on a poultice she was making.

"If he hasn't left me behind, I will do."

The old woman lifted a brow at that and snorted. "Unlikely."

Siobhann chose to ignore her and returned her attention to Kit. She forced the terseness from her voice and drew a deep breath as she pulled a stool to his side. "Please tell me what you can."

He recounted the full story from the minute he left his mother's house bound for Elder Holtmann's door. "They came upon me on the forest road that first night when dusk fell, before I had a chance to make camp for the night. They seemed to know I was there. Followed me, I suppose."

The healer stepped forward to place the poultice, careful to interfere as little as possible.

Kit went on. "I woke in a darkened shack with several others. Bound with ropes and forced to walk from one shack to another, several days' walk apart, always under threats. Others ran away. Most were brought back beaten, with whispers of their accomplices being put to death and left for the forest animals. I tried only once and failed. That's when I caught the attention of that one guard...."

Siobhann placed a hand on his. "He's dead."

Kit swallowed and nodded, his expression haunted.

"There's no need for you to talk about that, unless you want to." She glanced up at the silent militiaman.

Kit closed his eyes and shook his head. "You'll need to know about what their plans are."

"Yes."

He opened his eyes and turned his face toward her. "Most of them didn't talk in front of us. They went off a ways to talk to one another. But there were a couple, like the dead one, that liked to talk. But I don't know if what he said was true or just made up to scare us."

"Can you tell me?"

He huffed, not quite a laugh. "He said he was toughening us up for the Torgolis, that they wanted tough men to work the mountain stone. Which didn't make any sense to me. Aren't they strong enough to do that themselves if they wanted to? And why would they want to? They're Torgolis. They're beasts."

The militiaman shifted his posture at the mention of the Torgolis.

"Did they mention any places?"

"Car... Carlane? Does that make sense?"

She nodded. "That's what Nate said."

Holtmann's eyes widened as he struggled to sit up. "Nate?"

"Yes." Siobhann reached out to stop him. "I'm going back for him. You just need to rest and recover so you can return to your family. They've been trying to find you."

"The other men. They all have families, too."

"Can you name them?"

"Aye, most." He listed a dozen names and where they came from. "There were more, but they kept separating us and I began to lose track."

"You mentioned Lucas from Meiville?"

He nodded.

There were several names from other districts.

"I will report all of this, Kit, don't worry. The militia have been seeking these young men. We just didn't know where to look," the militiaman said.

Siobhann rose from the stool. "Rest now, but if you think of anything more, you let someone know."

"Aye. Thank you."

"Thank Nate Kirin when I get his sorry ass back to his wife." Kit laughed.

Elder Bruner walked her to the door. She kept her voice low as she spoke to Siobhann. "I've got him stable, but he'll be needing more treatment when he goes home. See that you tell his family to find him someone close."

Siobhann searched the old woman's solemn features. "His uncle has one of the best living next door."

The healer nodded, accepting that. "I see ye've done some dream work, which is right. The sense of ye feels different. Very different. Just... just be careful."

"No need to worry about me." She stepped down the steps when the older woman's hand caught her shoulder.

Siobhann turned, "There's really no need to worry, mistress. And I will tell everyone I know you're the best healer, with the best prices." She smiled.

"War mages are volatile. Dangerous when out of balance. Mind yourself."

The smile fell away at the woman's hardened tone. She nodded. "I will."

Satisfied, the older woman returned to her home and her patient.

Siobhann descended the steps, glancing up and down the road. Seeing no one, she shielded her eyes as she turned them to the treetops.

A black smudge launched itself into the sky. She extended her arm, inviting Moa to land.

As soon as he alighted onto her wrist, he croaked, ruffled his feathers and nibbled at the buckles on her bracer.

With her free hand, she opened the cylinder attached to his ankle and freed the rolled strip of paper.

Deciphered, the instructions read: 'Eterssal immediate. ~Arbitor.'

Ghalen.

Eterssal. Not the capital.

A war council?

She desperately hoped it was, and that it wasn't.

ATOP KELSTORM, LOADED WITH the supplies he had acquired, Erevan followed Siobhann and Odyn's lead toward the fortified city of Eterssal.

He'd had plenty of time to work through his new worries regarding her power and his.

Siobhann's mother hadn't bound her power because she was dangerous. She had bound her because she was in danger from others.

He'd wanted to help her, but the rise of his dragon's voice had put a hard halt to those desires. He needed to think this through.

And events with Nolgan and Kossa rose to the forefront of his thoughts again and again.

Still he struggled to accept and believe. For so long, he'd been tracking them. Over foreign lands, across oceans and deep into more foreign lands.

Had they been here so long that they had played a part of Siobhann's family destruction?

The timing made it possible. During those years, he'd been way off track, chasing sold artifacts in wrong directions. So much time wasted.

Had he followed the right leads, he might have caught up to them.

He might have been able to prevent those terrible events.

Might have allowed Siobhann to grow up with her family and the guidance she needed to become all that she was destined for.

He'd failed her, just as he'd failed his own clan.

Erevan needed the stolen tomes, now more than ever. He needed to know what they said about the Dragon and the Phoenix.

And dreaded that Nolgan was right.

At the iron gate, Siobhann identified herself and Erevan. The guard inspected her crest and asked a few more questions, before he moved onto Erevan, eyes narrowed. His suspicious gaze took in Erevan's markings and the brooch on his cloak. "I've seen the like afore. Years ago, mind." He turned back to Siobhann. "I've orders to direct you straight to the Arbitor on your arrival, mistress. Ensure your guest stays with you at all times, and he is to be presented without delay to the high council."

"The high council? Here?" She shot Erevan a glance over her shoulder.

Erevan tightened his hands on Kelstorm's reins.

If he proceeded through the gate, his life would quickly become more complicated as he was about to be pulled into the political realm.

His gaze swept the battlements above, with the archers surveying the open fields leading up to the walls.

*I could just go.*

Siobhann had given him the name of a guide. He had supplies.

She turned in her saddle and met his gaze. Her lips parted. He knew she was about to tell him to go.

"I will meet with your council," he said before she could voice the words and he could change his mind.

Her lips compressed. She glanced at the guard, who watched their exchange with a keen eye. "Wise choice, sir."

Erevan suppressed a sigh as he met Siobhann's eyes again.

Perhaps fate had a use for him yet.

# TWENTY-ONE

Sɪᴏʙʜᴀɴɴ ʜᴀɴᴅᴇᴅ Oᴅʏɴ's ʀᴇɪɴs to the stable boy and cast Erevan a glance.

*He should not be here.*

She straightened her shoulders, trying to roll the sudden tension out of them. Her gut told her something was wrong, if she was ordered to present Erevan.

Ordered, not requested.

Surely Donnen had sent correspondence to Ghalen, and he was fully aware of Erevan's intentions.

She glanced at his profile once more while his attention was on Kelstorm.

*What have I pulled you into?*

He'd already delayed his journey to help her find Nate and transport Kit to safety. Surely he should be continuing on, and not entangling himself in her responsibilities any further.

Had Erevan registered himself as a magic user in this realm? Somehow, she doubted it.

Having seen what he could do, they would no doubt see him as a threat.

Could they have somehow found out about his fire magic? About hers? Not that she actually had functioning magic, just a connection to a magical entity that had started communing with her since the Elven ritual.

Like she was being cast thoughts. Shown things that she should know but could not remember.

But there was no time for that. Not now.

Nate's life was in jeopardy, and that mattered to Darya. As for everything else, that was for others to deal with.

*I'm not a soldier.*

*'Soldier, warrior, mercenary, they're all the same'*, the old healer had said.

"We should have parted ways at the inn," she murmured as she led him through the entry to Eterssal's main hall.

"I'd have quickly become bored without your company. I never know what the day will hold when you're around."

She shot him a glare. "There's that funny elf-man again." But her lips twitched against a smile. "I suspect they'll interview you."

"Interview." His tone told her that he knew exactly what that meant. "Bound to happen sooner or later." He shrugged as she led him through an arch and along a narrow corridor.

She lifted a brow as she reached to knock on the door. She paused, drinking in his features once more.

*Any moment could be the last for us.*

They could separate them right here, send her on a mission and detain him or send him back to the border.

Though, she hoped they wouldn't. She hoped that Donnen would have spoken well for him.

He met her gaze.

She felt as though he caressed her face, the way he looked at her.

No, they weren't done with one another yet. Not yet.

Her knuckles struck the wood.

"Enter," Ghalen's voice was muffled through the thick door.

She grasped the handle and preceded Erevan into the room.

Three men stood clustered together over a table similar to Donnen's war table in the Kemberlan library.

Ghalen stood at the centre, looking for all the world like a more rigid version of Donnen, dressed as a politician, with a man she'd met only once before to the left. Ambassador Pailis and—.

Her breath stilled.

*Garioch.*

Not the fourteen-year-old warrior from her vision, but her full grown elder brother, whom she hadn't seen in several years.

Pleasure to see him warred with her concerns at his presence. Here, and now.

Her eyes met his and held his gaze for a long moment before she turned to Ghalen. "Arbitor," she nodded, then greeted his companion and Garioch. "Ambassador. Elder brother. It is good to see you all again, though the news is dire. Please welcome my travelling companion, Erevan ap Brodin y Draighdoine of Myst Innys."

Ghalen nodded and stepped forward, along with Pailis, to greet Erevan with an extended hand. "My brother Donnen informed me we had Elven royalty visiting our lands."

Erevan glanced at their hands, but shook each in kind. "He was generous with his hospitality and aid in my journey north."

Siobhann stepped back, observing the exchange. No formalities here, or titles. They were to be direct.

Ghalen and Pailis observed every detail of Erevan's person as their conversation continued, introducing themselves and their roles on the Council.

Garioch met Siobhann's gaze and held it as the others spoke. His eyes darted to Erevan and back to her. He wanted to speak to her afterward. She gave him a light nod and returned her attention to the meeting at hand.

"Siobhann, please report to Ambassador Pailis and me on the task you took on in relation to your sister."

Her gaze flicked to Garioch before returning to Ghalen. Erevan stood at her back as he'd done since they set off together.

She took comfort in that.

"Darya came to me about Nate Kirin's arrest over an accusation of a minor infringement that should have resulted in a warning and a fine, if found guilty. Instead, he was jailed without just cause, then transferred to the district court wherein he was decided to be guilty of a larger infraction. He was sent for imprisonment at Ondaggan prison. Before reaching that compound, he was transferred to slaver overseers, bound for the Shield."

"Go on," Ghalen said.

"I meant to extract him from the slavers when a young man, known to him, was discovered. He was close to death, so Nate bade me rescue the young man in his stead. He had confidence that we would go in pursuit while he gathered information about the slaver's network and base of operations."

"Darya's going to have your head for leaving her husbandless so close to her delivery time," Garioch muttered.

"I know it. Still, if a man refuses to be rescued, there is only so much I can do. Omi is following him."

"Omi?" Pailis asked.

"One of her ravens." Ghalen clarified.

Pailis nodded. "How does His Highness come to be your companion on such a mission?"

"He volunteered to help, since all other Kindred were out on assignments; mostly for the Empire, I believe Domini Kember said."

Pailis and Ghalen exchanged a glance. "Yes, that is right. Still. An Elven prince, volunteering for a dangerous quest such as this?"

Erevan turned to Pailis. "I offered my skills so that she would not be alone since no other Kindred companion was able to assist with her sister's plight. Besides, when we left, the original plan was to speak with the reeve and sort out the misunderstanding. Neither of us could have guessed the situation would escalate as it did."

"Skills?" Garioch homed in on that single word.

"I am a trained war mage, sir."

Siobhann's body prickled with shock that he would reveal himself like that. Her eyes snapped toward each man's face.

None of them gave away their thoughts as they studied the two of them. No surprise, no concern.

"We heard murmurings of a group of victims meeting a terrible, fiery death in the midst of the forest between here and the prison."

"We were attacked. By design," Siobhann said. "I believe the administrator working at the district magistrate's office fed information to the slaver network, alerting them of our presence. Had Ere—His Highness not drawn on his abilities, we'd either be enslaved or dead."

"There was no mention of a Royal Elven war mage registered at any Aelozian check points. Nor did my brother mention anything of your magical ability," Ghalen said.

"I did not share this information with anyone since leaving my home realm," Erevan said. "Mistress McLeighan knew nothing of it until the night of the attack."

Pailis nodded, accepting this. "Might I inquire as to why you chose to travel incognito, sir?"

"I'm tracking two kinsmen exiled from Myst Innys."

"Our authorities should have been notified of your intentions."

Erevan met his direct gaze. "I have been tracking them for several decades now, across many, many realms and oceans and more realms yet. I have not bothered to waste my time to retell my mission at any of them. There would be nothing to gain from it."

Pailis and Ghalen stiffened at this.

"An Elven war mage in our realm is a considerable threat. Especially with an unsanctioned mission on behalf of his crown within the bounds of our borders," Garioch said, voice quiet.

Erevan remained calm; his expression unconcerned. He'd expected this.

"And of your kinsmen? Would they be the same Elvenkind reported to be amassing a Torgolis army to descend on Aelozian citizens? I suppose you're not going to join them in their cause?" Ghalen's voice was dry, brow raised.

Ice slid down Siobhann's spine as she resisted the urge to turn to Erevan.

"I have not seen them or had direct communication with them since they were sent into exile. Not before our inventory clerks had discovered just how much of our heritable artifacts were stolen. Much more than expected. I have no information on what this *cause* you suspect is."

"But *you* have suspicions," Garioch pressed.

Siobhann's head jerked in his direction.

"I do."

Now she did turn to look at Erevan.

He met her gaze, expression calm, as though recounting a trip to the market for a new pair of shoes.

"My cousin is deranged, with the notion that the new Cycle is about to begin. He believes that he has some grand part in the ancient legends."

Siobhann casually linked her fingers in front of her to still their sudden trembling as her heart pounded.

"What do *you* believe?" Garioch pressed.

Erevan blinked, something flickering in his gaze as he looked at Siobhann. Regret? He swallowed before answering. He turned away from Siobhann to face the men. "I believe that he is driven. I have been told that these Torgolis are dangerous." Erevan shrugged. "If these Elvenkind are indeed my kin, then I will be involved with their capture. If they're not my people, then I have no idea what their intentions are. I would expect you would know more than I as to who your enemies and neighbours are. And which Elven realms you have poor relations with?"

Siobhann's gaze darted to Pailis and Ghalen, both of whom scowled.

It wasn't an unfair assessment. Aelozia was known for its appetite for land acquisitions these last few generations.

But her mind was alight with meaning. Erevan was tracking kin who were searching for the legends connected to the Great Cycle and they were in the Shield. He was searching for the Temple. He knew she had bound magic.

He'd seen her magic.

*He knew.*

Erevan knew what she was—saw what happened. And every step of the way, he'd been encouraging her to set her magic free.

What else did he know? Was he part of their deranged plan?

Her eyes locked on Garioch, who was watching her with keen eyes.

Perhaps these elves in the mountains had nothing to do with Erevan and his quest.

*'I have been tracking them for several decades now, across many, many realms and oceans and more realms yet.'* he said.

*Decades?*

Her mind went grey as she swayed on her feet.

*Torgolis.*

*Temple.*

*Decades.*

She turned to look at him again and saw the sadness in his expression as she did. He knew what connections she was making now, with just those few sentences.

Had he targeted her? Had he chosen Arlyss's tavern specifically to find her? How could he have known?

He couldn't have known.

*She* hadn't known.

Suspicions blew through her thoughts like the raging storms that destroyed the roofs of Kemberlan.

*Home.*

*I'm supposed to be on respite.*

She nearly laughed aloud.

*I should have bedded the louse-ridden warrior and stayed home, isolated, to pick the vermin out of my hair for the next week.*

Erevan watched the naked thoughts flickering across Siobhann's face as she stared at him.

He read every unspoken question. The suspicion in her expression sliced through him.

*I should have told her.*

*But how could I?*

He hadn't spoken to anyone about it since that day in his father's administration chambers, before he embarked on his own lonely exile.

Decades? Yes.

Decades of chasing someone that had betrayed him and caused his life to fracture. Because of a story.

A story he hadn't believed in.

Until he'd met this fiery tempered human that so intrigued him.

He'd refused to acknowledge the parallels until he no longer could deny them.

The ritual had sealed it.

As much a revelation for him as it was for her. And he'd needed to time to absorb what he'd seen, what it meant, and how to manage what his own magic was telling him. She had awakened something in him, that day she'd sat next to him.

The magic had been dormant. Quiet since his training. Content to work with him when called.

She'd awakened him, too. His magic.

His heart.

That expression on her face when she looked at him was betrayal.

He knew that look intimately.

It had changed his life.

Kossa's inability to deny her brother's jealousy had cost him his honour. His half-siblings had cost him everything.

He closed his eyes, dispelling those ancient memories.

Right now, he was the cause of that betrayal mirrored in Siobhann's eyes.

The men beside the war table were speaking to one another in hushed tones. He heard every word, though he remained focused on the woman before him.

Her face was ashen, her green eyes seemed larger, her stature smaller. She reminded him of the child of her memory.

It was in that moment that he understood she felt deeply about him, in order for him to have wounded her so, though she'd never hinted at it.

He'd felt it. Felt it in the way he'd caught her looking at him. The way she gave herself to him so easily, though he'd always thought that was just her way.

And perhaps this was the very moment she was finally understanding it, too.

What he'd already known.

That they were destined.

But he'd somehow damaged that thread, and he already felt her pulling away, as she'd done in those first days.

His throat closed.

He no longer cared if she was a phoenix and he a dragon.

He only cared that he unknowingly held her fragile heart and carelessly cracked it.

"Siobhann McLeighan, these are your Imperial orders to accompany a scouting party to Carlane fortress with members of the Kindred guild to assess and report. Your guild mates are in the barracks, and you leave before dawn," Ambassador Pailis said, extending a narrow rolled parchment. "It is essential we retrieve our general before the enemy realizes they have an individual of his rank, and intimate knowledge of our realm, in their midst. Troops are already mobilized for a siege. You will precede them. If Kirin cannot be extracted, he will be eliminated with the other prisoners."

Erevan would not have believed Siobhann's face could turn any whiter as she spun to face the Ambassador. Her brother, Garioch, also looked ashen as he processed the Ambassador's orders. Kirin was his brother-in-law, too.

Arbitor Ghalen Kember's voice was grave when he spoke to Erevan, "If you would accompany me, Your Highness, the other council members wish to interview you during your time here, as our guest."

He curled his hands into fists.

They meant to imprison him and send Siobhann to a frontier she was terrified of, vulnerable and without access to her power.

She was a seasoned warrior, but he'd seen through her eyes the size and brutality of the Torgolis that she was meant to spy on with a scouting party.

"I will go," he said to Siobhann.

Her brows knit together as she worked to understand his intention. His motivation.

"We will discuss your future in Aelozia soon, Your Highness," Pailis said. "McLeighan, you are dismissed."

"Use the talisman if you need it," Erevan said as she turned to obey the Ambassador's order.

She glanced back at him, her expression shuttered. She didn't stop as she opened the door and disappeared from his view.

Her brother followed her out with a final curious glance at Erevan.

"Now, shall we begin in earnest?" Pailis asked, clapping his hands together. "Do you care for a glass of wine? Kember has a fine label…"

# TWENTY-TWO

"Siobhann. Siobhann, stop!" Garioch's voice echoed along the corridor outside of Ghalen's chambers.

The emotions that roiled through her chest required vigorous movement. At the moment, that meant walking. Walking before she struck something or someone.

His fingers gripped her arm, forcing her to spin around. "I haven't seen you in years. You can at least give me a few moments."

She seethed. But was any of this his fault?

Her logical mind said it wasn't. But her angry heart said he was guilty by presence.

"Everything is going wrong! I'm supposed to be on respite from a job that earned a few coins for the goddess-damned roof, yet here I am, summoned to a war council and being packed off to the goddess-damned Shield!"

Garioch leaned his head back from her voice blasting up into his face.

She went on, "Nate is fucked. Darya and her children are fucked. Aelozia is fucked, and that elf fucked me over with his goddess-damned woo-woo, and the roof is still crumbling!"

"When hasn't Kemberlan's roof been crumbling?"

"That isn't the fucking point!"

"Isn't it? It's your home and your world is upside down."

She stared at him. He somehow made sense, but she wouldn't tell him so.

Her eyes stung. "My home should have been with you and Darya."

The words erupted hot from her heart through her mouth.

Garioch winced.

"Yes, it should have been," his voice was soft as he opened his arms to her.

Maybe it was the recent journey into her worst memory, and seeing him as that fourteen-year-old boy defending his family and her. She fell into his arms in a way she hadn't done since she was five and heartbroken because Orlan didn't have time for her that day.

She didn't cry. Even if she'd wanted to, she couldn't. She just stood with her face buried in her brother's chest.

His arms wrapped around her, holding her close, his chin resting on the top of her head. "We need to talk."

She drew a deep breath and expelled it with, "I know. I did an Elven version of a dreamwalk."

"Fuck."

"Yes. Fuck."

He squeezed her before releasing her so that he could lead the way down the hall to his own chambers. "Dwarven whiskey?"

"How many bottles do you have?"

"Two, but I'm saving one." He closed and locked the door behind her.

"Whatever for? Never mind, I don't need to know. Do you want me to use a glass?"

"What, and miss the chance to share slobber again?" He handed her a bottle as they settled on three-legged stools next to a small table.

"I don't slobber." She eyed him, pulled the cork, and swallowed a very long draw. She came up for air, gasping as it scalded its way down to her toes. "Oh, that's good," she wheezed.

"Grimms'." He nodded before drinking, eyes closed.

"Talk," she ordered, taking the bottle for her next turn.

"You first."

She sighed, setting the bottle on the table, but kept it in her grasp as she levelled her gaze on him.

He stared back, patient.

"I've never been able to remember all of it. What happened."

Garioch nodded. "It was a hard day."

"And you and Darya remembered it all?"

He reached for the bottle. She let him take it.

"In our own ways, yes. We've discussed it just enough to know that the other remembers. No heartfelt conversations, if that's what you're wondering."

Siobhann shook her head.

"I was so angry with her for doing it. For doing that to me. She didn't tell me that Mother forced her to focus that last bit of her life energy to do it. Mamma's last heartbeats were devoted to ensure I had no magic to be found."

"They were looking for you."

"Do you think there's any chance they're Erevan's kin?"

"Only he knows that."

"My gut tells me he thinks they are. He came to Donnen for a guide into the Shield. He said he was seeking the Temple."

"And you happened to be around?"

"Garioch, I've been with him every day since he came into Arlyss's place looking for the way to Donnen. He kept his business to himself, but I never once had the feeling that the meeting was contrived, though I will admit it seems suspicious now."

"You care about him."

She snatched the bottle from him and took another long swallow.

"Fuck." Garioch said.

"Yes." She handed the bottle back to him. "He knows everything that I know about that day."

"That makes him exceedingly dangerous."

"I know it."

Erevan met with the emperor's council at Eterssal.

The Aelozian military headquarters nestled in the central foothills of the Shield, stood guard to the southern mouth of the mountain range's subterranean caravan route to the northlands beyond.

He'd learned long ago that all the Elven maps of regions beyond the oceans were useless except to depict the terrain. The names and borders had all changed over the thousands of years since they were inked, and the elves had retreated to their corner of the world. According to the annals, the previous cycle had been hard on them.

Especially when the dwarves took it upon themselves to bury the sacred mountain temples in opposition to the desires of their Elven friends.

Friends no longer, after that.

He drew a deep breath as he surveyed the scene through the glassed window outside the quarters he'd been given in the keep. Soldiers mustered, dismantled siege weapons were carefully stacked on specially built carts and sledges. It would be hard going to get those monstrosities up into the mountains to Carlane.

Donnen's gazette still had the stronghold labelled as Aelozian, though abandoned. Taking that into consideration, how defensible was it still?

Dwarven built to safeguard the remains of the temple, it was already thousands of years old and meant to survive through the next cycle.

It would not fall.

The council meeting had him facing a bevy of old men with thin lips and suspicious eyes. All were younger than himself. He was learning the ways of the Elven court before their grandfathers were born. And even when he left his beloved Myst Innys, he was still considered barely more than a child.

And perhaps why his father thought this mission would be a good lesson for him. See the world, learn what is important, perhaps earn his honour back and return home ready to serve the clan.

He waded through their questions and suppositions until they convened on his fate.

Should they imprison him, though they didn't know it, he could allow it for a time to placate them and resume relations later. Or he could force his way out and join Siobhann and her guildmates' mission.

For now, his prison was a gilded stateroom, meant to impress upon him the wealth of the Aelozian Empire in their military headquarters.

Never mind that he'd already traversed much of the outer lands and the heart of the Empire, not bothering with the Aelozian capital.

Perhaps that's where the wealth was centred? He did not see a population cared for by the spoils of conquest.

He listened to the aside whispers of these men in their gold-trimmed robes.

"War mage... useful."

"We must do what we can, despite the emperor's illness."

"Elven politics..."

"Valuable hostage..."

"Dangerous..."

"Conspiracy..."

And on they went, heedless that Elvenkind had keen hearing, even across as grand a room as the central hall.

Until he interrupted their circular ramblings. "I have but one request, if I may."

They immediately turned; some curious, while others glared down their noses, and a few laughed. Those ones he suspected might have put forth the idea of ransom.

"Your Highness?" Arbitor Ghalen Kember stepped away from the group. They dragged like iron filings behind a magnet as he approached Erevan.

"I would join the scouting party. If my kin are indeed connected in any way to this army of Torgolis warriors gathering around Carlane, I would be useful in communicating with them. I know them. I could try to diffuse the situation and deal with them the Elven way. They are my responsibility."

"And if they are not?"

"I would remain an anonymous entity and follow orders like any other soldier."

One of the council members, a bald man with no eyebrows, whispered to Arbitor Kember, "Elves are not to be trusted."

"That would be wise, except in cases where there is a treaty. Elves always honour their contracts." Erevan looked the flushed councilman in the eye.

Kember's brow lifted. "An official agreement would be amenable."

Several councilmen nodded.

"Draft a contract and I will review and adjust as needed."

"The prince is our guest and must abide by Aelozian customs—," the bald man grumbled.

"Our Royal guest is a prince of his realm and would make a formidable ally and future trade partner. If he is so agreeable, he might graciously offer some insight on how our own war mages might improve their skills. Surely his ancient culture has learned a thing or two more than our own young dynasty, councilman." Ghalen held Erevan's gaze as he spoke.

Erevan tilted his head. "I would consider this, should we come to an agreement that is desirous for Aelozia, as well as Myst Innys, on the impending matter in the Shield."

"That would be very gracious of you, Your Highness."

None of them needed to know, even if Kember might suspect, that while Erevan maintained the title and markings of prince, he would never ascend to the Myst Innys seat of rule.

Not as a war mage.

# TWENTY-THREE

THE LONG, NARROW CORRIDOR tilted as Siobhann made her way through the garrison and the fortress toward the guest staterooms, grumbling at the distance they kept the soldiers from the guests.

After imbibing with Garioch, she had made her way to the barracks to meet with her guildmates quartered there.

The Dwarven whiskey softened the sting of Erevan's revelations.

It didn't matter anymore. She was going north. Without him.

"So ye've been gallivanting across the countryside with an Elven prince," Veira said when she appeared in the open door of the lounge.

"Aye, saving lives and takin' coin. Where've your sorry arses been, that I had to take up with the likes of an elf?"

"Spying and creeping, as we like to do." Nirran handed her a mug of ale.

"Room for one more?" She accepted the drink with a salute and a long gulp.

"As long as ye're the plus one. No room for a fancy elf."

"I am, and he's not so fancy."

Lorne lifted a brow with a sly grin. "Aaaye. I'll bet."

Veira settled next to her, giving her a little shove with her elbow. "Do tell, do tell. Are elves as good as dwarven or human men? Function the same and all that? One lass to another."

"You know mercenaries have strict confidentiality agreements with their patrons. What happens in the forest stays in the forest, and all that."

Veira rolled her eyes.

"Oh ho! I suspect ye tumbled yerselves right out of the forest. I hear he's put up in a stateroom. Everyone's been talking about the highborn prince that you dragged around Aelozia. You should pay him a visit before we set out. Might be yer last chance at a soft bed for the foreseeable future."

She snorted, but didn't rise to their teasing.

"Unless you're done with him? Then I'll give him a try. Or does he only like red heads?" Lorne winked at her, running his fingers through his long, blond hair.

Clutching her tankard, she rose from the bench. "I'll be back later. I'm going to see a few friendlier faces that have no interest in my bedding habits."

"You mean we'll see you fully sated and exhausted in the courtyard at dawn?"

"Same, same," she shrugged, and departed to more ribbing and laughter at her expense.

She stopped to greet some old friends and adventuring partners, and may have drunk a few more tankards over the course of the evening, before she mounted the steps to the guest hall.

She blew out her breath, guessing at which door might be Erevan's.

She meant to say goodbye. Even through the sense of betrayal, she needed to see him once more.

She tried a few doors, most were locked. One resulted in an accidental intrusion with profound apologies. There was only one left, right at the end. Of course. Likely the grandest chamber.

Whatever the legends were, she needed to focus on the task at hand if she was to rescue Nate and return his living body to her sister. She couldn't bear to face her if she didn't.

She remained outside the door trimmed with gold-leaf ornamentation.

She pulled Sendi's talisman from her pocket, where it now resided. Flipped it over and over in her hand.

Since the ritual, she sensed its power, where before it was just a bit of wood.

Her key.

He'd given her the key to unlocking a very powerful part of herself, and the desire to use it.

But for whom, really?

What would happen?

Who could control her now? She was a grown woman. No longer the vulnerable child from that memory.

*Perhaps I can find a High Priestess myself. Someone to guide me the way Mamma would have, had things gone differently.*

The question, then, was where to even start looking?

Would Garioch remember any of the elders from the old mountain community?

As far as she knew, they'd all dispersed after the attack. She'd only been able to find a few, such as the guide she'd recommended to Erevan.

*Maybe, once the siege is finished and Nate rescued, this foray into the mountains is the opportunity to find out what I am.*

With or without Erevan.

Preferably with.

She swallowed hard. If she were honest with herself, she desperately hoped so.

Siobhann squeezed the talisman against her palm.

She wanted to explore this unknown self, alongside him. She wanted him to teach her things, to show her how to have as much control over herself as he did.

To be her companion. Not just for the duration of the quest, but for always.

Or at least for the duration of her vital human years, until she became too old; because she would age and die, and he would go on.

*How old is he, anyway? Surely not nearly as old as Grimms.*

She wasn't sure she could bear that.

Brushing inconsequential thoughts aside, she shoved the talisman back into her pocket and knocked on the door, before she lost her nerve.

He opened the door. The corner of his lips uplifted, his skin flushed. "I wondered how long you'd stand out there." His silky hair fell around his bare shoulders and chest, light with air as though he'd been moving.

Her gaze trailed the lines of his chest downward. Her fingers itched to trace them too.

His usual cotton trousers hung low on his hips.

Whiskey and ale still swirled through her veins, muddling her thoughts.

She met his eyes. He knew what she was thinking as she licked her lips.

With one hand still on the door frame, he reached for her with the other and pulled her against him.

"How did you know it was me?"

"The way you walk when you're drunk."

"I'm not drunk. Just feeling good," she grinned. Her eyes flicked over his lips, so much closer now. Just a few inches away. "I came to say goodbye."

"There is no such thing for us, Siobhann."

His voice was low and husky.

She melted into him, her hands travelled around his waist and up his back as she rose up on tiptoe to brush her lips across his.

He closed the door behind her with a soft click and set the lock in place.

The hand on her back pressed her closer while the other cupped her face. "You know that, don't you?" His breath was silken against hers.

Her magic stirred in her chest, writhing around her heart. She nodded.

Heat flooded her as she inhaled him. Her own hands slid up around his shoulders to his nape, pulling him down to her level as she kissed him.

He returned her passion, reserve gone as he pressed her up against the frame with the full length of his body.

She wanted all of her clothes off, and all of his, too. To feel his body pressed to hers—within hers.

Was it the alcohol? Maybe some.

No, it was the knowledge of what lay ahead.

"It wasn't enough," she murmured against his throat.

"It never will be," he brushed his lips over her temple. "Siobhann, if you want me, claim me. I will be yours."

Her breath hitched. Hadn't she already done that? Shared his bed, shared her memory?

"I'm not ready to unbind my magic."

"This isn't about your fucking magic, Siobhann. This is about you and me. You came here tonight for a reason. We could have left things as they were. But you didn't let them alone."

The thrill of his words surged through her.

"I didn't. I—I couldn't." She looked up into his eyes. They glittered as he stared intently into hers. She swallowed, trying to help her fuzzy mind catch up to what her heart knew. "You want me to commit to you?"

"I want you to decide if you want to commit to me."

She swallowed. "I want you."

"I would have you for always, Siobhann."

She shivered against him. The sound of her name on his husky voice next to her ear, his body pressed so intimately to hers.

And still, she resisted saying the words. Her heart ached with it.

She wanted him for always, too, but just couldn't say so. She didn't know how or why.

*Not yet.*

She looked into his dark eyes for long moments, watching the light play in their depths, reading every nuance.

As much as he wanted her to claim him, he wanted it to be a true commitment from her. Anything less wasn't enough.

Perhaps in the next lifetime, if she didn't survive this mission.

She pressed her lips to his, hoping he would feel her heart in this last kiss as her fingers splayed across his warm cheek.

He accepted it, giving her back as much of his own as he eased away from her, leaving only their lips touching.

She released him, raising her eyes to his as he stepped away from her.

He was right.

There couldn't be a goodbye.

Or anything else.

Finally, she broke eye contact, turned, and let herself out of his room, heart breaking as she strode back along the hall toward her assigned cot in the barracks.

No one questioned her early return.

Or her silence.

HE'D KNOWN, AND HE'D said the words, anyway.

Erevan had asked too much of her.

He stared at the closed door, body alive from her touch, heart rending from her departure.

His fear of losing her was real.

He'd meant what he said, that there couldn't be goodbyes between them.

If he lost her in this lifetime, he would find her again in the next. But that could be an eternity from now.

He'd gambled, pressed and failed.

Erevan wanted her commitment to bind him to her so that he would know, that no matter what, she would want him to return to her. To find her. To be her life companion.

He'd agreed to the Imperial contract, and would participate in the journey to Carlane, but not as part of the Kindred contingent. He would be attached to another unit, belonging to Eterssal itself; a group of highly trained soldiers, designed to infiltrate the fortress from a secret point, to flush the Torgolis out.

He had his magic.

She had her axes.

Erevan turned away from the closed door and strode back across his room to resume his meditative ritual.

Trust.

He had to trust that she would survive.

He had to trust that the Goddess would protect her.

He had to trust that they would find their way back to each other.

In *this* lifetime.

# TWENTY-FOUR

THE ARMY WAS ON the move, and the generals had called all leaders together at the encampment midway to Carlane from Eterssal. Their voices, raised in argument, bellowed through the canvas tent walls. All commanders and first officers were inside, discussing the best tactical moves while everyone else paced outside.

Siobhann and her fellow Kemberlan warriors were waiting in a nearby tent, with tankards in hand, when the courier found them.

Lorne read the message. "We move out now. The rest of the companies have amassed their siege equipment and weapons, loaded onto all available wagons for transportation." He glanced up at the others. "They're just a few days behind us; do a final supply check. Siobhann, there's a note attached for you."

She accepted and unrolled the small scroll from Donnen and read aloud, "Child safely delivered."

She smiled as everyone shared their well-wishes at the good news from the safety of home.

They needed to keep it that way, by stopping whatever the Torgolis had planned.

She could only imagine an avalanche of the beastly enemy sweeping down the mountainside for the Aelozian foothills, destroying everything in their path.

She closed her eyes, stilling the persistent image that had been hounding her since she set foot back within the bounds of the Shield.

Instead, she turned her attention to the task at hand. The Kemberlan force had brought little with them beyond their necessary battle gear, for travel speed, since they acted as one of the scouting groups. They slept rough during the wee hours, always on alert. All the scout units fanned out, arching a path toward their goal.

Siobhann's raven, Omi, circled above.

Nate was nearby.

They'd failed to intercept the slavers en route to Carlane, but were able to determine which mountain trails they used.

Too often her thoughts turned to Erevan. Before they left, she'd heard that he was assigned to Eterssal's special unit.

Her hands shook. She quelled the tremble with a flare of anxiety, harnessing the fear in the tight ball of her fists.

Images of Torgolis warriors springing from every shadow to slay her companions weighed on her mind.

Fear for Erevan and his scout unit travelling in the opposite direction compounded it.

She prayed the Torgolis were too busy doing whatever they did to be exploring the surrounding mountainside forest.

She'd removed the talisman from her pocket, woven a thin leather thong around it and, with a few twists and knots, tied it around her neck so she could tuck it inside her tunic for better safe keeping.

Food stuff for herself and Odyn packed, she double checked her inventory of arrows, the state of the handle bindings on her throwing knives and various other equipment, including her chain mail hauberk, still freshly oiled and packed since her arrival back at Kemberlan.

It was all she'd had time to do during her brief respite by the riverside when she'd sharped her axes. Her beloved Sally and Trish. *Assailant* and *Attrition*. Crafted by none other than Grimms himself.

There'd been no messages from him, safe and sound at Kemberlan with Darya and Sendi.

She mounted Odyn and mustered with the others at the edge of camp.

Nirran, their head scout, was adept in his field and Siobhann remained outwardly calm under his leadership. Despite her heightened fear of the Torgolis, she forced herself to believe he would bring them to their position safely. He always did.

She travelled with her fingers burning to grip her weapon hilts. To let the infernal fear transform to anger, flow from her heart through her nimble limbs like quick-fire, and seek release in the comfort of battle. It gave her focus and calmed the whirlwind of doubt in her mind.

For days, they treaded lightly along the wilderness trails, constantly aware they could be watched or followed. Nirran remained ahead of the group at all times to decide which direction would keep them undetected, and to alert his companions of ambush.

The group made it as far as the outer forests of Carlane before they spotted any signs of enemy proximity. They immediately surrounded and eliminated a spy before they could give away their presence. Lorne searched the body before concealing it deep within a thicket grove, where only small animals and crawly things would find it. He handed the stained message to Veira to decipher as they set up to watch the keep.

Once she finished, she read it to the others, voice tight. "Activity in the Eastern crags promising. Send for more slaves."

"We still need to unravel their network," Siobhann said.

"Perhaps we should leave that to the local militia while we focus on our campaign," Lorne suggested. "We can't divide our attention."

Veira looked between Lorne and Siobhann. "The Eterssal unit is on the east side, whereas we intercepted our message here in the west. I think we do need to watch for them. Incoming slavers could alert the Torgolis to our advancing army."

It took four more days for the rest of Aelozian army to arrive. Nirran reported sightings of prisoners being held within the thick walls. Siobhann marvelled at the heights the man could climb to obtain optimal vantage points for his spyglass.

Nirran recounted seeing hostages dragged out for entertainment in the courtyard, bound hand and foot. Torgolis wandered around them, tormenting at will.

By now, she had to accept the reality that Nate likely was inside Carlane's walls, if he was still alive.

"Fuckers," Siobhann muttered, stomach tight as she listened with the others.

There was no mention of human slavers, or elves.

The days rolled on as the small Kemberlan force carefully maintained the frail veil of ignorance of their army's movement, intercepting enemy messengers until the day before the Aelozian forces arrived.

The enemy had little time to prepare for the mostly human army knocking at their imposing gate, but as soon as they sighted the siege weapons, they geared up for battle.

Still, the Kindred maintained their cover in the immediate forest, observing the siege camps surrounding the face of the fortress. By night, they moved like shadows along the perimeter, seeking weak points of infiltration.

From her perch upon a high, tree-lined crag overlooking the Aelozian camp, she watched the hundreds of soldiers preparing to lay siege to their enemy. There were more still to join them. This was the first few of many companies to come.

The pounding of the massive rams on the vast gates had begun. They expected the Torgolis would not remain inside for long. The Torgolis always fought with the full force of their savageness, without honour or mercy.

Siobhann settled by the small campfire to sharpen Trish and Sally's edges.

In a few hours, Kemberlan's small band would leave for their nightly trek through the woods. She slid the whetstone rhythmically along the edge, catching her reflection in the polished side of the blade. Pausing, she considered the hardened image that stared back at her. Would she fight honourably? Show mercy? Did it matter?

She shook her head, knowing herself better.

In their brief reunion, Darya's unrelenting worry lingered in Siobhann's mind. The fever of heartache was evident as she struggled to maintain rational action while her husband was missing.

The scent of ash from the logs beckoned the image of a burning farmhouse.

Quickly returning her gaze to her ministrations, she honed the blades to ensure they would slice through bone as well as sinew.

The image of Erevan's beautiful face, curled lips, silky hair and hard body relieved the fear of impending battle. She allowed herself to revel in the intimate memories when it was quiet.

They weren't foot soldiers, but battle would come.

She could no longer avoid facing Torgolis.

It didn't matter that she held no belief in the notion of Fate, because Fate had found her and dragged her right back into her past.

She pressed her face to Odyn's neck, leaning into his strength. He leaned back with a sigh. With a final pat, she left him picketed with the other horses and followed Lorne and Veira through the dark trees.

An hour later, Nirran's figure loomed up out of nowhere in the inky shadows, nearly making Siobhann loose her bowels.

"Movement," he whispered, signalling for them to follow. He led them along a cliff face above the northern edge of the fortress. "Listen."

She strained to detect sounds above the wind through the rattling tree branches and the usual night creatures.

After a while, she heard it.

Chains. The steady shuffle of many chains. Following the sound, she spotted the nearly invisible line of men emerging, two by two, from a gap in the rock below them to the east.

"Let's go," Lorne signalled to Nirran.

Nirran nodded and picked the way down, halting before they emerged from the dense brush. "Shit."

They had intended to follow the line of slaves ever closer on their approach to Carlane, not expecting to find a hidden door in the cliff face itself.

A tunnel cut through the rock into the fortress?

The prisoners waited outside a reinforced gate as a horde of Torgolis rushed out, turning east.

Siobhann's heart pounded in her ears as her fingers curled around Sally and Trish's hilts.

"That's a fuck-ton of Torgolis," Lorne breathed. "Where are they going?"

"Flanking our army?" Veira offered.

"Hush," Nirran warned.

Siobhann imitated a night-bird's call, while searching in the darkness for one of her ever present companions. The hush of silky wings signalled their arrival. In the darkness, she composed her cipher, stuffed it in the cylinder and cast Omi toward their allies.

Surely he was faster than the enemy. She swallowed, praying, as Nirran signalled for their group to proceed, now that the horde had disappeared into the darkness. The slaves resumed their forward shuffle, with the chains masking Kindred's presence behind them.

# TWENTY-FIVE

Nolgan looked up from his collection of scrolls as Kossa blew into his chambers again, breaking his concentration.

He cursed inwardly at his ineptitude in deciphering the ancient texts.

He leaned back in his seat, giving his sister his full attention.

The Aelozian army was massed at their doorstep, and she was anxious.

"I told you, the fortress is Dwarven built, the gate will hold," he sighed as she rushed toward him.

Since the humans had appeared, she'd been peeking out from one of the covered tower parapets, hands wringing, as she counted the siege weapons.

"He's here," she snapped, pacing the length of the room. She wrung her hands, then flicked them out as though shaking her nervous excitement.

"He who?"

Kossa stopped moving to give him a baleful stare. "Erevan."

Nolgan grinned, elation and concern at war within his chest.

She nodded, turning back toward the door. "He found us. I should pack our things."

"Yes, be ready, but we won't leave. Not yet."

She spun toward Nolgan. "Why not?"

"I've been reading through all the texts, and I'm sure now that we need him. Oh stop fidgeting, Kossa, what do you think he's going to do to us? He won't kill us, especially not you. So stop wringing your hands," he lied.

He theorized their need for him, based on the few words he thought he understood, along with the diagrams. The statement about Erevan not killing them was also a theory. Erevan had gone to great lengths to ensure that Kossa escaped execution.

Though that was decades ago, and perhaps his anger had hardened and now sought revenge.

Nolgan certainly would have. And was plotting just that.

She snarled back, "You're not the one they will execute if he drags us back to Myst Innys. You're just an exile."

Nolgan compressed his lips, seeking patience. "He's after the tomes. That's all. I've left him just enough evidence of our trail to guide him to us."

"You what?" she gaped, her eyes wide. "They want to execute me for *your* actions, and you leave him a trail to find us? And you think he'll just let me go? After tracking us for this long? After what you did to him? You destroyed his honour, Nolgan. Erevan won't forget that."

"I've also piqued his curiosity and forced him on this journey with us. Kossa, we're so close. *So* close."

She stared at him, shaking her head. "You've lost your mind."

"So you keep telling me." He stood, rolled the scrolls, and placed them next to the texts. "I've requested more slaves since our allies refuse to do manual labour, even at the behest of their Goddess," he nodded toward Kossa.

"They're getting harder to control and I can only hold the illusion for so long. They keep demanding longer prayer rituals, which taxes my magic."

"Hmm, yes, have you practiced the other spells I taught you?"

"Which, Nolgan? You've given me lists of them over the years." She crossed her arms.

"The direct mind tap." He ignored her acerbic tone.

"I've experimented with a few of the slaves and some of the dying Torgolis."

"And?"

"It's better with the exchange of blood, but it's disgusting, Nolgan. I don't like tainting my blood with theirs just to perform your experiments."

"But it *works*!" He clapped his hands, rubbing them together as his excitement escalated. "This is fortuitous news. And the others?"

She shrugged, "Some work, some don't. I've kept logs as requested."

"Why haven't I seen any of them?"

"You've been busy. I've been busy, and I don't care to chase after you to give you the information that you want."

"You've been busy? With what, stealing my slaves from their work?"

"Nolgan, I get bored out here and the Torgolis stink. At least I can have a human bathed ahead of my entertainment."

Nolgan turned up his nose. "There are more important things than your entertainment."

"I'm here at your request, brother. Keep me from my boredom or I'll move on to some more hospitable climate with more agreeable populations."

He was on his feet and loomed close to her face. "We both know your threats are empty, Kossa. You *need* me. You're incapable of caring for yourself and revel in the attention of someone else seeing to all of your needs."

She turned her face away, dropping her gaze under the force of his sudden show of temper.

"I have taken care of you all these years. All I ask of you is to use your power now and then to facilitate our mission."

"Your mission, Nolgan. I never wanted any part of this," she mewled.

"I don't know how you fail to understand that this is for both of us. To secure our place. Myst Innys didn't want us. We'll claim a realm of our own to rule." He leaned back, granting her some breathing space. "You, my dear, control the Torgolis as their goddess. We control the Torgolis, we control their territory. Anywhere they abide, we rule. And they're keen to sweep into the human domains to the south. There you'll have your agreeable climate, luxurious castles to choose from, and lush forests and rolling hills."

"And you'll have the magic you crave?" She lifted her eyes to his, her tone even. Careful.

He wasn't sure if she was seeking confirmation that he would be successful or if she mocked him. He nodded. "With the fulfilment of the legend. Where was Erevan seen? I want to send the Torgolis out to capture him."

"While the humans have besieged the front gate?"

"It won't matter once we access the temple."

"Which we haven't yet." Kossa ground her teeth.

"Soon. I know it."

Kossa eyed him.

"Have faith in me, little sister."

"I've had to have faith in you, since we betrayed Erevan's trust."

"It was necessary." He reached out to place a hand on her shoulder.

She glanced at his hand, then to his face. "How much longer, Nolgan?"

His gut wriggled at her tone. He searched her face.

*I'm losing her.*

He had to choose his words carefully as he studied her face; he understood now that he couldn't string her along indefinitely.

Anyone else would have abandoned him years ago.

*I still need her.*

He needed her magic to control the Torgolis. And to perform the rituals he would need to secure his own power as soon as they found the temple. Which he knew, more than he'd ever known anything else in his life, that they were on the cusp of discovering.

"Just days, I'm sure of it."

Uncertainty flickered in her gaze.

"Your constant understanding and loyalty and sisterly devotion has meant the universe to me. Everything that we have achieved has been down to you, Kossa." Nolgan swallowed the rising bile at his own words.

*If she needs empty words, I will do what is necessary.*

Though, he was sure that they were close—in that he was firm.

# TWENTY-SIX

Hidden in the trees, Siobhann waited quietly with her party as they watched the chained group.

In the distance, the crash of boulders and assorted war missiles striking the gate echoed along the cliff face.

Once they were sure the majority of the horde was out of sight, they began their approach. Crouched with weapons in hand along the cover of the shadowy stone walls, they waited for Nirran's signal. Each of them was aware that they could easily be overwhelmed as they attempted to sneak into the keep behind the Torgolis warriors, should they turn back for any reason.

She stared at the weapons in her trembling hands, hoping she would succeed in recovering her kin alive.

*Please let us get the hostages to safety. I can't face Darya if I fail again.*

Dressed as they were in forest green and black clothing and leather, they blended well into the shadows circling the mossy walls.

The signal came.

Nirran had dispatched a guard just inside the reinforced door, creating a safer passage for his kinsmen. Once through, they closed the door and hid the bar so that it could not be secured.

Following the prisoners at a distance, the stench of the place nearly drove them back, with more force than a dozen Torgolis could have done. Adjusting, they continued on in the dark stone tunnel leading toward the heart of the fortress.

Ahead, dull light illuminated another opening into a brighter area. The prisoners filed through, disappearing around the corner.

Siobhann paused, allowing her eyes to adjust at their approach. The door opened into a side yard between the wall they emerged from and a section of the keep, similar to the nook where Grimms kept his forge at Kemberlan. Guards forced the prisoners toward the larger courtyard inside the keep.

Across the short side yard was a set of stone steps that lead up to a door and a walkway that wrapped around the interior face of the keep. Nirran led them up, ever watchful.

They ducked, covering their heads as a misaligned catapult shot crashed off the side of the keep above them. Broken stone rained down around them, covering them in shards of missile slate and structural granite.

"I expected there to be far more Torgolis here," Lorne murmured, shaking off the debris.

Siobhann mounted behind the others, to creep along the keep's face, mindful of Torgolis inhabitants. Hesitating a moment to cover her nose and mouth, her eyes slid around the courtyard below in disgust at the refuse piled and spread without shame. Squinting, she noticed movement in one of the farther corners. One of the Torgolis grabbed hold of a hostage, dragging him through a dark doorway.

"There!"

They scurried through the shadows around to the far door and followed the inky corridor down into a series of dungeons.

Torchlight flickered at the bottom of the slippery stairs and screams echoed along the walls.

Above, the siege continued to pound the front gate and battlements.

The stench of decay and refuse was stronger here. The sounds of battle faded as the small group pushed downward toward the dim light. Barred doors lining the dripping walls came into view. The Torgolis grunted and snarled, lumbering back and forth, dragging prisoners around by whichever limb was most convenient.

Leading the small group past the prison cells, Nirran eased forward to glance inside the space where the Torgolis were. The way he jerked his head away from the first room and struggled to control himself made Siobhann's heart lurch.

*Nate?*

Pushing her way closer to Lorne's position, she scanned the room in horror. Veira gripped her arm, pulling back. Blinking the tears from her eyes, she straightened her spine and readied herself.

It wasn't Nate. Whoever it had been was an unrecognizable mess with blond hair, whereas Nate's was dark.

At the edge of the shadows, the room opened up with large tables and other equipment used for interrogations. Beyond that, more cells lined the rock walls where human slavers were transferring prisoners from their chain line to the cells.

Two Torgolis, larger than most others of their kind, were busy with captives in the central area, preparing to strap a few to the tables.

Nirran gave the signal.

They rushed into the room, weapons drawn, engaging the oversized Torgolis butchers.

The floor was slick with the blood and torn remains of the dead, making their task more difficult. The sheer size and brutality of the Torgolis meant they were slow to die as they tried to batter and crush the small group of fighters.

Prisoners able to move away scattered to the edges, or grabbed knives and other instruments from the tables. A few tried to help in the fight, hindered by their chains, while others used them against their human slaver escorts.

Veira concentrated on evading the charging Torgolis' fists while striking with her deadly ironwood staff.

Nirran rapid-fired his bow alternately at each of the Torgolis engaged in fighting with Lorne and Siobhann. His steel-tipped arrows embedded in their thick skin, leaving pinpricks of fatal poison.

Siobhann swiftly jumped clear of a number of hits, but was still knocked to the slimy floor. Nimbly regaining her footing, she whipped her axes through the air, slicing the Torgolis' flesh. She lost her concentration when she heard a shout and saw Lorne go down, losing his sword. The Torgolis raised great fists above his head to crush him with a single double-fisted blow.

"No!" Siobhann's lightening movements plunged her toward the Torgolis. She jumped, bringing down her axes with the full weight of her body. She felt the crunch of its skull as her blades separated the bone and sank into the mush of its brain, halting its movement.

It staggered, swinging a great fist to swat her away. She flew back into the bars.

The other grunted, struggling furiously against Veira and Nirran to attack Siobhann, who crumpled in a daze, close to its mammoth foot.

Lorne regained his sword in time to join the others, swinging it in a great arc downward through the Torgolis before it reached her.

The four Kindred gathered themselves together, struggling to ignore their injuries in order to free the remaining prisoners and get them to the safety of the tunnel before they planned their next moves.

Nirran retrieved the keys from a dead Torgolis to unlock the prison doors. He swung open the second door and froze.

"Siobhann." His voice was so quiet, ice crawled along her arms.

She rushed past to see what had stopped him. Horror and relief washed over her as she looked over her brother-in-law's battered body. He lay on the filthy pallet, unmoving, his breath a shallow rasp. She rushed to his side.

Veira followed closely. After a few minutes of inspection, Veira leaned back on her haunches. "He may live," she said, grave. "We need to get him out of here."

Quickly, they gathered the few remaining prisoners. There was no time to make a stretcher. Lorne and Nirran supported Nate under his arms. Veira and Siobhann led the small group out into the courtyard, weapons ready.

There were only a few Torgolis up on the walls, firing bolts down on the Aelozian soldiers beyond. No one guarded the gate. "Here," she whispered, unlooping the leather necklace holding Sendi's talisman. She threw it over Nate's head, grabbed his hand, and closed his fingers around it. "Nate! You know how to use this. It's Sendi's token." She hoped he'd hear her through the haze of pain keeping him inert.

His fingers twitched at her words.

"Don't die," she ordered, stepping back from the group.

"Where the hells are you going?" Veira demanded, eyes flicking between Siobhann and the direction she stepped toward. "You're not going alone, you fucking lunatic," she hissed, glancing up at the preoccupied Torgolis.

Siobhann grinned, raising her brows.

She couldn't have explained the sudden change. Perhaps it was the long, long days of constant terror of facing the Torgolis warriors again. And not dying in the dungeon. Perhaps it was the nearly successful rescue of her sister's husband—they still had time to fail. Or it was altogether something else that she couldn't name.

Perhaps it was just the fight, and her father's Baerskyr heritage had kicked in, goading her onward.

"You have no idea how terrified I am, but if we can get to the release mechanism unseen, we can end this."

*And I can find Erevan, and help him find the Temple, and get some answers.*

"And if we can't, we're dead." Lorne growled.

"*You,* are taking *them* to safety," she nodded toward the shivering, bent prisoners.

"I don't agree with this plan, Siobhann," Nirran said. "It's—,"

"Reckless. I know. I'll wait until you're out of sight before I even twitch in that direction."

"We. Before *we* even twitch." Veira corrected, hefting her staff. "If we live, you owe me big for this."

Siobhann nodded. "I sure will."

# TWENTY-SEVEN

KOSSA REMAINED AS SHE was, hidden in the shadows of the parapet she used to spy on the fortress and its surrounding countryside.

Cloaked in the illusion of her environment, she mused on her conversation with her brother.

She knew he was using her. There was no way they would have reached this point without her magic.

But what else was she to do?

While she had the gift to conjure and make people see what they wanted to see, Nolgan had the gift of convincing people of what they wanted to know.

How easily he lied.

She knew he plied his trade with her, too. She just didn't want to admit its truth: How deep it went, so that she could no longer tell if there were any truths in his words. If there ever were.

He was the reason she was judged for execution, and now an exile for all these years.

She'd stolen the tomes for him.

Their father's heritage and property of the clan.

Their father and Erevan's father.

Due to her and Nolgan's human mother, they were never in line for succession, even though Nolgan was older than Erevan.

All because they were begotten on a concubine of non-Elven blood. The children were allowed to stay, while their exceptionally beautiful mother was gifted to a neighbouring clan leader during their centennial negotiations.

"The clan would never accept you as their king. You do understand, Nolgan," she'd overheard Father say to him when she'd hidden under a table in the corner of the chamber.

She was good at hiding, always had been.

That was the first day that things changed. That Nolgan changed.

From then on, he spent every hour he could in the library, searching. Then to the vaults, searching still. Then he somehow gained access to the king's personal collections. Those were the ones he craved. There was no way to remove them unseen to study, so he would sneak in to steal any moment he could, with parchment and charcoal to copy the pages. The drawings never looked right, and he couldn't decipher the words, which frustrated him all the more.

They were his obsession.

He complained constantly that their father refused to allow him to learn the old Elven languages which the full-blooded royal children were forced to know.

Then came the day she had discovered her magic. She'd begun to ask questions that raised brows. Nolgan had demanded to know more.

She told him, and the very first thing he did was convince her to steal something for him.

"Steal it, or I'll tell everyone your secret." Reinforcing the fear that she mustn't tell anyone.

She stole a scroll from the library's special area and the guilt and fear of discovery overwhelmed her.

That's when Erevan found her crying in a corner, behind one of many the spiral staircases.

He'd always been kind to her. He treated everyone with respect. Even Nolgan, though he often didn't deserve it.

"Hush, little Kossa," he placed a hand on her shoulder. "Don't be afraid. I have magic too. We can share that secret. When you are frightened, you can talk to me, and one day when we're brave, we will go and present ourselves to Father to decide what our fates will be. We can learn to be brave together."

She looked up at him then, sniffling. "Fates? But aren't you to ascend?"

"I don't think I will be allowed to. Not with magic like this." He flicked his fingers, producing a small flame like that of a candle. His royal markings glimmered with their own inner light as he ignited the magic.

Kossa and Nolgan had no such markings as half-elves, even though they too had royal blood.

She gasped, eyes wide, reaching for it. "Is it real? How does it not burn you?"

"It is real, and I don't know. I hope to find out one day."

Her fingertip made contact with the orange edge of the flame, and she jerked her hand back to her chest.

"We must tell Father?" she asked him.

"Yes, but not just yet. Shall we tell him together, you and I? One day when we work up the nerve?"

She half nodded, believing he would suggest the best course of action, but also wishing never to reveal such a thing that would mark her differently—even more so than she already was.

She wanted to keep her secret, for always.

Nolgan had too, until she refused to do his bidding and foolishly spat that Erevan never used his magic for devious things, nor would he ever ask her to.

Her second mistake, and the next change in Nolgan.

Not only did she have magic, while he didn't but Erevan did too.

Anger twisted his face for several intense moments, then, just as suddenly, he relaxed and began to ask questions.

She heard nothing more of it until the day came that Nolgan again asked to be allowed to study with the other royal children, and was again refused.

Father had stopped to visit them in their section of the study wing.

"That is the privilege of the heritable line, Nolgan. I've already explained this to you many times."

Nolgan's eyes narrowed as he shot Kossa a sly glance. "Then why should Erevan be allowed to learn?"

Father waved a hand, "As primary heir, it's expected. Stop with your ridiculous inquiries. Ask your Maester for more learning materials that are appropriate for your station."

"Even as a magic user?" Nolgan shot.

Kossa stopped breathing, her fingers icy, her eyes darting from her brother to their father.

Father scowled at Nolgan, brows descending over the bridge of his nose.

"Maester's teachings had several chapters on the roles for Elvenkind. Magic users and Inadepts." Nolgan tapped a finger to his chin. "Magic disqualifies an heir from ascending, yes?"

Father's frown deepened as he studied his progeny, lips compressed.

"They're considered too dangerous to rule over other elves, should they misuse their power, right? Like in the old tales of the Heroes and Villains of the last Cycle." Nolgan drew a deep breath, his expression taking on an air of sad compassion. "As a war mage, linguistics is a thorough waste of his time, father."

"How do you come by this idea that Erevan has magic?"

Kossa's chest tightened as Nolgan turned to her.

"Kossa told me."

"Kossa?"

Father's stern voice made her body go rigid. She gasped, eyes pleading with Nolgan to take back the words.

Father barked her name again, pulling her attention back to him.

"Y—yes, Father. Erevan can do tricks."

"Tell me."

"Just a little trick where he made fire appear from his fingers."

Her stomach tightened painfully as Father's complexion went white.

"You saw this?"

She nodded.

"Why? Why did he show you this?"

She shook her head, slowly lifting a shoulder. Her mouth opened to answer but words stuck in her throat. She wanted nothing more than to hide, but knew that to use her magic to escape her father's glare would be unwise.

"Perhaps to frighten her?" Nolgan blurted.

Father straightened.

"Is that true? Did he frighten you?"

"She was very frightened, Father. He told her to keep it a secret." Nolgan spoke for her.

The following morning, Erevan was sent away.

Nolgan didn't get his language lessons, but he still seemed content.

He continued to force her to use her magic to steal things for him. More scrolls, tomes and tablets.

Erevan was permitted visits. The first time he returned, Kossa experienced the sickening weight of her guilt.

When she came to the hall to see his arrival, his gaze found her. Betrayal flashed across his features before he turned his attention from her to their younger siblings.

His rejection twisted her heart.

Nolgan adopted it as another tool to control her.

Their entire lives at the royal compound revolved around each other. They had limited contact with their full Elven siblings. Servants were cool and distant.

She was lonely.

As long as she did as Nolgan wanted, she wasn't alone.

Now, as she stared out over the courtyard with revulsion, she wondered if any of it was worth it?

She hoped the Torgolis didn't harm Erevan.

Perhaps, if he didn't hate her completely, she could leave with him and find somewhere new to live. Returning to Myst Innys would never happen. Father would not overrule the council's judgment. He believed her to be the thief that Nolgan forced her to be, and worse. She'd had to use her magic to impersonate one of their younger siblings to gain access to the language texts Nolgan coveted.

She'd been able to steal and hide one before she was caught through carelessness.

Deemed untrustworthy, with her access to the royal family and their holdings, her judgment was harsh.

The palace guard launched an investigation to inventory everything of value throughout the entire complex.

Most of what she'd stolen was noted.

Nolgan somehow managed to hide almost everything from recovery. She had no idea how or where. But on one occasion, they'd searched his rooms and found some of the items, including the missing language tome.

He was sentenced to exile as her accomplice.

Erevan was summoned to the palace. As a member of the royal family, he was expected to bear witness to the sentencing of his half-siblings.

His own infraction had never been made public, though she could not imagine why.

The day before she was to be put to death, Erevan made an announcement to the people of Myst Innys.

He chose to abdicate his right to rule in favour of his younger sibling. He declared this was of his choosing as was right for a member of the royal family to follow an alternate path and serve his people as a war mage, rather than their prince.

The declaration shook the foundations of their father's kingdom.

Questions rose, Erevan disappeared.

Kossa was sent into exile with her brother.

Nolgan retrieved his hoard of stolen artifacts and priceless heritage pieces and led the way out of their realm, bound for the coast.

Whatever he told her, she just accepted at face value.

She recalled what the human slave escort had told her the week prior, in his report regarding their journey. They'd had considerable delay recruiting new men after an attack by an

Elven fire mage and a red-headed human woman with twin axes and a bow.

Her first thought had been Erevan, but then she'd discounted it. Why would he be here, of all places?

Nolgan's admission that he'd deliberately left a trail for Erevan to track them, while insane, made some sense now.

# TWENTY-EIGHT

"You're a fucking, fucking lunatic, Siobhann McLeighan," Veira muttered again and again.

"I will point out that you're right here alongside me, Veira Valkyr. What does that make you?"

"Your fucking saviour."

Siobhann snorted.

Veira punched her arm for silence as voices sounded nearby. They crouched lower in their slim corner, shielded from the courtyard torches. It was full night now and thankfully the moon slumbered behind thick cloud cover.

"We have to get this done before that wandering horde returns."

"'Cause then we'll be even more fucked than we already are."

Siobhann glanced at her diminutive partner. "Veira, our exploits only go wrong sometimes, and we always make it out alive."

It was Veira's turn to snort. "What is it Arlyss calls you? Right. A fucking cat. And one of these days, you're going to run out of lives."

Siobhann quirked a brow. "I'm bound for great things, Veira, I don't have time to die just yet. So you're in luck, too. There's a gap, ready?"

"As I'll ever fucking be." Veira gripped her staff tighter, eyes darting to every corner of the yard.

There were still Torgolis on the wall, firing bolts at the army, and prisoners being dragged from one end to another.

"Go." She sprinted from their corner to a cracked barrel and paused as Veira arrived two heartbeats behind her.

"Shit." Siobhann's gaze darted from object to object from this new vantage point.

"Yeah, no kidding."

The next obstacle that could provide them cover was, in fact, a massive pile of dung and not a stack of *anything* else that they might have hoped for.

"Hold your breath," she muttered, and scuttled toward it with the wall at her back, glancing up enough to notice another guard entering the yard.

"Fuck me, that's bad." Veira's face screwed up, trying not to gag. "I don't think that's horse or cow manure."

Another boulder went sailing over their heads, bouncing off the keep. Broken chunks of stone fell on a Torgolis.

"It's not," Siobhann assured her, "Don't ask. We're almost there."

They ducked as the newcomer lumbered around the perimeter of the yard, extending their stay behind the dung pile.

As soon as he was far enough away, Siobhann risked rising out of her crouch to peer at the mechanism for the gate. "It looks like the one that Grimms rebuilt at Kemberlan."

"I remember. I helped him set some of the pieces in place." Veira nodded. "You're taller, but I'm stronger. We'll figure it out."

Siobhann peeked around the steaming pile with the back of her bracer pressed against her nose.

"One shot."

Veira nodded. "We have to do this before the rest of those big fuckers get back to slaughter and eat us."

"You'd give'em indigestion," Siobhann cracked as she dashed for the shadows surrounding the empty guard post where the mechanism for the gate was. Heart pounding, she flattened her back against the stone wall, making room for Veira to move in around her.

They immediately set to work on the windlass, drawing the portcullis up.

A great cheer resounded by the soldiers on the other side, drawing the enemy's attention to the gate.

Just as Veira hauled the bar over to prop the portcullis, a Torgolis saw them and charged forward.

With one foot on the windlass, Siobhann gripped Sally and Trish by their handles, ready to swing. "Veira!" she screamed as the Torgolis worked up to speed, ready to swipe her with its clawed hands.

Evading the first swipe, she struggled to hold her position.

Arrows whistled in through the open gate, striking the Torgolis, pulling its attention from Siobhann.

"Got it!" Veira scurried inside and ducked into the guard post as soldiers poured in through the gate behind her. Retrieving her ironwood staff, she cracked the Torgolis in the face, making it scream. "Fucker!" she screamed back.

Erevan disliked leaving Kelstorm behind, but his group leader had insisted they needed to scout this region on foot. They moved up into craggy, narrow paths too dangerous for their horses.

In the distance, the crash of siege missiles striking the fortress echoed across the plateau in all directions and up the mountain face. Every few minutes, the sharp strike punctuated the necessity of their mission to take the fortress from the Torgolis before they could descend on the Aelozian citizens inhabiting the lands to the south.

Torgolis scouts were sighted exploring in numerous directions from Carlane.

Eterssal scouts split up to follow some of them to determine their destination. One appeared to be a courier between the fortress and the remnants of a burnt-out homestead, while others meandered through the crevices and caves, seemingly at random.

He was part of the contingent that went to the homestead. He recognized it immediately from Siobhann's memories. Now his memories, as they'd become part of him during that ritual.

The site had been cleared of snow and stubborn winter ice. Charred house beams stood stark against the backdrop of the white mountains behind them. The ground and stones remained blackened, with nothing growing in the subsequent years. The scene had an eerie quality to it, while the atmosphere held an otherworldly charge. It made his magic prickle to the surface.

After that, they inspected other locations the Torgolis had searched.

*They still haven't found the temple.*

Siobhann knew where it was.

His thoughts constantly returned to her, hoping that whatever situation she found herself in that she would remain unscathed. He meant to reunite with her when this was all done. Surely she would accompany him to the Temple, and together they could discover their shared mystery.

Maybe they'd find nothing but ancient stories etched in stone, admire some crumbling Dwarven architecture, and return home—his home, her home—he didn't care which.

Just together.

A low, constant rumble resounded, echoing off the mountain stone. Moments later, the ground beneath them trembled. The lead scout's hand shot up, halting the squad on their narrow track.

Along a hard-packed road above their current position, the sounds of many feet running past them left them immobile, breath held. The lead scout eased to another position within the cover of nearby foliage to get a visual confirmation.

Torgolis.

From the reverberating ground thunder, several dozen, Erevan would have guessed.

While they'd been successful in a few small scuffles with no more than four or five Torgolis at a time, there was no hope against such a large number. Were his squad comprised of Elves and Dwarves, perhaps. But the humans, no matter how seasoned many of them were, did not have the augmented strength, dexterity and senses that their older brethren benefited from.

The horde disappeared around the bend in the road; the rumbling grew fainter.

The lead scout signalled to continue on. They were to monitor the state of the siege and check in with the forces outside of Carlane, somewhere below their current position, where he hoped to meet with Siobhann.

Their path veered up toward the road. Still the rumble continued, reverberating off of the surrounding mountain.

He looked back toward where they'd lost visibility of the horde. Surely, they should no longer hear them.

The lead scout was about to escort their group across the open road.

The rumbling grew louder.

Erevan realized his human companions could not hear it as he could.

"Stop, there are more coming," he reached for the soldier ahead of him, unable to call out, but it was too late. Their leader scurried across the road to the brush beyond. Several others made it after him. Finally, hearing what was clear to Erevan, a younger man froze at the edge of the road.

Too late, he retreated, slipping on the loose ground, causing branches to crack as he struggled to catch his balance.

It was enough to draw the approaching Torgolis' attention.

Exposed and separated, they had limited options.

The second horde was as large as the first.

Erevan drew his sword, determined to give his companions a breath of a chance of escaping.

He curled the fingers of his free hand, drawing on his magic as he shouted. "Run for safety, alert the siege company!"

The two men closest nodded, understanding that the army needed to know that the Torgolis were on the move in large numbers. They could outflank and slaughter the Aelozians.

The others had already engaged the oversized warriors, outnumbered. The Aelozians were dedicated to fighting, even to the death.

They would kill as many of the enemy as they could before they fell, to protect their families.

KOSSA SAW IT ALL happen so fast, it took her some time to understand what was happening.

One moment she observed the disgusting habits of their Torgolis allies in the courtyard below from the safety of her preferred hiding spot on the parapet. In the next, there were two figures scurrying toward the unguarded gate post.

She meant to call out to stop them but had to duck as another boulder whistled over the wall, crashing into fragments against the keep.

By the time she re-emerged, the scene below was crowded with human soldiers flooding in through the open portcullis, swarming and slaughtering the Torgolis like angry little ants.

*Lost.*

Below, one of the human slavers ran toward her brother's quarters, screaming for all to escape.

She stepped forward to run, but doubled back as more soldiers suddenly ran past her position, seeking enemy warriors to engage.

*They're all gone.*

Her heart sank, recalling that Nolgan had sent them after Erevan, leaving the keep unguarded.

*Nolgan had failed to consider that the stronghold could be infiltrated.*

She wrapped her cloak tighter as she pressed her back to the shadows of her nook.

Her heart hammered in her chest.

*Think!*

*Stay hidden, escape when the time is right.*

Nolgan would go down into the hidden tunnels he'd found while excavating the Dwarven vaults. They proved to be collapsed, but would still provide a secure hiding place until the Torgolis returned to retake the fortress.

*If they return and don't just leave us. Simple beasts.*

*Surely they wouldn't leave their goddess incarnate in the hands of their detested human enemies?*

At least the infernal pounding of the ballistae had stopped.

Kossa twisted her fingers to reinforce the magic echoing the illusion of the surrounding stone in the narrow guard post at the north-western corner of the parapet.

# TWENTY-NINE

"I RECEIVED YOUR MESSAGE regarding the departing Torgolis from Omi. The Eterssal scouts are working that sector of the mountain, and should report on their movement soon." Gari-och said as he and Siobhann walked the top of the wall together in the aftermath of their army overrunning the courtyard and keep.

They had slain every Torgolis that they couldn't subdue and imprison. All humans working for the enemy had also been taken prisoner.

"Nirran and Lorne got Nate and the other prisoners to the safety of the camp. He was immediately transferred to the care of a healer. It appears that little talisman gave him enough vitality to hold on."

Siobhann nodded. "They'll take him down the mountain."

"The generals assigned a special escort to take him straight back to his wife. What a mess they got themselves into."

"She was just trying to protect Sendi from my fate."

Garioch's lips compressed as he turned silent.

Siobhann looked up at the sky and breathed deeply. The clouds had cleared, revealing a bright full moon.

Aelozian soldier activity kept the courtyard alive despite the late hour, and the moon provided some extra light for their work.

They continued walking along the high wall, surveying both the courtyard and the landscape beyond.

She glanced inside the empty parapet guard post and turned her attention back to her brother as they looked out over the mountain plateau.

"You should go back," Garioch said.

"Back to what?"

"The Temple. Pay your respects to Mamma and Father and the Goddess. And see if there's a way to fix what we did to you."

"Garioch, you didn't bind my power."

"I was part of your fate. It was necessary. But I'm just sorry that things went so badly for you, the way they did."

"You couldn't have known how bad the orphanage was."

"I'm just glad that Grimms found you." He gave her a side-long glance.

"Grimms found me? I picked Donnen's pocket and Grimms called me out."

Garioch's eyes twinkled. "Mhmm."

"What? Don't 'Mhmm' me, Garioch." She pushed his arm. "What aren't you telling me?"

"You'll have to ask Grimms when you see him next."

"Which will be some time. He never leaves his forge."

"I wouldn't be so sure about that."

"What do you mean?"

A flash of orange in the darkness pulled her attention toward the distant trees lining the mountain roads. "Did you see that?"

Garioch turned, squinting in the darkness.

"There," she pointed to a flash lower down the mountain than the first. "It's moving."

Another.

"It's getting closer."

A fist wrapped around her heart.

"Prince Erevan?"

"I hope not," she said as she rushed off, back along the wall to the nearest stairs down to the next level. As soon as her feet hit the level walk, she sprinted the perimeter of the winding path.

"We can't go out there without knowing what that is," Garioch shouted after her, then screamed for archers to double up on the walls.

EREVAN DROPPED TO HIS knees, scrambling for the cover of nearby bramble bushes. He shoved himself back against the sharp branches and closed his eyes, attempting to control his breathing. In the moment it took to regain control of his body, his thoughts automatically fell into place.

Without the deafening thunder of his heart in his ears, he could now pick out the faint noises of pursuit back in the direction he had come. Through the tangle of foliage overhead, he could see the crisp, clear sky, with stars twinkling and the moon at its zenith. A time when his powers should be their strongest.

He struggled with the grief that struck him as he finally acknowledged to himself that he could be the last. His scouting group, unprepared, had met the horde of raiders intent on capturing him.

"That one, with the fire hands! Capture him for the glory of our goddess!" One had shouted in the mountain language.

Erevan witnessed each of his few comrades fall to claws and blades, trying to protect one another and hold off the impending attack on their precious lands over these last weeks. He looked at his empty hands shaking upon his lap, resting on bloodstained, tattered clothes that were normally pristine.

*I lost my fucking sword.*

He'd run it through a Torgolis throat and lost his grip when it sent him flying backward down the steep decline with a hard kick.

He'd tumbled ass over crown, hitting a fallen log with a hard, breath-knocking stop.

They'd pursued him down, and chased him still.

He had nothing left but his fire magic, which he threw at them in fierce blasts as he retreated.

Had the other two men made it? The two that he'd sent off to alert the army?

If he drew them down the mountainside, making as much noise and lighting up the forest, it might alert them to trouble.

A branch snapped close to Erevan's left side, forcing his breath to stop. He closed his eyes once more and kept his mind open as he focused on pulling energy from his surroundings and from within himself. His fingertips tingled, then his palms itched as he forced discipline on his thoughts to draw the powers of the elements.

He planned his moves, aware of the growing sounds of predators. Back straight, despite the sharp twigs tearing his clothes and flesh, he was nearly surrounded by the stench of these evil creatures come to conquer the plateau.

Just outside the protection of his bushes was an organized ring of marauders.

Would the army even notice him, occupied with pounding the hells out of the front gate? He hoped one of the scouts would see him.

*I have to try.*

The fate of the Aelozian people was at risk if the army was flanked and destroyed.

*Siobhann is at risk.*

A large grime-covered foot stomped the ground close to Erevan.

He had to go before they could sever his path.

Moving into a crouch, he balled his fists, constantly gathering energy to himself. Images of his lost companions flashed through his mind, bodies broken in battle. They'd killed some of the Torgolis, but not nearly enough.

And then the vision of his love hovered before his eyes, giving his heart the crumbs of hope and determination to go forth and complete the task.

While the forest provided him cover, it was also an obstruction for his plan—if he could do it in time.

His toes gouged the soft earth below him as he shot from the bushes toward the clearing outside the fortress wall. His eyes never left the distant fires lighting the guard posts, and his ears were trained on the heavy feet in pursuit. Erevan dared not flinch as rough arrows whizzed past his head, striking trees around him. Shouts spurred him on until he was mid-way from the forest to the stone walls, where he drew to a stop and listened to the shadows thundering from behind. Out of range from wall-top bolts, but near enough to make use of the great wall itself.

He slammed his palms together with so much force that a burst of fire was struck and contained between his fingers. He stood his ground as it shook beneath him. Sweat tickled down his brow with the strain of drawing and harnessing more power than he had ever prayed for.

With a final flick of his fingers, a ring surrounded him, flipped, doubled, tripled and flipped ever faster.

His timing had to be impeccable, else he couldn't divide the spell correctly. Erevan drew his right hand back and pitched forth a great ball of fire, eyes closed in concentration. His magic twisted into a bright flash that illuminated the walls. The ring of a sword being drawn directly behind him broke his concentration as the force of impact sent the immediate lines of Torgolis attackers flying back toward the bush from where they had emerged.

AGITATION PERMEATED SIOBHANN'S BODY as she paced the ramparts like a caged lioness, eyes trained on the dark void before them. Tension knotted her stomach. She stopped her movement to stare a moment at the heavy moon and offer a prayer to Ashiel, Goddess of the Lost. Its silvered light lined the treetops and mountainside surrounding the fortress, but could not reach the interior of the forest. The bright flashes had stopped, making her worry all the more.

*Erevan.*

She hoped it was him returning to her and yet prayed it wasn't him engaged in some fiery battle.

A cold twinge swept down her back, making her shiver. She shifted her shoulders to shake the annoyance out from beneath her light chain mail as she continued along the stone walkway. A shadow emerged from the trees, making a rapid path for the wall.

Her stomach knotted, but she hesitated for only a second.

"Movement!" she shouted, taking up her bow in case the shadow proved to be an enemy scout.

She watched the swift motion of the figure coming closer. Her bow wavered, then lowered slightly.

The figure stopped.

Her gaze shot to the wave of darkness that flowed from beneath the trees.

She couldn't breathe.

*Gods!*

"Erevan!" She screamed when breath rushed back into her lungs. "Erevan! Run!"

By now, the guards lined the ramparts, their arrows notched, ready to fire. They watched in disbelief as the figure stopped.

Everyone saw the tiny flint glow, and then the flare which appeared and grew between Erevan's palms, even at this distance.

Siobhann screamed in frustration that he was not coming to safety.

The glow surrounding him intensified.

Immense.

He drew and harnessed the power he gained from the elements around him.

It pulled at her.

Her beast rose to the surface, imprisoned by her flesh and bone.

She burned from within.

Her magic screamed for freedom, stretching toward the call of his magic.

Her heart was on the brink of exploding as the enemy rumbled closer in thick masses toward where Erevan stood.

Siobhann heard Garioch rapidly shouting orders to the marksmen to fire at anything that approached the wall.

Everyone rushed, torn between bracing for the attack and wanting to go to the prince's aide.

Siobhann's hands pounded the thick stones, frustrated that Erevan could not hear her, nor could she get to him in time to help.

His hand drew back, preparing to pitch his massive fireball.

She felt herself separating, as though her spirit was trying to shed her useless body to get to him in time to stop the inevitable.

The screaming beast in her head was deafening.

The roar of sound enveloping her became a murmur.

She stopped shouting.

Motionless, time crept around her.

The wind blew her hair, stroking her face.

The moon illuminated Erevan's form within the surrounding blackness.

A stray moonbeam glinted off the steel that unsheathed somewhere behind him.

"Down!" A blast of light exploded from Erevan, roaring across the ground between himself, the forest, and the keep, forceful enough to send Torgolis troops flying in all directions.

The glow of the moon, the light of Erevan's fire, and the blackness swam around her, revolving faster and faster.

Eyes closed, she saw nothing but an inferno filling the space between wall and forest, as her heart raged against the loss of her love.

Her powerlessness to save him.

Weightless, arms spread, her chest arched against the pain.

Her mind remained calm, retreating as the beast took over.

She saw the world through its eyes.

It fought against Mamma's magic, stabbing and twisting with its beak, finally snapping its aged and thinned threads.

The binding fell away like spider silk wisps on the moonlight breeze.

Siobhann revelled in its power, like the ultimate Baerskyr battle fever, but so much more.

She embraced its rage as it sought revenge on the little stinking beasts, for daring to hurt those she loved.

They would burn.

All of them.

They would burn for taking her love from her before she and he could fulfil their destiny.

For daring to imprison her.

Something struck her back, cool and light, and stung like a poisoned tether hook in her spine.

"No!" She and her beast screamed. "No," she sobbed, knowing well the rasping pain of a new cage.

Everything went black.

The fire winked out.

Her body of flesh and bone hit hard stone. Things cracked, blood seeped.

She didn't care.

Erevan was gone.

Her beast was again trapped.

She didn't care anymore.

# THIRTY

EYES OF MOLTEN GOLD filled Siobhann's vision.

The hungry eyes of a predator intent on destruction so complete it could raze the world.

She was afire, with its talons sunk into her chest, determined to rip out her pounding heart and devour it.

Like it had when her family was slaughtered.

*No.*

Pain stole her breath away as she resisted the onslaught of memory. The talons sank deeper still.

"Don't resist. Let me take it from you."

Siobhann shrank away from the voice like nothing else in her life.

It was terrible. A demon emulating the voices of her dead mother and beloved sister, Darya.

*No! Leave them be!*

She struck out against the sound that brought with it the image of her dying mother, devoured by agonizing flames. Her younger siblings and father had already been consumed.

*No, that isn't right. That isn't what happened.*

Heat infused Siobhann's chest. So intense, she had the sense it should have scalded, yet it was somehow soothing.

MAGIC RIPPED THROUGH THE night air, slamming Kossa back against the stone wall of her little guard post, high on the parapet.

She could never have guessed that Nolgan's proof would stroll right past her, ignorant of her presence, speaking of the Temple and the Goddess's power.

The true goddess.

Not Kossa's illusions.

Her skin prickled with her newfound knowledge.

She'd stayed where she was until she could be sure the way was safe. She had been about to sneak out amid the chaos when the shouts rippled throughout the Aelozian army that the Elven prince was outside.

*Erevan.*

Somehow, she *knew* it was him.

Protective magic forgotten, breath held, she emerged from her hiding place. High up as she was, she witnessed it all.

Erevan's explosion.

And the emergence.

Captivated.

Yet dimly aware of the shadowy movement on the ground.

Blinking against the brilliance of the swirling flames rising into the sky over the fortress, she glanced down as wounded, but mobile, Torgolis lunged forward, retrieving a body from a crater in the mountain plateau.

They disappeared into the forest.

No one noticed them.

Every soul on that wall was captivated by the sight of the swirling bird of fire in the sky with a human woman at its heart.

The inferno screamed, setting the ground afire where the Torgolis scrambled to escape.

Her breath hitched.

Her own imagined illusion was so very pale compared to the true goddess.

Nolgan's copied drawings could never capture the essence of what had been in the original tomes. She'd glimpsed their pages on a few occasions, but never enough for a clear study.

She stared, breathless.

Her heart twisted as another figure, positioned on the lower wall, shot a beam of magic toward the glorious bird of fire.

It screamed, terrible and deafening.

The light anchored into its back, reeling it down, diminishing its glory until it faded so that the human dropped onto the stone below her.

"No," she whispered, devastated to see it disappear. Contained. Imprisoned.

Again.

The Temple.

The Goddess.

Kossa shook herself, glancing around. She remained undiscovered as she flicked her protective magic back into place and made her way, slow and sure, back to her brother.

# THIRTY-ONE

ALL SOUND WAS MUFFLED as consciousness returned to Erevan.

He opened his eyes enough to see more darkness. His skin registered dampness, the air heavy with it.

Shackles weighted his wrists and ankles.

Muscles stiff, he jerked his fingers in a simple pattern that, with the slightest intent, should have produced an illumination.

He tried again.

The magic struggled to obey, but it was exhausted.

He blew out a breath, sagging against the moist stones below him.

*Siobhann.*

*Is she safe?*

Had he got their attention?

Could he bear it, knowing he'd failed?

To exist without her. She may not have committed to him before their parting. But his heart was fully hers long before that.

Despair threatened him with images of his companions falling to the Torgolis soldiers.

Some images taunted him with Siobhann's face on their bodies.

*No.*

No. Not that. Her worst fear. Never that.

He drew a deep, steadying breath despite the musty particles weighing it. He blew them out on an exhale, seeking his balance, whispering to his magic.

Making amends for pushing it to its precipice.

*We're not done. Not yet.* He found it, wounded and withdrawn.

He would have to cajole and cradle and treat it with care until they regained their strength.

They would because they had to.

If Siobhann wasn't dead, she would need him.

And he had to believe she wasn't dead.

SIOBHANN LAY ON HER side, curled into herself, facing a stained stucco wall.

Every time she fell asleep, she gasped awake from within the confines of a buried temple and the words *'Find it,'* echoing through her mind.

Awake, she was met with the memory of Erevan's explosion.

She stared at the wall, her heart a limp mess in her chest.

*He's gone.*

*The beast is imprisoned.*

She'd felt it. It had encompassed her with its spirit, its power, its devotion.

They'd been one.

Until someone separated them again. Still together in one body, but barred from one another.

Who would dare?

Who would have the power? The knowledge?

Darya?

Would she have dragged her babies all the way to a war zone? Garioch had told her that Nate was on his way to her.

"Was it necessary?" Grimms' voice was barely audible, but unmistakable.

"The time was not right. She was out of control, Jelani." A woman's soft, rich voice eased over Siobhann's wounded heart. Familiar, but distant.

"What a sight she was." A third voice, similar to the second, said.

This one Siobhann knew.

Kwayssi. Was Darya here too, as Siobhann had guessed?

She kept her back to them, eyes burning with betrayal.

Her heart still did not stir. It didn't have the beats to care.

Empty.

"She could have burned the entire mountainside to nothing," the woman said, "Including all of us."

"She would never," Grimms growled.

"She witnessed her destiny fall before her eyes and was powerless to save him. Revenge follows such devastation; complete and blind destruction."

She wasn't wrong.

She and her beast hadn't cared that there were friends and allies on that wall.

*Garioch.*

He'd been right next to her.

Again.

A twinge of grief pulled at her.

*Veira, Lorne and Nirran.*

Examining those moments with raw honesty, she would have allowed them to fall, too.

"No." A sob escaped.

A warm hand rested on her shoulder. Large and so work-worn, she could feel the calluses through the fabric of her tunic.

She squeezed her eyes shut.

"We'll give you some time," the woman said. The sounds of swishing fabric and light footsteps followed her out. A door clicked shut.

For the first time since before Siobhann lost her family on this very mountain, she began to cry.

Grimms gently pulled her shoulder, rolling her away from the wall.

Limp, like a broken child, she allowed it.

He pulled her into his arms, cradling her like her father would have.

"I should have been there earlier, lass. I should have taken you in sooner. Hells, we should have been there long before they came for you. If we had been, we might have prevented all of this. Moira sent for us, as others have before her. We thought it was another false report. We should have at least come to see for ourselves."

With her ear pressed to his solid chest, his rumbling voice was so sad, his words so confusing.

"How could you know any of this?"

His body lost its rigidness as he sighed.

"We didn't think the Phoenix would awaken yet. It was too soon, according to the annals we protected. But apparently someone miscalculated. Or the Phoenix rises when she pleases, regardless of what the calendar says," he huffed. "We'd seen the glimmer in Moira's eyes as a lass, and her grandmother before her. Maybe it was your father's Baerskyr blood. The battle fever. Or the attack. Or both all at once."

She sat up, pulling away enough to look into his dark, tired face. "What are you saying? I don't understand."

"We thought she'd gone back to sleep after that, when Moira performed the Gabhaile to bind her." He laughed a bitter grunt. "And then a young elf of the old bloodline shows up on our doorstep. I had to bring Nadzia to see for herself. And nearly too late too. Ah, lass, I'm so very sorry."

She scowled at him, suspicious. "I've never seen you sorry for anything in my life."

He held her gaze, direct and unflinching until his words wormed their way through her.

Her heart pounded in her ears. "You *knew*. All this time? And all of this could have been avoided? My family could still be alive."

He nodded.

Her breath rushed in and out of her as a new betrayal flared through her. She shoved herself away from him.

Pacing, she spit angry words at him.

Still he didn't flinch. He maintained that same unwavering expression he always did when she raged.

"*Say* something!" she snapped.

"We made a mistake."

"A big, fucking mistake," she nodded, temper flaring higher.

The door opened. Wordless, Kwayssi stepped inside.

Behind her, the other woman filled the doorway with her presence, despite her diminutive size.

Siobhann stared down into her eyes.

The woman stared up into hers, unblinking.

She bore the same ritual markings that her mother did, only more of them.

A priestess.

"My ex-husband is a good man, Siobhann McLeighan." Her voice was like diamonds rubbing together. "Jelani Egrimmbe did his best by you. Now I will speak, and you will listen."

Siobhann's gaping mouth snapped shut. She sat on the cot next to Grimms.

"The others return and this fortress will be reinforced against the Torgolis. Garioch told me that Aelozian spies suspect Elves of organizing this gathering."

Siobhann glanced to Grimms then spoke to the Priestess, "Erevan thought that if they were his kin, they might be here for the temple. He feared they could be responsible for the first attack on our farm."

The Dwarven woman's gaze flicked to Grimms and back to Siobhann.

"The Aelozians will be preoccupied with routing the scattered Torgolis, to keep them from heading south. Our concerns are here."

"During that first attack, Mother was worried that the Empire would find me."

"She bound your power so that you could not be molded into something you were never meant to be. I have done the binding this time and it will hold. You mother's life force stopped feeding it with her death. Darya's magic at the time was young and not yet strong enough to hold it as it was meant to be."

"The magic can't break free again?"

The priestess chuckled. "A goddess cannot be contained indefinitely. You have not had the training you need. There are rituals you should know for your own safety; of your body and of your mind so that you are not overwhelmed, as you were. Uninitiated, you are weak and chaotic and dangerous. Trained, you are stronger."

Images of Erevan's morning ritual came to mind. The easy flow of muscle and breath, to balance his body, mind and magic.

An ache set into her chest. "Erevan meant to teach me how to balance. I still don't understand what any of this means." She turned to Grimms. "I understand why it was kept from me, though it frustrates me that it was. But what do I do now? Those elves haven't been found, have they? Erevan said his kinsman was deranged and determined to find the temple. Has Erevan's body been recovered? Shouldn't we perform a death ritual? Do we bury him here or send him back to his clan?" Her throat tightened on the words.

"Nirran, Veira and Lorne are still searching for him."

Siobhann jumped to her feet, flashes of the blast reeling through her mind. Her gut twisted.

"There is no trace of him, Siobhann. The remains of the Torgolis are there, but he is not."

Her heart stammered. "He survived?"

"We don't know." Grimms got to his feet. "I must go and see which of the Dwarven tribes have answered the summons. There will be much argument over what to do next. The temple was buried for a reason."

# THIRTY-TWO

Kossa slid onto the cot to sit next to Erevan's inert form.

One of her humans placed a small table by her knee with a bowl, a blade and a linen. She waved him out. He bowed and locked the door behind him, as previously instructed.

She studied Erevan's face for a long moment.

*My handsome half-brother.*

He didn't appear any older after these last decades, nor did she. But he was different in the set of his mouth and the deepened lines between his brows.

Her chest constricted.

How different things would have been, had their mothers been of the same people.

But hers was human, his Elven.

*You did try to protect me. Though it wasn't enough.*

*Not with Nolgan.*

Nolgan.

She sighed and swallowed as she picked up the linen, spread it over her lap, and placed the bowl atop it.

Kossa cradled Erevan's hand in hers a moment. The last time they'd held hands was the day that sealed both of their fates.

Nolgan had never touched her except as a means to intimidate her. Never in kindness or affection.

Erevan had held her hand, then embraced her as any older brother who cares for a younger sister would when she's upset.

Kossa's heart flipped.

*My fault.*

That day changed everything.

Her gaze swept his unconscious face, wondering how long he would remain so. That blast outside of the fortress had taken substantial power. She hadn't realized just how much power he had until then, and it sent a shiver up her spine.

*Hopefully, you will sleep yet, brother.*

She picked up the small, razor-sharp blade with one hand while her other smoothed over his palm and fingers, memorizing the texture of his skin and bone against hers.

Leaning, she pressed her lips to his brow.

As she straightened, she began the chant. Small slices at key points along his fingertips, wrist and palm. She did the same to hers on the opposing hand, so they aligned.

Blood trickled from the small wounds.

She pressed their corresponding slices together, then reached for his other hand, balancing his forearm across her shoulder so that his hand rested against the back of her head beneath her hair. She supported his arm with hers as she slid her hand through his silky hair, pressing her fingers and palm against his scalp.

The words continued and repeated until she felt her position was correct.

Once she was sure, she closed her eyes and called on her magic.

First to bind the spelled words to her power, then to twist the magic toward her will.

She didn't have his shared power pushing the spell forward, nor his consent, both of which would tax her all the more.

Her survival depended on this.

There might not be another chance to learn what Nolgan needed to know to secure their future.

She had to know what Erevan knew about the Phoenix. What he knew about the kind of power that Nolgan sought.

Dragon Magic.

The source of Erevan's magic, so Nolgan had explained to her many times over the years. It was right there in the depictions.

Some of the drawings showed elves paying homage to a great beast.

He'd said the great beast had bestowed magic upon their clan. The Dragon clan, to do its bidding.

If Erevan had the power, Nolgan should be able to access it, too.

And show the world what it meant to be a dragon mage.

Not like Erevan, who hid his magic. Or their people, who lived diminished at the far end of the world.

This, she wasn't so sure about, but if it meant they could secure their future and live comfortably, then she would help him.

She ignored the twinge of guilt and spoke the words with more force, pushing the magic through her body, through her blood, seeking a connection to Erevan's blood and to this magic.

As soon as their life forces were close, they snapped together, recognizing her blood, like for like.

She gasped as Erevan's magic took hold of hers and surged through her body, through his and back through hers in a self-sustaining loop.

The rush made her light-headed, igniting and overloading every physical sense in her body.

*So much power!*

Jealousy and awe ripped through her.

She trembled, struggling to control her breathing to focus on the spell. She was already weakening, her magic a watered-down version of his. Sweat slicked her skin.

*Focus. Hold. Seek.*

Once she got her toe hold, she homed in, wasting no time to direct their magics and burrow deeper.

She flicked back through memories, seeking anything to do with the Phoenix or the secrets of his magic.

Their magic.

She prowled the images of his interactions with the red-haired woman.

He had recently performed this ritual with her.

The vision of the child incinerating Kossa's Torgolis allies sent shivers throughout her body.

*So much destruction!*

She hadn't expected the emotions to accompany the images. The sounds of the dying, the smells of their burning corpses.

The rage, the regret, the burden of guilt.

Shoving all of that aside, she continued back, and back, and back, to before their worlds collapsed.

Erevan's mage training. The discipline, the logic and control. All of which Kossa had had to learn on her own.

She stopped.

There it was.

Her breath rasped as her body shook. Sweat trickled down her temple.

Kossa stepped into the memory, within a great cavern.

Erevan, not yet full grown, faced a great reptilian beast, petrified. Behind him was a door bearing the seal of their house.

His young face was white and strained.

The fear took her. His fear.

She trembled as he trembled.

*'Find her.'*

The great beast pushed thought through the cavern until it penetrated his consciousness.

He nodded his understanding.

The next thought was the image of a magnificent temple.

Kossa dimly recognized the mountain plateau that Carlane sat upon, from its surrounding faces and peaks.

There was no fortress.

Instead, many buildings stood, with one glorious central open-sided structure rising out of the carved mountain stone. At the highest point, a stone phoenix poised in flight, supported by a single claw gripping the tail of a curved beast resembling this one. Its body surrounded the temple, as its wall, rising from the ground.

At its centre was a great stair-lined well that descended deep into the mountain's core. Deeper than the mountain was at its tallest point.

*'Protect it.'*

Again, Erevan nodded woodenly before the terrible thing.

Kossa gasped as the beast drew a breath and opened its maw to expel a great rippling cloud of magic. Bits of it spun out in all directions, finding its way through crevices and currents at will.

Most of it surrounded Erevan, saturating his flesh, burrowing into his bones, infusing his mind.

He screamed as it overwhelmed him.

*Power.*

The instinct to destroy and take and hoard gripped Kossa as it had gripped Erevan.

He struggled against it. Against the deep-rooted desire to use this power over everyone and everything.

His soul stood strong.He would not.

*Can I steal any of his power for myself?*

Kossa reached out, fingers stretching toward the source of the magic.

The beast's eye rolled, pinning her.

*'Thief! You are not worthy.'*

She reeled as it sent her careening upward, sure she would slam against the roof of the cavern.

Instinct took over. She threw up a barrier to hide herself from the beast.

She did not strike the cavern ceiling, but she jerked out of the ritual with a hard snap.

Pain overtook her as fire shot through her entire body, so great it stole the breath intended for a scream.

Breaking contact with Erevan, her curled fingers were blackened. Every incision was cauterized, the blood smoked everywhere it trailed.

Her darting eyes found Erevan's face.

He looked up at her with eyes of molten gold.

Kossa turned her gaze away, trembling and mewling, extending a shaking hand toward Erevan's forehead for one last attempt to defend herself against this attack.

She found the memory of when he'd found her crying behind the stairwell, seeking to subdue him with sympathy.

Instead, she belatedly made the connection of her terror of that day in discovering her illusory powers, as the memory ricocheted back through time to that moment.

That very same moment when magic struck her, causing her body to mimic her surroundings so that she nearly disappeared.

Then the day she tried to use her magic to scare Erevan's youngest sibling into giving her what she wanted.

It overlapped with the vision of the beast's great maw turned in her direction.

She dropped to her knees beneath the stairs. Both adult and child Kossa.

The memory duplicated and separated into two distinct events, looping one into the other.

She tried once more to create some form of protection for herself, from herself, and it only caused another split.

She clutched her knees, her breaths in gasps, large eyes fixated on the image burned into her mind.

EREVAN'S EYES SNAPPED OPEN, heart pounding. Molten gold filled his vision, not the usual fire glow when his magic sparked to life. This was closer to the moment when Siobhann's power flared through Kemberlan, igniting him.

But more. So much more.

He staggered to his feet.

Power surged through his body as the vision of that first encounter with the dragon flooded his memory, when it had been locked away for so long. A whisper in his consciousness all his life. Now it howled through him, unrestrained.

*Kossa.*

He looked down at the floor.

Eyes wide and unseeing, her body crammed up against the stone wall. Her pulse ticked at her throat.

*'Inconsequential,'* the voice said.

The beast.

*Kossa, what have you done?*

He bent to rouse her, but she remained enraptured, seeing only what she could see.

*'It does not matter. You must retrieve the stolen texts so that your people may prepare for my awakening.'*

*Siobhann.*

He still didn't know if she'd survived the Torgolis attack.

Turning, he found the locked door.

He pressed his palm to the ancient oak, infusing it with the power flowing through him. In moments, the dense wood turned to brittle carbon. It struck the passage wall and crumbled when he shoved it outward.

A human backed away from the wall, eyes wide, flicking from the collapsed door to Erevan's face, to the chain that hung from Erevan's cuffed wrists.

"Where is Nolgan?"

The man's terrified eyes darted toward the stone corridor behind him, backing away from Erevan.

Erevan snatched up the chain in his fist, heating the links close to the cuffs until they fell apart. Crouching, he did the same with the chain between his ankles.

"You know where the Aelozian army is?"

The man nodded.

"Go."

Erevan left the man behind as he went in search of Nolgan.

He encountered one Torgolis warrior, who raised a battle-ax bigger than his head. His eyes trained on Erevan's glowing ones.

The ax dropped inch by inch.

Erevan conjured a ball of fire from his left palm and a smirk.

The Torgolis' beastly face registered terror as his eyes widened before he dropped to his knees in supplication.

Erevan barked, "Nolgan."

The Torgolis scrambled to his feet, casting surreptitious glances at Erevan's bouncing fireball, keeping a safe distance between it and his oily fur as he led him through the winding tunnels.

They rounded a corner to a large semi-finished room carved into the stone; the tunnel continued on. Tables had been set along the walls with lanterns. Books, maps, scrolls and various other scraps of parchment littered their surfaces.

Erevan observed Nolgan for a long moment as he darted between the tables, scribbling notes.

"It's been a long time, *brother*."

Nolgan spun at the sound of Erevan's voice echoing across the space, his eyes flicking to the Torgolis and the empty space between him and Erevan, with his bouncing ball of flame.

"What did you do to Kossa?"

"She is where you left me."

Nolgan's eyes narrowed on Erevan. "Not dead."

Erevan shook his head as he studied Nolgan's expressions. No concern, just pure calculation.

Nolgan assessed the ball of fire and the Torgolis warrior, eyes narrowed. "If you wish to claim the South Lands, you will have to subdue this one." Nolgan backed toward the tables, gathering up all the bits of parchment and tablets, shoving them into worn leather satchels. "He will take it from you and destroy all of your brethren just to cow you."

Erevan could set the tables ablaze, but the Beast had wanted the texts preserved.

He'd spent decades chasing his half-siblings across the world to retrieve them.

*I can't lose them now.*

He ignored Nolgan's movements, turning toward the warrior who was considering his options with the battle-ax clutched in his fists, eyes on the flame.

The Torgolis drew a deep breath and roared at Erevan, stomping a foot. The sounds echoed back along the tunnels.

Nolgan's frantic gathering continued behind him.

"Don't kill him. Kossa failed, so I still need him to find the Temple."

Erevan laughed. "You still haven't found it?"

The thunder of many feet rumbled toward them from the passageway.

"Clearly not, but I'm close," he spat, clutching his satchels to his chest, struggling to loop their straps over his shoulders.

Torgolis filed in around their comrade, facing Erevan with his flaming palm.

Their eyes registered the fire, but still they moved in closer with their weapons, determined to capture him.

Nolgan had offered them the southlands and threatened Erevan against their people. They would fight.

The extra power surging through him from the Beast would incinerate the horde. And while Erevan could create a shield around himself, the heat from the inferno would destroy the artifacts in Nolgan's possession.

He backed away from the Torgolis inching toward him.

The sound of heavy wood screeching over stone drew Erevan's attention as Nolgan shoved at a hidden door large enough for a crouching dwarf and crawled through it.

The Torgolis advanced.

Nolgan was escaping, which was a boon for the preservation of the scrolls and books.

He wanted the temple.

He'd get the fucking temple.

Erevan dropped to a knee, slamming his palms down onto the stone, startling the Torgolis, who instinctively backed away.

The Beast's power surged through his body, downward, seeking.

Alone, Erevan could never had done this. He wouldn't have had the strength or the understanding.

The ground rumbled. First from the downward force, then with the upward pull from deep, deep down, once the magic found its source.

The stone beneath their feet cracked as the cavern shook. Bits of rock dropped around them.

The Torgolis closest to the exits fled, leaving room for others to thin the herd.

The one that had dropped in supplication, then roared for his brethren, stood transfixed, seemingly unsure what to do.

The Beast within Erevan pushed the magic through the mountain's faults until it found the molten core flowing deep below, creating space for it to flow back up.

"The Temple must be protected," the Torgolis growled in the mountain language. He stepped toward Erevan, battle-ax raised.

The ground continued to rumble as rock shifted little by little, making room for new growth, as the Dwarves would have called it in the legends.

Erevan stretched his fingers over the stone. The Beast's magic pulsed one last time, cracking the stone and creating a blackened fissure between them. From the growing crevice, the stench of sulphur preceded the appearance of liquid earth flowing along the space, oozing over its edges.

Finally, Erevan stood, allowing its natural course to take over as he turned for the small door to pursue his half-brother.

# THIRTY-THREE

Siobhann followed the Dwarven High Priestess along the carved stone corridors beneath Carlane, descending ever lower.

Grimms preceded them both with a lantern, Kwayssi and Garioch trailed behind. All armed except for the Priestess.

They started on the journey after Siobhann had recounted her experiences with Erevan's magic and the dreams. She described the temple and the order to *'Find it'*. Whatever *it* was.

"I didn't know these tunnels were here," Garioch's whisper travelled along the stone. "Mother always brought us to the temple through the access at the farm."

"I don't remember any of it," Siobhann said, trying to ignore the fact that they were far deeper underground than she was comfortable with. She forced her gaze downward from the rock suspended over them, supporting a fortress full of people, supplies, livestock, and siege gear.

"That is understandable," Kwayssi said. "Such events tend to bury themselves until we are able to heal from them."

Siobhann's laugh was bitter as she gripped Sally and Trish's handles where they rested, suspended from her hips. "I'm not sure I'm ready for this."

"No one ever is, my dear," the priestess said. "Fate often chooses for us."

"Not so long ago, I would have told you that I don't believe in Fate."

"And now?" Kwayssi strode alongside her.

"Now I no longer have the choice to not believe."

Garioch snorted.

Siobhann shot her brother a scathing glance.

"You likely won't either, young Garioch," the priestess said over her shoulder.

Siobhann raised a brow. "Oh? How interesting. What mythological creature lives inside my brother?"

"His path is entirely different from yours, but you all play a critical role in the coming cycle."

"Ever cryptic," Grimms muttered.

Kwayssi's laugh echoed up the tunnel.

A deep rumble echoed back, halting the group in their tracks.

The ground shook again. Rock dust and pebbles loosed from cracks appearing in the stone over their heads.

"What the fuck was that?" Siobhann's heart tripped.

"Jelani, we must hurry," the priestess said, resuming their journey. "It has begun."

"According to your astrologers, it's too damned early."

"It is, but that no longer matters."

"What was that?" Garioch repeated Siobhann's question as they all jogged down the tunnel, mindful of stones littering the ground.

A third rumble shook the surrounding stone, widening the fissures.

Siobhann stumbled to a stop to observe the red, gold and white liquid oozing along the cracks in the walls around them. It resembled the ingots that Grimms fired in Bella's open belly before the hammering began. "Grimms?"

"I see it, lass. Keep going."

"It isn't overflowing,"

"I know it, now move."

"It will only go where it must," Nadzia said.

"What is causing it?"

"Your young Elven friend survived the blast outside the wall, after all."

"Erevan is doing this?" Siobhann staggered, catching Garioch's shoulder as they moved faster still, ever downward. Her heart hammered with elation.

*He's alive, and melting the fucking ground!*

"Not on his own, I should think."

The memory of her beast staring eye to eye with Erevan's with only a thin barrier between them. The barrier of the binding that ultimately crumbled under the power of the Phoenix.

Fear rippled through Siobhann. She struggled to control it as they ran further down the insides of the mountain, deeper, putting even more rock over their heads.

*I'm going to die.*

*We're all going to be crushed by the mountain, looking for a temple I'm supposed to find. The prophecy will end before it could start.*

Stones shook loose, falling around them.

*Don't look up!*

"Jelani, go left," Nadzia ordered as they met an intersection. As soon as they were around the bend, the ceiling behind them collapsed.

"Ashiel's fucking toes!" Siobhann yelped, glancing at the debris. She slammed into Garioch's back.

"Move," Nadzia barked, hand outstretched toward an oak door with heavy bolted bands across it. Grimms and Kwayssi slid out of her way as she chanted, eyes closed.

The ground continued to shudder around them.

Grimms handed Kwayssi the lantern.

Loud clangs echoed as Nadzia's spell triggered the locks inside the iron bands holding the door in place. "Now, Jelani!"

Grimms heaved the door open. Nadzia immediately shoved Kwayssi, Garioch, and Siobhann through it.

The second she stepped through the door, Grimms let go and scrambled over the threshold with her. The door suddenly disappeared downward, scraping the sole of Grimms' boot as they teetered in place with the sensation of the ground rising.

They were at another intersection. More doors.

Siobhann's heart was in her throat as she grabbed Garioch's hand.

She clung to the knowledge that Darya and her children were safe at Kemberlan, far, far away from an imploding mountain still crawling with Torgolis.

What if they hadn't found them because they, too, were somewhere below the mountain?

Nadzia stood, eyes closed, whispering before the banded doors. One before them, two on either side.

Siobhann swayed as an image of the doors flashed through her mind. The same images that she saw in her dreams. "That one," she pointed to the one they faced.

"You're sure?" Garioch asked her.

"Fuck no, but it's what I saw in the dream."

"The dream that ushered us down here in the first place." Garioch's wry voice elicited a huff from Siobhann.

Nadzia slapped her palm on the wood and began her chant again. The bolts slid free for Grimms to heave open. They ran through, but nothing collapsed behind them this time.

"Nadzia, what is this?" Grimms asked his ex-wife, awestruck, as he stared at the mountain over their heads.

"It is the beginning," she smiled, with as much awe as certainty in her wondrous voice.

Siobhann looked up with the others.

The stone was alive, glowing, writhing, and swirling across the expanse and down the sides, churning.

At the centre of the expanse stood a wall-less temple with an elaborately carved bird, one foot supported by the tail of a dragon encircling the space.

Nadzia looked at Siobhann.

There were no words.

# THIRTY-FOUR

Erevan crawled along the lightless narrow tunnel on his hands and knees after Nolgan.

He would not evade Erevan, no matter how deep into the mountain he went.

Erevan finally had him after decades of pursuit.

He would take the texts from him, he knew. What he didn't know was what he would do with Nolgan afterward. Or Kossa, if she wasn't trapped or crushed by the twisting mountain.

They crawled along an escape shaft, meant for a crouching dwarf and not an elf.

The air thinned the deeper they went.

The dwarves had buried it specifically so that Elven kind would not corrupt the temple, as they had in the last cycle.

He would not allow Nolgan to do that.

He could not allow him to corrupt Siobhann the way he'd corrupted Kossa.

Erevan didn't fear for himself. He'd seen how the Beast had repelled Kossa for even thinking of stealing its power for herself. It would not grant Nolgan his demented dream.

It could not, surely.

Unless there was some larger plan at play that Erevan could not imagine.

If it was destined, there was nothing he could do, but he would not simply *allow* it.

The sounds of grunting, cursing, and thudding drifted up the shaft toward him.

*Seems he's found the end.*

Nolgan's frantic breathing echoed along the narrow space. "How can this be? It was open before!"

*Collapsed wall. Wonderful.*

Erevan paused where he was, rather than scramble right up to Nolgan's arse. Neither of them was going anywhere without backing out.

It would be foolish to blast the debris without knowing for certain there was somewhere for the rock to go on the other side. While he could protect himself from the magic, he couldn't escape an all-out collapse.

Nolgan's breathing increased. "I'll die before I let you take me back to Myst Innys. I'll destroy the texts."

"Silence, Nolgan, I'm trying to concentrate. Besides, I could leave you here to suffocate and take them from your dead hands, anyway."

"You—"

"Shut. Up." Erevan squeezed his eyes shut, seeking, as the Beast had done, to awaken the living rock below the mountain. Stretching his magic out, he followed the natural paths of the earth toward its molten essence. A living thing with a purpose of its own. Expand, create new rock and reform the old. It wasn't yet finished what it had awakened to do.

He sensed it gathering around a central point somewhere beyond the blocked shaft.

There was a seam of molten rock flowing past their shaft several inches within the wall.

*Will it work with me?*

Pushing his magic out, he did his best to coax the flow to expand, melting the surrounding stone.

The air continued to thin, and the shaft grew warmer as the rock between him and the flow dissolved. Erevan increased the magic surrounding his body, protecting him from the effects of the heat.

"What are you doing? It's stifling in here." Nolgan's nasal voice was closer now.

The side of the shaft glowed before it crumbled into the flow beside him like a slow-moving river.

"Give me the satchels, Nolgan."

"I will never—,"

"Like I said, I can just take them from your dead hands. Your choice."

"Is it?" Nolgan spat.

Erevan waited. "Give me the satchels and you can back out of here. Maybe your Torgolis allies will help you. If they haven't yet realized what a liar you are."

"I will go with you as your prisoner. I request safe passage to Myst Innys."

Erevan laughed. "You have been gone a long, long time, but they will not have forgotten that you are an exile. The humans here might put you in one of their prisons."

"I'm Elven. We're kin. Brother, you can't just—,"

"Silence, Nolgan. Decide now."

There was some shuffling as Nolgan wriggled out of the satchel loops and shoved them along the shaft toward Erevan, then gave them a final kick.

Erevan collected them, slung the straps over his own shoulders and gripped them tight to his chest. "Nolgan, I don't have time to deal with you now, but if you and Kossa do escape, I will come after you for what you did here."

Perhaps the Aelozian army would capture them or the Torgolis would seek vengeance for their deceit.

Nolgan sputtered more words that Erevan ignored as he clutched the satchels and rolled into the molten river. His barrier held as he rode the current toward its convergence.

It brought him free of the black rock, where he dropped into an open chamber surrounded by the liquid fire. Catching his balance next to a carved dragon head, he took in his surroundings as he released the magic barrier that protected him from the flame.

It was the temple complex that the Beast had tasked him to find. Scanning the landscape illuminated by the fire flow, he caught sight of a cluster of individuals near the phoenix sculpture.

His heart soared.

*Siobhann.*

He'd found her. Alive.

Her eyes were round as she stared back at him.

He grinned.

What a sight his entry must have been!

He ignored her companions as he strode toward her, removing the straps from his chest. He dropped the bags at his feet as she met him, arms encircling his waist, face pressed to his chest.

"I thought I lost you."

"I told you I was capable." His arms pulled her against him as he pressed his cheek to the top of her head.

She laughed against him. "Arrogant elf."

"I don't deny it." He leaned back to look down into her face.

Hers upturned, the emotion writ across her features was unmistakable. Tears spiked her lashes, though they did not fall.

He cradled her face in his hands so that she could not escape the kiss he meant to place on her lips. He needed her to feel what was in his heart as his lips ghosted hers.

She rose up onto her toes to seal and return the heartfelt greeting.

Her fingers traced the lines of his jaw and cheekbones so that he could not escape her any more than she could escape him.

Finally, he released her lips, pressing his forehead to hers. "We have much work to do."

She nodded against him. "Any idea what we do next? I'm not sure we should leave the place like this?"

He chuckled, raising his head to look at her companions. His gaze lingered on the Dwarven woman with the distinctive symbols of her status. "Good, you have a priestess. Perhaps she can help us make sense of the documents Nolgan gave me."

"Gave you?"

"Yes. He's escaping in a shaft somewhere. Hopefully, he'll find his sister and I'll round them up later. If the Torgolis don't get to them first." He clasped her hand, interlinking their fingers as he bent to retrieve the satchels.

"I see."

The priestess approached with a Dwarven warrior and a healer behind her.

Erevan nodded to Garioch.

"Your Highness." The priestess greeted him with a slight bow of her head.

Siobhann quickly introduced the rest of her companions. "He's retrieved the lost Elven texts. Perhaps with your knowledge of the temple, we can figure out what to do with this." She waved a hand at the liquid fire coating the walls and ceiling over them. "Maybe before we're roasted."

Erevan passed the satchels to Nadzia. She brought them to a nearby stone bench that was part of the temple proper. Flipping through the pages, fingers scanning the diagrams and texts. "Jelani, what do you make of this?"

Grimms peered over her shoulder, and they whispered between them. Now and then he'd look over at Erevan and Siobhann. Their discussion grew a little fiercer.

"We're supposed to protect the place from another rogue elf and here you want to hand it over to another rogue elf?" Grimms growled.

"Jelani, a rogue elf would not have just handed me the most sacred of texts."

Grimms turned with a brow raised. "It could be a ruse."

Nadzia rolled her eyes, turning away from Grimms to Siobhann. "I must release the binding so that you may complete the ritual."

Siobhann's hand tightened against Erevan's. "I can't, Nadzia. I can't lose control."

The Dwarven priestess stepped toward Siobhann, looking up into her eyes. She reached out to place her hands on Siobhann's arms. "You won't because your dragon will ground you and provide the balance you need to soar."

"I don't understand." Her gaze flicked to Erevan.

"Let go of the fear and trust in the magic."

Erevan squeezed Siobhann's hand as her frightened gaze found her brother's. Her throat worked as she pressed her lips together.

"I think it's time," Garioch said.

Kwayssi took Grimms' hand, with her other, she reached out to touch the centre of Siobhann's chest. "We'll be here, Siobhann. Let the fear fade away and clear your heart."

Kwayssi's white-green light magic rippled through Siobhann and encircled Erevan.

"Best go find somewhere safe where fire won't fall on our heads," Grimms said, heading toward a door at the far end of the temple compound. "Just in case."

The priestess raised her arms toward Siobhann and Erevan's faces. They bent at the waist so that she could touch their foreheads. "May your vision be focused with the clarity of your hearts." Her palms glowed with an indigo light. "Your mother should have guided you through this. But I am glad to have the honour of being here in her stead."

Her firm hands turned Erevan and Siobhann toward each other. She smoothed her indigo light over their palms before linking Erevan's left hand to Siobhann's right and placed his right hand over her heart. It beat a wild staccato.

Siobhann's free hand rested on his heart, her touch warm and soothing.

She met his gaze.

He stared back. The fear subsided, relaxing her features as her gaze fluttered over his face.

The priestess moved behind her.

Siobhann squeezed his hand and whispered, "I commit to you, Erevan."

Joy surged through him, making his heart patter beneath her palm. "I am eternally yours, Siobhann."

"I unbind thee," the priestess said in a commanding voice.

Siobhann's head jerked back, eyes squeezed shut, her breath hissed through her teeth.

When she had control of the pain, she opened her eyes.
They glowed like his, when his magic came alive.

# THIRTY-FIVE

GARIOCH'S HEART POUNDED IN his chest as he looked at the scene, hoping they weren't making a gross error in judgment.

Beside him, Grimms grumbled and Kwayssi shushed him.

"I never thought this would become reality. Not in my lifetime."

"Aye, nor in mine," Grimms said. "She's going to need us more than ever, whatever happens next."

"I will continue to do my part as long as I can maintain my presence at the palace. You make sure Ghalen and Donnen prepare the Kindred."

"No worries there. You focus on the emperor and make sure he keeps his greedy hands clear of her."

"Hush, both of you. We are the only ones to witness this in the thousands of years since the beginning of the last cycle, and thousands more before the next."

Garioch's gaze roved the roiling ceiling. Sweat slicked his skin under the dense heat. "I'm glad you're excited about this."

Kwayssi scoffed at him, but kept her attention focused on the trio at the centre of the temple. "It's beginning."

The priestess stood behind Siobhann, palm to her back. They were too far away to hear her words as her palm glowed white, as it had when she cast the binding spell. The glow soon turned violet, then a deep indigo.

Siobhann jerked in pain.

Erevan didn't let go of her as they faced one another.

*Goddess, let us all survive. Please don't let my sister blow the mountain apart.*

Siobhann's eyes glowed as she opened them.

Garioch tensed. The last two times he saw her eyes glow, destruction followed.

The priestess backed away to the edge of the stone circle marking the centre of the temple. She stepped off the edge and moved under the open temple where a statue of a pregnant goddess rested on a pedestal.

Air breezed past them, building and rushing, orbiting the temple.

Erevan's eyes glowed, as did his hands. Flames licked along his arms, travelling, seeking.

Siobhann's did the same until their fires mingled and encircled one another so that Garioch could barely see them.

The fire changed form, reaching for the rushing air to feed it, stretching.

The air moved faster, slowly pushing Garioch, Grimms and Kwayssi in toward the centre.

A bright flash blinded him for several moments.

The fire around Siobhann and Erevan intensified, stretching into two distinct forms superimposed over their corporeal bodies. The familiar bird of flame enveloped Siobhann, lifting her off of her feet. She hovered, anchored by Erevan's hand clasping hers; their palms remained affixed to each other's chests. A massive beast resembling the one carved into the stone surrounding the temple formed from his magic.

Garioch gaped.

The wind howled. The ceiling writhed.

Wings of fire extended from Siobhann, fanning the elements.

The temple platform groaned, trembling below their feet.

Garioch and his companions rushed for the temple where the Priestess stood, clutching one of the pillars, her face alight with awe.

No one had words.

They wouldn't have been able to hear them anyway over the deafening sounds of the wind and the rock platform sliding upward through the mountain.

Siobhann's phoenix strained upward. Erevan's dragon held fast, grounding her.

Slowly, the molten ceiling opened to the sky. The edges rippled, flowing and steaming against the mountain snow. The familiar face of the mountain cliffs loomed behind Siobhann and Erevan.

Garioch turned to see Carlane at his back. The walls were lined with gaping onlookers.

They had risen to the plateau where Erevan had loosed a fireball to save the Aelozian army from the Torgolis warriors.

The platform continued to rise until it rested at a new elevation from the original clearing. A river of liquid rock flowed around the temple base, cooling as mountain snow melted and rushed into the spaces, solidifying it.

The mountain ceased trembling as the winds calmed.

Siobhann's phoenix continued to strain for freedom.

Erevan's dragon growled, drawing her attention.

For several heartbeats, Garioch thought the phoenix would attack the dragon to liberate herself with beak and claws extended.

As she looked down at her dragon, her head tilted in recognition, beak and claws relaxing as she retracted her wings. Final wisps of flame floated away toward the mountain peak, dissolving.

Siobhann's body lowered to the ground of her own volition, still holding Erevan's hand. Erevan's magic circled several more times, also dissipating until it flowed down into residual cracks in the temple floor, sealing them shut.

Garioch breathed a sigh of relief.

No one was dead.

Siobhann collapsed into Erevan's arms.

Garioch leaned against the temple pillar, rubbing his hands over his face, trying to absorb what he'd just witnessed.

When he looked around him, every being on the plateau stared in open-mouthed silence. Many of them had witnessed Siobhann's destruction the night they thought Erevan was lost.

"That was a sight," Grimms' gruff voice finally floated to Garioch.

Garioch glanced to see Grimms' eyes shimmering with emotion as he leaned against the statue of the pregnant goddess at the centre of the temple.

It had endured several cracks under the pressure of the trembling rise and the extreme elements.

Regret twinged through his chest as he stared at the damage on the ancient carving.

In the distance, from the wall, someone cheered.

*They must have figured out what was going on, or they're all just happy the mountain didn't crumble.*

The cheer grew as soldiers threw their arms up. The sound rolled around the mountain peaks, echoing, reverberating back toward the temple.

Garioch grinned. Kwayssi and the Priestess smiled. Grimms didn't scowl.

Dropping stone dust startled Garioch, and he jumped away from the statue. The fissures grew and gaped. He tentatively pressed a hand to the stone. The sound of the people's voices vibrated through it.

More pieces crumbled. He wanted to silence them, but it was too late, as the statue of the pregnant goddess crumbled from the top down, past her rounded belly to her tilted hips, revealing another object.

"Ashiel's fucking toes," he breathed, glancing at Grimms. "That isn't what I think it is. Is it?"

Kwayssi approached, wide-eyed, fingers outstretched with her magic. She gasped, turning to Garioch in awe. "It's alive."

Grimms and Nadzia approached, the four of them surrounding the pedestal.

Nadzia pressed her hands to her heart. "I do believe it is."

"What are we going to do with it?" Grimms muttered.

"It must be protected," Nadzia said.

"I know it," he growled.

Garioch started to laugh, "I think Siobhann and Erevan just became parents." He laughed even harder.

"What's so funny, and what the hells is that?" Siobhann demanded, approaching with Erevan, hands still linked.

Garioch turned to see Erevan's mouth drop open when his eyes found the object of discussion and laughed even harder. "It's a fucking dragon egg, little sister. Congratulations!"

# THIRTY-SIX

Siobhann stood a step back from her companions, observing each of their faces, happy to be home. Even if the roof still needed repair and the walls still crumbled.

Home was home.

"Thank Ashiel no one realized that your oddly shaped rock was a dragon egg," Donnen stared at it in wonder.

It sat atop his map-strewn war table in the midst of his library, surrounded by most of the Kindred, gaping at it.

Sendi reached across the table to poke it. She giggled, "It wants to come out soon. Can I help it grow, Aunty Shebi?"

"No!" Everyone gasped.

Nate scooped her up into his arms before she could slap her palm on the alabaster shell.

"Here is your guide fee," Erevan dropped the familiar leather pouch of gems and titanium ingots on the maps next to the egg. "That should mend your roof."

"And more," Donnen chuckled. "I am pleased that you had the time to describe the lands so that we can fill in the blanks of our maps. This will be very useful in the coming years."

"Aye, especially since we don't know where the Torgolis have gone. They fled the fortress when the ground started to rumble, and didn't look back. We were all preparing to follow them, since it seemed as though the whole thing was going to collapse." Lorne said.

Dea tapped Siobhann's arm and signed, "They won't come back?"

"We think the Torgolis have had enough of Aelozia for the time being. And the individuals leading them are imprisoned until the Empire decides what to do with them."

"They are outlaws. Myst Innys won't have them." Erevan said, meeting Siobhann's gaze from across the room.

"What happens now?" Roan asked, eyes fixed on the egg.

"We protect the egg for as long as we need to. Erevan and I leave in the morning to return the texts to his father." Siobhann left out the part where they'd already begun transcribing them. Erevan had a fair enough hand with ink to copy the images. It would take time, but they had plenty of it during their travels.

"I'm going to miss you, but it's for the best that you are leaving before the emperor realizes the depth of what's happened and gets ideas for you." Darya said, adjusting her hold on her sleeping son.

"Garioch is already handling things as much as he can without raising suspicions." Ghalen said. "I will do the same with the generals. Nate, you'd do well to come to court and help me with this."

Nate and Darya exchanged a glance over the heads of their young children. "I will have my hands full, but we will consider it."

Alda appeared in the doorway. "Dinner is ready and Arlyss is here with pies."

"Pies," echoed through the library, which quickly cleared out.

"I will keep this warm by the forge until you're ready to go." Grimms reached for the egg. "Save me some pie."

"Roan will bring it to you later."

Grimms nodded, cradling the egg as Darya had with her infant, and left Siobhann and Erevan alone in the room.

As soon as they were gone, Siobhann turned to face Erevan, backing up to lean on the table.

He stood between her feet, slipping his hands around her hips. "I almost had you on this table that first night."

"Hmmm," she smiled. "I almost had *you* on this table." She pulled him closer to her.

"I don't think Donnen would appreciate us wrinkling his maps. Should we join the others?"

"I'm not hungry for food." She pulled him down to kiss her.

He braced his hands on the table to either side of her as he claimed her lips, deepening the kiss.

"We should find somewhere more appropriate to continue this conversation." He nuzzled her throat, sending shivers down through her body.

When her hands slid over his shoulders, he took advantage and scooped her up into his arms, as he had done that first night when she was too drunk to care.

She giggled as he strode out of the library, past the open dining hall—to many hoots and whistles following them up the stairs—to the guest room overlooking the garden.

He shoved the heavy door closed with his heel. He held her close until he reached the high bed and lay her on it.

Unwilling to relinquish her hold on his shoulders, she held him until he lay atop her, supported by his elbows and knees.

Her smile faded as she looked up into his face, her fingertips tracing the lines of his royal markings.

"Regret?"

She blinked. "For?"

"Leaving. Kemberlan is your home."

"We'll come back." She offered a weak smile.

His warm hands gently pushed the hair from her face as he studied her.

"Do *you* have regrets?"

"I've secured my people's valuable artifacts. We've stopped Nolgan and Kossa from encouraging the Torgolis to invade Aelozia." He smiled down at her. His fingers trailed along the fine bones of her face to her throat and along the edge of her shift. "And I found my destiny."

"You did. And a dragon egg."

"I meant you, Siobhann. You are my destiny." Golden light flared to life in his dark eyes.

She blinked as her throat tightened. "I know it." She pulled him so that she accepted the weight of his body against hers. "I know it," she whispered against his lips, claiming him so that he had no doubt that she did.

The Kindred Chronicles will continue...

...In the mean time, if you haven't read *Darya and Nate*'s story in '***Healer***', get it free when you sign up for my **newsletter** at **JodiKendrick.com** or **find** it at your favourite retailer.

# Thank You!

Dear Reader,

Thank you so much for taking the time to read Mercenary. If you enjoyed it, please consider leaving a review on your favourite platform.

This story has been in the making for about two decades and has seen many iterations via short stories featuring Siobhann and Erevan that have never been published.

Back in the day, many many moons ago, I was a gamer immersed in the world of MMORPG wherein I was part of a guild called The Kindred (of DAoC and various other games) under the banner of the raven on a green and black field. They are my inspiration for this fantasy world that I have lived with for so long. They are forever in my gamer heart.

For free downloads, to join my newsletter and browse my growing library for more books with *Romance, Adventure and Passion*, visit **JodiKendrick.com**

-Jodi

# Author

Jodi Kendrick lives in Eastern Ontario Canada with her *Favourite Person* and chompy furbaby, while their adult children explore the wider world.

As a romance author, she writes in paranormal, fantasy, steampunk & gaslamp subgenres, and sometimes delves into urban fantasy and paranormal women's fiction. Her characters are often quirky, sometimes cranky, but they all woman-up and get the job done while their partners ensure they survive with all their bits and bobs attached.

A history enthusiast and word dabbler most of her life, she enjoys exploring 'beyond-the-everyday' and the 'time-before-now', discovering relationship threads weaving individuals through time and place. She's rarely seen without flashy notebooks and colourful pens.

**Follow Jodi on Social Media:**

## Dragon Island

Dragon Heat
Dragon Rogue
Dragon Blood

## Enchanted Ardor

Wish

## EveL Worlds : FUCN'A

Tough Nut
Diamond in the Ruff
Honeyed Nut
Gorilla in the Hiss
FUCN'A Collection One
Pedigree Collection

## Finely Aged

Dragon Steel

## The Kindred Chronicles

Healer
Mercenary

## Global Paranormal
## Security Agency

Awakened
Surfacing
Polestar
Aquatic Investigations
Prowler

## The Nightshade Guild

Destined Time
Trial by Blood

## The Soaring Dragon Chronicles

Return Flight
Changeling

www.ingramcontent.com/pod-product-compliance
Lightning Source LLC
Chambersburg PA
CBHW032243010726
47494CB00002B/604